Song of the Crow

Song of the Crow

LAYNE MAHEU

UNBRIDLED BOOKS

2006

UNBRIDLED BOOKS
Denver, Colorado

The epigraphs to Book I, Chapter 1 and Book II, Chapter 11, reprinted with permission from Lawrence Kilham, *The American Crow and the Common Raven* (College Station: Texas A&M University Press, 1989).

The epigraph to Book I, Chapter 4 is taken from *Tommy McGinty's Northern Tutchone story of crow: a First Nation elder recounts the creation of the world,* by Dominique Legros, Canadian Museum of Civilization, 1999, p. 59. © Canadian Museum of Civilization.

The epigraph to Book III, reprinted with the permission of Simon & Schuster from Adult Publishing Group, *Noah's Flood*, by William Ryan and Walter Pitman. Copyright © 1998 by Walter C. Pitman III and William B. F. Ryan.

Library of Congress Cataloging-in-Publication Data

Maheu, Layne.

Song of the crow / Layne Maheu.

p.   cm.

ISBN 1-932961-18-6 (alk. paper)

1. Noah (Biblical figure)—Fiction. 2. Bible. O.T. Genesis—History of Biblical events—Fiction. 3. Noah's ark—Fiction. 4. Deluge—Fiction. 5. Crows—Fiction. 6. Religious Fiction. I. Title.

PS3613.A34933S66 2006

813'.6—dc22   2005035594

1   3   5   7   9   10   8   6   4   2

Book Design by CV•SH

First Printing

To Frank and Allie, young Spenny, and young Sam

Song of the Crow

*A big black bird is making the most gawd-
awful racket, for no apparent reason, CAW
CAW CAW!!! his entire body bouncing
upward with each caw. Perhaps he is singing.*

—BEN JACKLET, "CROW MYSTERIES"

Prologue

Happy Noah, singing Noah, eager to do God's bidding without a single drop from the sky. There's the story of his miraculous birth, that he came into the world already circumcised, with a full head of hair all long and silver and already combed, and at the age of three could stand and deliver speeches on the virtues of his all-powerful moral authority in the sky. But if it were true, that he was born with the pale signs of Misfortune already sprouting from his head, he wouldn't boast, not even at the age of three, because it is a wellspring of sadness that grows there, and to carry it around with you always is a burden no one would wish for.

How would I know? And why was I summoned to keep an eye on this peculiar example of his species? It was in my stars, in my sky, and in my bones, and is the story I'm about to tell.

I.

Nestling

Suddenly the ocean waters began to break through over the westward hills and to pour in upon these primitive peoples—the lake that had been their home and friend, became their enemy; its waters rose and never abated; their settlements were submerged; the waters pursued them in their flight. Day by day and year by year the waters spread up the valleys and drove mankind before them. Many must have been surrounded and caught by that continually rising salt flood. It knew no check; it came faster and faster; it rose over the tree-tops, over the hills, until it had filled the whole basin of the present Mediterranean and until it lapped the mountain cliffs of Arabia and Africa. Far away, long before the dawn of written history, this catastrophe occurred.

—H. G. WELLS, *OUTLINE OF HISTORY*, 1920

Crows, and with them I include ravens, seem as though by convergent evolution to have something in their psyches corresponding to something in our own.

—LAWRENCE KILHAM,
*The American Crow and
the Common Raven*

1. Keeyaw the Terrible

I remember the nest that hatched me. My mother lined it carefully with the fleece of human and sheep, mane of horse, down of dogwood, but mostly the fray of twigs and grasses. At first that was the world to me, until I was strong enough to look out over the tangled latticework of twigs on the outside of our nest.

Then I discovered the sky, spread out above our cedar roof branches.

And from the sky came our mother's call, low and urgent and gurgled through the broth of freshly dead things in her beak.

"Grow! Grow!"

She lit, a black ball of rattling feathers, scanned all around her, then lowered the quick clippers of her beak, smeared with blood and slime and victuals.

And my brother and I, we opened our beaks to the sky.

"Me! Me!"

We cried, naked and fierce.

"I Am!"

Until we were just blood-red little holes crying out for the minced guts of life.

Her beak worked in fits, shaking the foodstuff into us, then pushing it further with her tongue. That became all of the world to me. That and sleep. Sleep, and feeding, and our mother's low mewing call.

Then I began to wake to other sounds, other crow calls, and our mother flew off to meet them. When the calls were near enough, I saw how the rest of my family would feed her, and how she'd dive back down to the nest and give us their offering. Before long I began to realize when it wasn't Our Mother of Many coming down to us. The others were longer and more luxurious in the air. Our Many flew as if perpetually landing—the air and everything in it between her and wherever she wanted to be. And if she found our father or one of the other siblings feeding us, she'd look us over afterward to see if we were still plump and juicy, as if their inept feeding had sucked the vital juices from us. Her eyes told us she was the only one with enough patience and wisdom and past to love us, as if she were nourishment itself. Through the ragged fall of her feathers, her eyes peered down at us, cloudy sky-yellow orbs of concern, the only thing about her that was calm.

But when the others left and Our Many leaned low to nudge us, or cooed down at us with her horn barely parted and trembling like two reeds, a wondrous warmth filled the nest. A blue-black cast spread out and covered us like our mother's worn patch of brood feathers, and sitting over us, she hummed out slow winding histories, or ballads of the afternoon, or long ancestral songs of nothing but names that repeated and trailed off and left me dreaming my baby bird dreams in a tree.

My Other woke me up for no reason—or the only reason—hunger. I found him ripping at the frayed weave of our nest's inner bowl. He gulped on the air. *"I'm hungry."* He clicked against the waddle. *"I'm hungry! I Am!"*

"Me, too."

I looked up.

Above us, no mother.

No crow with worm in the sky.

Only emptiness.

Only a peaceable sun-filled blue. As if that were the sky's natural state.

Then the sky sent a panic of bushtits our way, along with a lost little kinglet whose crest flared up into a red eye of agitation. He seemed even more lost, hanging on to the mixed flock. Their fleeing only excited my hungry brother. His eyes blinked, and his veins pulsed, and he flapped his naked elbows, ready to fly off to wherever small birds go. He wanted to eat them and become them and cry out their wee bird calls. There was no way he could have scared them, not with his round, splotched head much too big for him, wobbling around on a skinny neck without much control. His stomach was already engorged, but he kept stuffing it so that his twiggy legs could hardly lift him, which they did only so that he could get to the food before me. The points of our new pinfeathers did nothing to cover our gray and brown, liver-spotted skin. I laughed at the sight of him, but in pained recognition. Was I really just like him, so naked and helpless? No, worse. I was afraid of everything. A leaf blew past our nest and I shrieked and hid myself down in my own dung. But My Other saw it as an opportunity to fill his belly and raised his gaping beak to the sky, crying, *"Me! Me! I Am!"* as the leaf blew past, tumbling.

Then a disturbance took hold of the leaves.

The wind flew round in circles and gave no sign of going anywhere else. It grew in force until it shook the trees. They groaned. Their ancient arms whipped around in different directions, clacking against one another, making the sound of knocking antlers. Above us, the sky rolled up into a dark cloud mass and whispered along the limbs. Everywhere the wind said *yes,* first *yes,* then *no,* then *yes* and *no* in rankled argument with itself, pushing our tree as the sky and the leaves hissed.

A crow I'd never seen before hung onto the sky, blown sideways without making headway, calling, *"Keeyaw! Keeyaw!"*

"What? What do you see?" I asked.

Down in the familiar crags and burrows, I always asked my hungry brother what he saw. Because My Other was destined to be a crow of Pure Flight, at least in the eyes of our father. Already My Other could travel to the extremities of the nest and beyond, almost. He was an early hopper and climber and full of reckless curiosity as he teetered on the uppermost twigs of our nest. Above all things, our father valued this ability, as crows who possess it fly practically in legend. No other bird from our aerie had it. But My Other, he showed potential.

"What do you see now?"

The winds toppled him down beside me.

"Nothing," he said, kicking his claws to stand back up. *"I was looking for Our Many through the trees."*

"So was I." I hoped it was our mother who'd frightened off the flock, bringing us more good gorge and spittle. *"What's taking her?"*

But I already knew. Far back in the darkness of the egg, I'd felt the blows that landed in the forest and sent a tremor through our tree. I'd thought it was some dark force of the weather. But I knew now it was not only a beast but a beast human, Keeyaw the Terrible, doom of the trees, and I knew there must be others, all sorts of Keeyaw-looking creatures, chopping and mauling, driving a wedge into the pulp of the woods. But no. There was only one. One old, hairy curse on two legs, Keeyaw, the grim reaper of our trees, hunkered over the roots of the Giants, assailing them with his anger and dragging them away to the underworld. The thud of that beast working was like the struggle of my own beak, trying to muzzle my way out of the eggshell, or the clap of the flicker, drumming away at the bark, or the rhythm of the wind, my mother's song, the pause of nightfall. The noise of him felling trees goes far back in my mind, to a time before sound and memory, where the boggy water never stirs.

I didn't know if my hearing was getting better, or if Keeyaw was getting closer. But the crunch of his stone ax grew tremendous. With each blow, our tree quaked, and the wind scattered his hammering and brought it back again as if he were attacking all of the giants of the woods at once.

"Get up," I said. *"Get out there and look."*

"No one's coming," said My Other, kicking his claws to get back up. *"He's too close."*

"Close?" He's chopping us down."

2. Fall of the Giant

"Fly off!

"Fly!"

It was our mother. But from where? Where? Who could tell with the wind chasing her calls?

I saw her, a few trees away. She appeared on one branch, then another, then in an altogether different tree. But it was just the *yes* and *no* of the wind heaving her perch and whipping her feathers into a confusion of leaves. Why didn't she swoop onto the nest and stuff food into us?

"Fly!" she kept calling.

"Fly!"

So what choice did we have? Though I'd never left the deep of the nest, I reluctantly climbed up to the fatal jump. There was no way we could survive it, but Our Many must have known there was no way we'd survive the falling of Our Giant either. And to die at least trying, even though you couldn't fly yet, was a way to fly off to the Tree of the Dead. Any death before that was no death at all, but only a quick flight into whatever fate befell you—flies and maggots and stiff feathers and dust. The only way to become a true crow was to fly. Until then you were nothing, without a name; flying was all.

My Other was still in the deep of the nest, trying to stand back up, while I picked my way through the hurling twigs and stuck my beak into the head-winds. They howled *yesss* across my face. They howled *yes* and *no* in biting, utter cold. I'd never felt anything like it. But then, this was my first experi-ence beyond the bowl of our nest. As our tree bent, the underworld was thrown into view, first one side of our nest, then the other. I was so scared and astonished, I would have kept going if it weren't for my enormous bony feet holding me back. Below was a mad sea of branches thrashing every which way. What lay below all the layers of bushes and vines I could not see. But I was hungry to fly. Or fall. Or eat the air. I had to wrap it in my wings, if you could call them that, just bare bones and points. For this very reason, infant crows are discouraged from the edge of the nest. Some just cannot overcome the urge to lunge out and grab hold of the wind and plummet, or whatever the feeling is that takes hold of your wings, even though there are no feathers anywhere yet to fly.

It was worse than I could imagine. Our mother still urged us out.

But I found myself awed and calm in the stinging headwinds and wanted to take in as much as I could before casting myself down into the depths of a short life in the unknown.

The whole world swayed on its stem, complaining.

There was no bottom to the world, while our nest was filled with stuff from down there, or so I was told. I looked and saw only the green hurling movement below. Until I saw a sight yet stranger still.

Through the flying leaves and broken branches, I finally saw him, the mon-ster, the mythic, the beastman, Keeyaw. He was much farther from our tree than I had thought. Not an army, or a gathering of many, as I'd learn was the case with his kind, but just one, one beastman like no other, separated from the rest of his kind, Keeyaw of the lank figure and mournful mustaches, low, groveling, hunkered over from the weight of his implements and the white, colorless beard that hung from his face in a way he had no control over. It just hung there and swung as he worked. And his eyes—those suspicious, unseeing orbs he occasionally turned to the sky as though he were about to be scolded and were constantly being watched—how could eyes sunk so far back in his skull ever see a thing? And his tools—they say he was the first to use tools, that he invented them. According to the lore of his kind, this was his gift to the world. And it was always upon us. All around us, the trees had been severed from the air and hurled to the underworld. And somehow I took a strange pity on this supposed *Doom of the Trees*. It seemed his grim hacking away at the Giants gave him no satisfaction whatsoever. Instead he seemed trapped in a landscape of irritable brooding, and taking his anger out on the mute Giants gave him no escape. Still, it was his only answer, which he repeatedly struck.

My Other finally plucked his way up to the nest top. He perched much closer to the edge than I did and spread his prickly wing points out to catch hold of the howling, but he failed to jump. He just crouched low and did what I did. We sat there and wondered about this Keeyaw creature from the heaving edge of the nest. Then My Other picked himself up and whipped his tiny bones in the direction of the powerful gusts.

"*No! Stay there!*" cried our mother, seeing his brave little twigs flapping. "*Stay in the nest!*"

I realized she'd wanted to join us at the nest but didn't want to reveal our whereabouts to Keeyaw.

Though we thought Our Many had been calling us out to *fly,* she must have meant it for Keeyaw. Crows have no alarm call for *walk off,* or *grovel your way back across the underworld. Fly* was the only call she had to drive Keeyaw away.

And she dove down to mob him, strafing his whiskery head. But the wind weakened her attack. When she dove after him a second time, a sudden gust nearly pushed her up against the trunk. So she hung on to the trees between us and the beast, looking at him, then at us, then back to him, full of hesitation, until it turned to weary patience.

"Get back inside," she called, mute and panicked

So I dove back into the safety of our nest's inner bowl and closed my eyes, until I felt more acutely the heaving and roiling of Our Giant through the air. My fearless Other, who was already practiced in the ancient art of imitation, stayed up in the headwinds and made the sound of Keeyaw's ax just fine. But no crow could imitate the sound of a tree falling, like the rippling of violent thunders, darker than doom, worse than the end, broken limbs, loose leaves flying. Frightened birds and creatures took off. Then our mother fled. The branches of our own tree sank, and there was a silence, like a weight falling in my chest. We felt the whole world tilt. When the Giant hit, the woods exploded. Each bounce brought more thunder, until it stopped.

The forest was never so quiet as then.

Except the cooling of the wind. And the murmuring of the *yes.* And the murmuring of the *no.* And the sighing beneath the leaves, waiting for the final word.

Soon the rhythm of Keeyaw's ax resumed.

And the wind picked up, arguing again through the grizzled mat of the beastman's beard, and My Other could imitate, with the high, nasally pitch of parody, the sound Keeyaw made, hacking away at the underworld, rending the tree of its branches, and the beastman would hesitate and look up, full of woe and worry, swinging those awful implements over his head and then down again. *Tunk, tunk, tunk,* sang My Other. And Keeyaw's mournful mustaches shook.

*We're told that his understanding of nature
was so exact that he could select the tree,
specifically a cedar tree, or a kind of cedar
tree, that in the course of one-hundred and
twenty years, once planted, could grow to the
height of fifty meters, which is the measure
he needed for the construction of the Ark.*

—AARON TENDLER, *Noah and the Ark,
Voyage to a New Beginning*

3. Mother of Many

Another tree gone, and the sky hung lower.

The Giant lay dead, dumb, and naked, and Keeyaw kept smacking it, ripping the limbs free until the trunk lay wasted in the clearing. He went after the branches with the same grim intensity he went at the trunks, lost in mossy arboreal sadness, and he kept hacking away until he was further hidden from sight. Only then did our mother find it safe enough to fly to the nest. Her eyes, leaking the ancient ooze of her years, took us in lovingly as she lowered strips of half-chewed frog gut into our gapes. Then she cleaned the nest of our dung sacks, flew away with them in her beak, and then came back.

Every once in a while the winds threatened to argue all over again, but the sky let out a long sigh and the wind went on its troubled way, leaving us to the devices of Keeyaw.

My hungry brother and I strained above the nest to see what Keeyaw was up to.

He heaped all of the severed branches into a loose, snaggy pile.

"Is he building a nest here?" I asked.

I waited for an answer, staring at Our Many's claws, scaled and gnarly and clutched to the nest at my face. Above her hooks, her squat old body blocked out the sun. But then she *was* the sun, dark with love, ragged with comfort. As if she were well-being itself, we longed for the blue-black, worn-feather protection to come shining down over us. But she bristled now from wounded authority, and her beak kept working away at the unrest in her coat.

Then *"Eeiiwaaack! Eeiiwaaack!"* off in the distance, soaring.

Whereas most creatures flee the sound of Keeyaw, my father flew in, desperate for a look. *"Fly Home!"* Whenever our father heard the beastman's attack fall over the woods, he cried out in alarm, but also in eerie exultation. *"Fly Home!"* Was it a welcome? A threat? He flew in wild and large and threw his hooks out to land—even though the tree was no longer there— as if in denial of what Keeyaw had done. He must have thought his own absence had allowed the tree to fall. He lit far from our nest and let Keeyaw have it. He bobbed with each caw and his feathers flared as if Keeyaw were directly below, and the strange, terrible beast answered with the gnawing of his ax.

"Me! Me!" cried My Other. *"I Am!"*

But not even the begging of his favorite could bring my father to the nest.

Instead, Fly Home stayed where he was, leaning and lunging and spreading with each call, and our mother flew to the outlying woods to meet him. But their greeting was clipped and afraid. Our father had a huge, swimming brow of crown feathers where all his distant thoughts could live, and our thick old mother stretched herself up as best she could to rearrange his scattered brow.

"Can't you see?" she said. *"What's happening to the woods?"*

"Has he touched Our Giant?"

"No," she said. *"I won't let him."*

And they quieted even further as if suddenly realizing the good luck that our own tree had been spared, and silently they watched Keeyaw, turning their heads, pecking at their perch, while the beastman walked in and out of the Giant's arms, carrying cracked sticks and heavy fans of cedar leaf.

"So. What did you bring us?" Our Many finally asked with a quiet sweetness. *"From far off, from far off."*

"Open your beak, and I will show you."

My father gave a gentle tilt to his horn and shook the offering down into the sweet food pouch of her throat.

Then he flared up and leaned into the wind.

"Meet me in the sky," he said, which was a common enough farewell among lovers but was especially gallant in the falling woods.

Instead of flying away, though, he perched just above the downed Giant and began yelling again at the beastman.

And the wild-haired Keeyaw stopped what he was doing long enough to poke his head out from underneath the heavy weeping of the tree as my father grew even more menacing with pride. But Keeyaw showed no fear and only blinked and squinted with a look of vague curiosity, as if he had bad eyes, or my father's attack was baffling him. My father continued harassing him with his hackles extended and his brow fierce. Keeyaw was about to creep back into the injured Giant when he stood back away from it. He walked up and down the entire sprawling length of the trunk and moaned, flummoxed by what he'd done, as if the whole thing would not release him from its enormous burden. And he took his frustration out on his beard, pulling at the bits of bark and leaf stuck there. When Keeyaw looked up again at my father's territorial bickering, the white-haired creature had a sinking expression, even in his beard. Was it understanding? Had Keeyaw had a change of mind, or whatever it was that drove him at the woods, bent · on destruction?

With defeated shoulders, he took the reins of his mule and walked off, dragging the animal away with him into the woods.

My father swooped over him, assured of his prowess. Over and over again, he mobbed the man, and Our Many's eyes followed them, piercing into the unknown beyond the limbs of our spiny tree, where my father called from even farther off, from beyond the beyond, until his echo could no longer be heard.

In Keeyaw's absence, the woods remembered their silence.

It was the hot, brooding silence of insects, and the silence of small song-birds high in the branches of the sweltering heat. They remained hidden from sight as if the treetops themselves chirped vacuously back and forth. And a strange inner weather began to affect Our Many's eyes, the spell of an old mother crow, which was what she was. Later in life, I would find the large winter roosts filled with elder siblings of mine, crows from all ends of the wind, all of them singing out variations of her song. Our mother had lived long enough and had enough nests to be known as a mother of many, a great-grandmother over and over again, and though I have yet to meet another mother of many, I've heard of others. Every crow's song includes at least one. Our stout, imperious mother had outlived two mates. Our father was her third. And like gurgling water from a waterfall, Our Many came down to us, and my brother and I—we opened our beaks to the sky, and waited.

When all the food was gone, she sang.

The bristles around her beak were thin with age and her eyes milky with cataracts. But when she opened her ancient horn, out came the call of fledges from innumerable nest times, from the seasons beyond counting, with a random whirl to the call, or the way she got stuck on one. Over and over again she cried out, "*Sable . . .*"

In a muted, dreamy voice, since she was just over the nest.

"*Where are you?*"

She answered her own call.

"*Plucked away by owls.*"

She fanned her wings open and flew down onto the abandoned tree, stretched out across a bed of scrub and fern. She bobbed there and sang into one of the few weeping branches that remained. She cawed inwardly, lunging with muscles of grieving gut, as if regurgitating her song, as if feeding and singing were one and the same.

"*Nestor!*" She called to some fledge of her memory, now lost inside the tree.

"*Where?*

"*Where!*

"*Bloated by rain.*

"*Kettle, flung by the wind, eaten by mice, by flies, by maggots.*

"*Fledges snagged by hawks, by angry gods without names.*"

Since crows can count up to seven, any bird beyond that in age is from the seasons beyond counting, and though it wasn't always true for my mother, the seasons beyond her counting were advancing. She could remember the many who had flown from her nest. She just couldn't tell how long ago they had come, or gone, or if they had gone, or where to.

Then Our Many flew back up to the nest.

Through her distant, cloudy blinking, I could swear she hardly saw us, but looked far into her song and whatever unfortunate simp her memory had conjured up just then.

Then somebody talked from the air. Maybe
it was Moses. He said:
"You build a big boat."
Crow did that and put the moose, the bear,
the caribou, the lion, and everything in it.

—TOMMY MCGINTY'S NORTHERN
TUTCHONE STORY OF CROW:
A FIRST NATION ELDER RECOUNTS
THE CREATION OF THE WORLD

4. *Treasure*

"Who? Who dares attack the Giants of our song?"

Fly Home called his threats to the sky.

Then he called softly to Our Many, *"Why the sad song?"*

Soon he and Our Many were both above the nest, leaning over with a foodstuff so wondrous that Fly Home must have flown far to find it. Often our father returned with strange delectables from the human roost: meats made dark and rough by fire, sweetmeats wrapped in leaves, nuts and figs soaked in juice, and a thing called bread that my father liked to dip in fresh rainwater. He had a keen eye for all things human, and such offerings were his specialty.

"What?" I asked. *"What is it?"*

Our Many hushed me in discouraging whispers, as if Keeyaw were still near. But our father said, *"From the beastman. By the sea."*

"Keeyaw?" I asked.

"No," said our father. *"I don't like his nest."*

Our Mother of Many gave him a look as if to say—what? *"You spend all of your time watching him, and you forget to raid his food stores."*

There was something about Our Father's long, perching silences that made me and My Other strain our necks and blink out over the twigs of the nest with expectant wonder. Our father sat like a bird who had been long by the sea, who could swoop down and pluck things up from its briny depths. Not just clams and bright, juicy fish with wounded gills gasping on the sunlight. But utterly useless things. Shining metallic things. Like treasure. And nothing less.

"Me, Me, I Am," cried My Other. *"I Am."*

My hungry brother ate the most, yelled the most. He cried the most. He turned his baby's blood-red beak to the sky. My father loved that beak and dangled food just above it. *"Of course, my brave little flier, of course."* Fly Home laughed the deep, reedy laugh that was part of his song, and down came the food to My Other. Of course our father would prefer that beak; as it was the nourishing vessel to the promise of Pure Flight.

History speaks of the noteworthy flier, the Old Bone of Misfortune, who could fly in his sleep. He chased hawks and molested owls all through the deep of night, as if his flight were a manifestation of some strange, powerful dreaming. We're also told of the remarkable abilities of the great flier Hookbill the Haunted, who flew not only in her sleep but while clutching tightly to the tree below her. Her soul took leave of her body. Thus unsheathed, she bore witness to amazing landscapes and events that far transcended the boundaries of the horizon and returned with news of these. She became a living oracle of sorts, dazzling crows and inspiring them with hope and awe. There were times when I felt My Other had inklings of this. He could see things just before they happened, like the great ones, said our father. In the promise of My Other's wings was also the promise of the future, somehow, in my father's eyes.

· · ·

Just then the woods sounded.

It was Keeyaw.

But he made none of his mournful hammering noises and so appeared with the impact of insects or grazing deer. Above us, Fly Home and Our Many pretended to look elsewhere, though all of their attention fell on the strange underworld animal. They watched as if taking in breaths without exhaling. Neither spoke.

We saw the hapless beastman scuttle out from under the bushes, peering from behind his desperate mane of hairy brambles. He seemed anxious, as if he'd forgotten where he'd left the fallen tree. Once he was in the clearing, though, he settled down and pulled his mule out into the open. He called sharply back into the woods, and a small group of Keeyaw-like creatures came to join him, a few of them with the same wild growth around their faces, but dark, like a crow's. Others had smooth, serene, hairless faces, and with them came a mixed team of hoofed animals. Before long they had an encampment set up with tents and campfires and cooking pots and their animals tethered to the trees. One of the beastmen was slight and half grown, with no trace of a beard on his face, and he dawdled behind the others, lost in childish dreams, humming to himself and cradling a jawbone ax with the teeth of a dragon, or an ox, or some other monster, over his shoulders.

That was when I climbed out beyond the nest.

I picked my way up over the barbed scratchgrass and forbidding sticks and my toes hung up. In the open air, I felt acutely my impish nakedness and the whole world swam into being. Cloud, hill, nausea, carcass, bloody grin, gravity, constellations, illimitable depth. Out farther, I hung on to the spongy green cedar fronds and bobbed above the heights. Everything was much clearer, but that was fear. Then my mother's beak hurled me back into the nest, and I hadn't traveled nearly as far as I thought. Still, my new perch had a much better view than before.

"*Careful,*" our father said to me. "*Careful. Watch your perch. Watch yourself.*"

"Cursed," cried my mother. "*Just like his father. Left on his own, he'd do nothing but sit around and watch the ways of that thing human. Why? Why is our nest even here? So close to the road?*"

My father only folded his wings into place. "*The babes will be able to fly soon enough,*" he said.

"*They'll need more feathers than that.*"

My father only tugged at his own feathers. When he wasn't off watching Keeyaw, he liked to watch the human go back and forth along a pathway made hard and barren by constant use, one man alone, or a small band riding other beasts, or whipping them, or traveling in great growing armies. If it weren't for the traffic along the road, I don't know if we'd ever have seen our father. For long vigils, he would sit in his tree above the road, his bulky brow stern and preoccupied. Just then he reached out for the air in the direction of Keeyaw's tents, ready to fly.

"*What?*" said our mother. "*Again? If you keep watching, you'll just lead him here.*"

"*Lead him here? He doesn't notice a bird. It's as if the trees fall down on their own. If we could lead the Keeyaw here, then surely we could lead him away. No. He comes here following his own madness.*"

Then Fly Home leaned again as if to dive into the wind but turned back to the nest. He bent his head far down to feed me again. But this time no food came from his beak. His sharp one-eyed stare watched me and watched me from different angles, then stopped watching me altogether, all except for the pale patch of skin just below my eyes, the patch where the white pinfeather grew. His glare was so fierce, I felt ashamed and had to hide my head down in my usual crags and burrows. The white feather's appearance was like grief stuck to my parents, but especially my father, because he'd seen it before, on the skin of a sibling from his very own nest time, the one known as Hookbill the Haunted, whose tree had been struck by lightning and who had lost her eyesight. Then, half-dead and half-living, she'd returned from the Tree of the Dead, where she had gained the powers of divination and prophecy, and began uttering cryptic speeches because she lived now close to the God Crow, Who sometimes spoke through her in Its heady God Crow speech. How did I know of all this? My mother and father had discussed it all before, that time when my father ripped out the white pinfeather at its first appearance and the blood trickled down and dried on my face.

"Why?" my mother had cried. "Why?"

"So it will never grow back."

But when the washed-out color reemerged, I overheard my father mumbling something under his beak, about how maybe I was a mockingbird, or some other foreign egg placed in the nest when no one was looking.

This time he lunged at the feather in one swift bite and pulled back on my face until my bones made a snapping sound. Now he had three pale pinfeathers in his beak and spat the two smaller ones out. I nearly lunged from the tree, hoping to catch a glimpse of one, having never before seen them or their color, stuck as they were just below my eye. I saw one, perhaps, a mere spindly blade of fluff. It dove as if injured, not quite a feather and not exactly white either, but a pale gray or absence of any color whatsoever and so an absence of Crowness and a portal to some strange otherness that would put the fear in my father and burden him.

"These are far too early," he said with his horn clenched, "for normal feathers. They're definitely not baby's down."

"I thought you were going off to watch the Keeyaws," my mother said.

"I was. But now I'm taking this confounded feather to the Old Bone."

"He is like you," said Our Many, "or how you should be, maimed by the beastman, always off watching him. What will that prove?"

"He is the only other bird around with the paleness. He'll know. He'll know what our wintry son is all about."

"I don't care who knows. Surely you can see with your own eyes. Why don't you help me find out what's happening to the woods? Find out where Keeyaw has and has not been. For when the babes are strong enough, we'll fly to safer woods."

"The Old Bone will know about that, too. Fear not."

The wind took his call and brought it back a second time, as Fly Home opened his broad, serrated wings until they covered all of our opening to the sky in black, and the sun shone through in iridescent greens and purples as they ripped through the air and were gone, throwing a sharp blast of air down over us.

"Fear not."

*Cooperative breeding behavior is rare in
birds. . . . I have seen five adult crows at a
single nest at once, all with their heads in the
nest feeding young.*

—KEVIN J. McGOWAN,
"FAMILY LIVES OF THE
UNCOMMON AMERICAN CROW"

5. *The Most Delectable*

From the sky came all changes: sea-salt winds, clouds in the shape of fishes, hailstones, thunder, tree-drenched water, and hard winds that drove misfortune in the face of hope. It wasn't unusual to have Fly Home gone all afternoon. But I had the unnerving feeling he'd be gone all night, and he'd taken the warmth of the sky with him.

Now the changes came from the deepest underworld.

Under a gathering thunderstorm, Keeyaw unhooked his huge, sullen land animals from their traces and gave up on trying to move the fallen Giant for the day. It had taken them all afternoon, and after much nervous yelling and flapping around, they'd managed to move the shorn tree trunk just a single length of itself in the direction of the highway. When the thunder rolled through the woods, it chased Keeyaw and his flock into their tent. I'd heard that there were fire breathers in there, which seemed true, as the smoke poured out of a flap on the roof and seeped through the seams. The sky was angry at only them, because they left their beasts outside, tied up, their backs to the storm and their ears flicking in the gray sheets of rain. Here and there the animals kept their unsurprised mouths busy on the wet leaves and grasses.

The sky flashed.

Thunder split the sky.

Perched far above us, encircling the nest, loomed a dark theater of crow faces, a council of gods staring down at our cold, water-wrinkled skin. These were the brothers and sisters from previous nest times, who numbered three, and who helped my mother and father in keeping the nest, since they weren't old enough to begin nests of their own.

"*Eeeeiiwaahh!*" The one known as Squall cried out in fear of the sky.

"*Don't crack an egg,*" cried Night Time.

"*Bring on his own heart attack's more like it,*" said Plum Black.

It was common knowledge that upon hearing thunder for the first time, some fresh fledges drop from the tree like wet, heavy fruit, then rot in the mud like fruit, too.

"*Let your heart attack this,*" said Squall.

And he pecked at Plum Black's shins.

When the thunder exploded again, Night Time made one of his wicked, uncanny mockeries and Squall stuck his beak down into his coat, wishing to fly off and hide.

"*Hush.*" Our Many cast a suspicious eye down at the hide tent of the Keeyaws, still full of humans, though the rains were letting up.

"*None of you brought any food?*"

"*I did,*" said Night Time.

"*. . . and . . . ?*"

"*It was delicious.*"

Night Time twisted his arrogant beak until it was right down over my face, and I thought I was going to receive a wondrous late-day offering, when he said, "*Hmmm . . . his affliction seems to have—cleared up—a bit.*"

"*Your father pruned him.*"

"*I suppose he's at all ends of the wind,*" said Night Time, "*where the Old Bone lives.*"

"*I've flown with the Old Bone,*" said Plum Black. "*I've seen him, and ridden with him, in the sky.*"

". . . and . . . ?" Night Time didn't hesitate to mimic even Our Mother of Many.

"*I can fly him to the ground,*" said Plum Black.

"*It's not how fast,*" said Night Time. "*But for how long? And how far? And from where? It's the intangibles.*"

"*Back when I was a fledge,*" said Our Many, "*the Old Bone was already old, and known as such.*"

All of my family turned their beaks to my face, and their eyes blinked and wondered.

Like the portent it might possibly be, the quills and absence of quills burned there.

Where they'd been plucked.

Below my eye.

Morning came slowly.

Constantly I listened for my father's return through the vaporous woods. Instead, I heard only the elder siblings call out and tried to guess how far. With time I could sense their wingbeats in their caws, and the ravines and open meadows had their resonant effect on their songs. As they moved in and out of earshot, I got a sense of our songscape and its traditional winds, long before I could venture out into it by my own wing power. Still, I heard nothing of Fly Home. Not even his far cry. Not even the dull echo of Keeyaw's yelling could summon him.

With the beastmen below, pestering the fallen Giant to move, no one returned that morning with happy amounts of half-chewed creature: no pieces of caddis fly. No carrion beetle. No grasshopper. No grub dug up from the underworld. No seed from the farmer. No nut. No berry. No juicy eider egg, or gull egg, or nestling.

Nothing. Not a drop.

It was as if we were still under a heavy rain, even though the morning sunlight warmed us and a steam rose up from the leaves and glistening tangle of branches. All around us the steam hung in the air. It seeped from the bark of the trees like a hunger.

Soon the Giant lay fully in the road, where the wooden carts waited, and Keeyaw stood high up on the trunk, one hand holding on to his whip-switch and the other on to an untrimmed branch, and he rode his land barge far into his squinty-eyed purpose. The only thing about him moving—unless you counted the occasional lurch of the Giant—was his weedy, sea-gray beard, blown stubbornly over his distant, scowling face.

"*Where will they take the Giant?*" I asked.

But Our Many acted as if Keeyaw no longer existed.

"*Where?*" I said. "*Where will they go?*"

"*Away,*" she said. "*Away!*" she yelled down at the beasts. "*Away!*"

Usually Fly Home announced himself from far off. But I heard only the click of his sharp hooks on the nest and looked up. High above stood the old bird, somber and remote, and his feathers gave a rustling sigh as they settled into place. The elder siblings all gathered around, but not too near, so they could caw out their questions and be ready to duck away in fear of the answer.

"*What?*"

"*What?*"

"*What of the pale feather?*"

"*What is the news?*"

They flapped and pecked at the air, and I wanted to crawl under Fly Home's wings and have him fly off because I wanted to be free of everyone's ill-feathered commotion. Our Mother of Many sidled up beside him and arranged his nape.

"*So, what took you?*"

"*What took me? How long will we have to endure him dragging our friends away? What took me?*" He kissed Our Many. "*Open up,*" he said, "*and I will show you.*"

Turning his beak sideways, he shook a sweet morsel of offering down into her throat. Whatever he fed her must have been the most scrumptious delectable yet, because he lowered his great curved horn to My Other, and my brother's eyes closed and his skin nearly changed color as if he were heating up.

"The news," said my father, taking note of the barking and yanking of Keeyaw at his animals, "is the army of beastmen traveling here along the road."

"Keeyaw?" she said. "Soon he will be gone."

"No. More are coming. More than Keeyaw, and less than him. These are the kind who do not fell trees, but who fell each other, in numbers too great to count, let alone chew into pieces and hide in the trees."

Squawks of giddy excitement came from my siblings as they shook their wings.

"So——" said Our Many. "What did become of the white feather?"

"I spat out. I had to. In order to bring back enough for an offering."

"And what of the Old Bone? What did he make of the paleness?"

My father mumbled something under his beak.

"You mean you were gone all this time and you never saw the Old One?"

"You know how it is. You can't just find the Old Bone; he finds you. It's like going out looking for the wind."

As Fly Home went on, his voice sailed far off into his resolve, far beyond the drudgery of Keeyaw.

"Last night, in the land beyond trees, I saw the great human masses and kept watch as they slept under the skin of dead animals. Today I followed them until I was sure they would pass by our aerie. It won't be long now. Soon the hills will shake."

The noise, the rumbling, it grew and grew and was still nowhere near. I thought it must be Keeyaw. But when I looked, it wasn't the one ruthless Keeyaw at all but a long procession of his kind, all beastmen, pure and simple. Instead of casting fear and worry, these humans caused a thrill, except to Keeyaw. Hearing the procession, he and his small clan fled into the woods, taking all their possessions, utensils, tents, tools, beasts, fire, any trace of themselves, except the felled Giant, which now lay stripped and up on carts in the middle of the pathway. They moved quickly, losing themselves in the brush.

"You see!" cawed my older brother Night Time. *"Where is the Tree Eater now?"* He mocked the hammering of Keeyaw. *"The many scare the one away."*

My older siblings flapped to the different trees above the road, calling back to the beast with names strange and wonderful to hear. While my father barely stirred, his deep-set features seeing all, telling none.

"Camels!"

"Oxen!"

"Elephants!"

"Armies!" my elders yelled over and over again.

"Armies of the beastmen!"

"When?"

"Where?"

"Soon!"

"I'm starved!"

Finally I could no longer stand it. I put myself in peril and climbed up out of the nest.

The beastman Keeyaw was a large behemoth of a thousand heads, all of them staying on the road, each staring at the one before it, mouth open, eyes vacant, feet trudging forward, animated by logic or some other force further hidden and dull. Some liked to just sit above a beast that did all the moving for them. One straddled an elephant laced with tassels and bells. But all the creatures, no matter how big or small, moved under the same dreary will. I could see now why my father liked to watch them so much; they were completely baffling to a bird.

When they came to the shorn tree trunk, they sent a search party into the woods after Keeyaw. They also tied a long train of their own animals to the sleeping Giant, and hauled it away.

Carts and all.

No more Giant.

The herd of a thousand heads glittered and clanked as it moved, and the trees still standing quaked in fear. With its many arms, it carried naked branches with sharpened points. It beat drums and cried out hoarsely and whipped itself. It seemed like an unbearable burden to move so slowly, unable to take leave of the earth and fly, vanquished to grovel, not only in the underworld but along that one deadened path. It took the herd of a thousand heads all morning to pass.

The wait, however, had its rewards. I learned that not all humans fell trees, and that the beast humans' army overflowed with the rich wounds of kindness. Less than a day's flight ahead was another such beast of a thousand heads, waiting for the time of the Great Offering, when the ground would swell with their numbers. For three days we feasted on nothing but the flesh of this tasty creature—eye tissue and innards and all sorts of tender delectables. And for days after that, strips of its fat and gristle hung in the woods all around us, hidden there to be eaten later.

One for sorrow.

Two for mirth.

Three for a wedding.

Four for a birth.

Five for rich.

Six for poor.

Seven for a witch—

I can tell you no more.

—English Counting Rhyme

of the Magpie.

6. Mark of the Blade

Keeyaw returned.

My Other and I watched the lowly beastman emerge from below the bushes. He wandered out slowly into the clearing, edging his mule along, as if something might rattle them both. When nothing happened, he began barking his commands back into the woods. This time only the boy came out, the youngest of his clan, humming as he pulled on a rope, followed by a tawny old ram. One of the ram's horns was broken, and the nap of its fur was scraggy and worn.

Keeyaw held the boy's hand, and the water of the mammal leaked freely down the boy's face. Keeyaw kissed the tears away, and made the boy stand near as Keeyaw dug a hole into the flank of the ram, stuck both of his hands into the bloody opening, and began pulling things out. Keeyaw acted as if he was showing the boy how to do it. He made the boy hold on to a long glob of gut, and the mass of it shivered as blood ran down the boy's arms.

Then Keeyaw held out a bowl for the boy, where they placed the viscera along with some fat, and set it all down beside a dried pile of sticks, arranged like a large nest across the ground. Keeyaw then took two stones from his mule pack and scared the fire out of them by striking them together. As the fire took hold, he bled the ram and collected the blood in the same bowl. Then Keeyaw poured the contents of his bowl onto the fire. The smoke twisted, dirty and black. Above the flames, he waved smoking stocks of frankincense and myrrh, then dropped them onto the fire and uttered strange sounds.

Still, the wild, white-haired beast could not leave the woods alone. He hacked away at the vegetation on the forest floor until he stood just below our very own tree and made low, exhaling grunts of approval. He yanked his mule over by the reins, withdrew one of his implements from the mule pack, and dug into the bark. He did the same to a neighboring tree. I didn't see it; I heard it, the nervous scraping away at the bark above the root.

"What?" I asked. *"What was that?"*

Keeyaw spoke again to the trees.

He even started to look like a tree.

Suddenly I could understand the mammal's moans and grunts and strange staccato sounds, though the meanings were mired in his mysterious ways. The thing about his language that I understood most was his insatiable sorrow, distorted and grotesque. He held his thin tree-branch arms out until they trembled, and he addressed the trees with the following words— perhaps he addressed the Tree of the Many Names—he called it "Amen," then "Yahweh," and "Neter"; he called it "Jehovah" and "Amon Rah." And he addressed the Tree in the following manner: "Deliver these, the last of the timbers suitable for a keel, to the long water house, and not again to the Sons of God and the Daughters of Men. Or is it Your plan that the Nephalem should sail away, and not us? Either way, I don't care. I don't care whom You choose. I'll just keep trying. What else can I do?"

Then, wearily, Keeyaw picked up what was left of the ram and tied the ancient carcass to his mule, and he and his son left our aerie, searching the woods and sky.

Raven and some crows go picking berries.
Raven eats the berries. He lies and tells the
crows that it was a band of raiders that took
them. He even plucks out his own feathers
and tries to make them look like the raiders'
canoes. The berry juice, he says, is blood
from the struggle.

—*Raven Gets Caught in a Lie,* LOWER
COAST SALISH OF VANCOUVER ISLAND

7. Into the Unseen

Gray morning, ashen fog.

In a whoosh of wingbeats came our father. Perhaps this time he'd made his pilgrimage to the Old Bone, because the news had deformed him. His beak seemed larger from having to deliver the horrid word, and the burden of knowing had turned him into a confused, lanky monster, shining like one of our family, only so many times larger, with wings as wide as the trees. One wing spanned our entire nest, and he hurled past us without landing. But the *whump* of his wings told us he'd stopped somewhere in our tree.

We could sense him in the branches above, waiting.

My Other cried out.

Then our father blew past us again, tumbling through the fog. He turned and lunged onto the nest. The news had completely outweighed his ability to land, and he warped the bowl-like shape of our nest, and Our Many wouldn't be happy about that.

My Other and I both looked up at the long, curving mandible that I hoped would give us food and not the horrid word. But then I realized that this was *not* our father. Perhaps it was the Old Bone of the Holy Realm here to pass judgment. The fear of my Misfortune burned hot across my face, and the great black bird gave me his one-eyed stare of mirth and scrutiny. The eyes that peered through his ragged mask were predators. He gulped and his beard rippled—an awful, hoary rippling of feathers with each gulp. Then his beak parted and he gripped my whole head in the vice of his horns. He bit down hard, with a force I'd known only from the time my father had plucked me. Was he plucking? Or feeding? It seemed he was tasting me, then spitting me out, and I felt the pang of rejection all over again.

"*Sorry,*" he said. "*You'll need plucking.*"

He spoke strangely, with a huge, slobbering accent. Still, the sage old bird beamed with pleasure. And I shrank into the nest, searching upward for a sign.

"*Me? Me? I Am.*" My Other stood himself up and opened his throat out wide.

"*Oh! You'll do.*"

The monster's beak opened, and down came his curved, obscene horn. With a sickening, slithering sound, the beak pierced right through My Other. Then the raven snatched My Other up with that eerie opening and flew off with him, leaving behind blood-stained twigs and feathers. I remember the heavy swooshing sound of the wings, *vwhump, vwhump, vwhump,* as he fled.

"*Fear not,*" My Other called out, clenched in the very horn of his death. "*I'll always watch over you.*"

I thought that those were his last words, but as the monster's beak cracked down on his tiny wing bones, my brave brother cried out to be fed, even as he was carried off to be eaten.

"*RAVEN!*" came the calls from my family.

"*RAVEN!*" hollered my father, who tore in from nowhere and speared the monster and kept after him. A whirl of black feathers erupted in the air, and as My Other was carried off in a tangle of wingbeats and cries, all that remained were a few feathers of the murderer, floating down in the fog.

Long after My Other was gone, my family shrieked and called and clapped their wings, going nowhere.

"Raven!" cawed my siblings, in calls that trailed off into disbelief.

"I Am," they cawed, in the same way My Other had cried it, but with a longing and loss that happens when a bird goes to the realm of song.

Our father came in from his futile chase and opened his maw in a rage, but no sound came out. He cleaned the slime of the raven feathers off his beak, scraping either side of it against the bark. He moved to call again, heaving and furious, but no sound came out. Then he flew next to our mother and tried to calm her, craning his head sideways and crouching low.

"I Am!" she cried and flew in a circle around the tree.

She landed above the nest and cried, *"I Am!"* gaping down, looking through me and into the soiled part of our nest. She took up a stone of old excrement and threw it in a hard, heavy chunk down her throat. She circled our tree and landed above me. *"I Am,"* she cried and flew around the tree. She kept circling and landing like that, groping through the fog.

The soul of Aristaeus, also, was seen at Proconnesus flying out of his mouth in the form of a raven; this subsequently gave rise to the invention of many stories.

—PLINY THE ELDER

8. Burnt Offerings

"Surely you are my last lovely simp, for I will not live to have another."

And though Our Many flew far into the tree of her sorrow, she never neglected her feedings or duties to me. When it grew hot, she'd fly back from the cold stream, moving her feathers as little as possible so that the water might drip from her wings and cool me. When the nights grew cold, she would ruffle her belly feathers down over me as if I were a clutch of unborn eggs, even though I was far too old for it, but since I was alone, it was tolerable, smothered up against the walls of the nest. While my own coat of feathers spread out dark and thick, hers grew prickly and slate-gray underneath and lost their luster in the hot summer noon.

"Oh my last, sweet last, hatched next to the Promise," and from her horn came sounds that made me doubt the very world around me and believe only in the pale shroud of her song floating between me and the woods, while I sensed My Other come back and sit in the nest beside me and cry out. Her fading loves, drifting in and out of her last season, were sung for my ears and mine alone, one nestled beneath the stray, washed-out emanation growing beneath my eye.

It rained without end.

The water came down in such thick sheets that my mother sat there bathing in sorrow. After the loss of My Other, she had many strange, bewildering episodes and I thought that this overwhelming water from the sky was one of them. She watched distantly as my siblings shook and flapped over the nest, shrieking as if that might empty it of water.

My father spoke. *"Oh, hapless bit of birdlife."*

I knew he wished I was My Other, so there still could be the promise of Pure Flight. Fly Home's feathers were slick and no longer repelled the rain. He nudged Our Many to save me from the water pooling up in the nest, but she only shivered, staring into the onslaught. Their feathers were so water-logged, their pale skin showed through, and it sickened me to see how much our skin was like the human's. Soon I had to strain my neck, unable to call or else have the foamy water rush down my throat. The water weighed me down and kept me from climbing up on the nest top.

That was when the terrible *whack* of Keeyaw's implement shook the base of Our Giant and moved through the branches. The pool of water in the nest shivered with each blow.

Our Many stuck her head beneath the fowl soup and dislodged some of the twigs and began throwing them over the edge. As the rainwater drained, she spoke. She put her beak right against mine and said these words: *"Now. It's time. I know it doesn't seem like it. But you've been able to fly for a while now. You're just shy of the wind. Don't worry. I'll stay over you until your feathers are dry. But be quiet when you're down there. Nothing. Not a sound."*

"After I jump?" I felt just like the worm, no feathers, no wings, no eyes, no feature anywhere except the twisting of my guts through the middle. *"What? What do I do then?"*

My mother leaned back so she could take me in with both of her eyes, blinking with her alert, cloud-yellow love. She slid her beak through my feathers and gave me one last kiss.

"Why—you'll be able to fly," she said. *"You'll follow us, through the sky. It's what you were born for."*

. . .

So I climbed my way out into the storm.

The rain seemed thicker but somehow warmer out here. I edged my way out along the branch that shook from the grim attacks of Keeyaw, and soon my family called from their different trees.

"Fly!" they called, and it caused a break in the rhythm of Keeyaw's implement. When I reached the edge of the heavy, sagging leaves, where it would be easier to jump, Keeyaw stopped, and through the spongy fronds, I saw him. He stood there staring at me in silence. My family stopped making their racket, too.

All that could be heard was the rain falling on itself.

In the dull calm, I spread my wings and flapped but still held on to my perch. The branch dipped menacingly.

Keeyaw was still looking up at me when he took his tool and slammed it once against the base of our tree, not in his usually pounding fashion but in anger, with just one arm. Then he threw his maul spinning through the woods. As if he'd suddenly proved something, he stood again in silence, staring at the woods all around him. Then he started to whack at the bushes in the vicinity of his tool. But the going was hard for such a lowly, groveling creature, and he stumbled. Falling made him angrier, and he complained, standing up against the rain. He stood stoop-shouldered and emaciated, with his clothes stuck to his bones and his beard plastered down to a thin rope hanging from his face. Waterlogged as he was, he reminded me of a tree with that likeness that always evoked such a strange pity, and I climbed even farther out onto the branch for a better view.

Giving up on his tool, he thrashed his way back through the bushes. From his mule pack, he pulled out dry grasses, kindling, and wood and placed all of it beneath a thick overhang of branches. He arranged his kindling as best he could and struck two stones together to release the sparks and smoke that hid within the rocks. But he couldn't summon his fire. Keeyaw blew over the strange source of smoke. Even his breath couldn't summon the fire, and the air was thick with the dampened smoke. The smoldering hung in the air all around him, staying below the overhang of branches like the anger of his predicament.

From his mule's pouch, Keeyaw pulled out a bright orange sucker fish with one whisker on either side of its face, giving it the appearance of wisdom, even though rigor mortis had set in. He hung the fish by twine from a low branch above him. He pulled out a chicken with its orange feathers still dry, and the chicken tried to fly out of Keeyaw's arms. Why did it even bother? Could I fly? If our tree fell? Keeyaw stuck its throat with a blunt knife, and feathers stuck to the blade as he pulled it out. Rather than cutting the bird, the knife bludgeoned it and the bird's head hung, barely attached. Then, out of the mule's pouch, Keeyaw pulled a large white goose with an orange beak, and he stabbed it, there in the crook of his arm. Even though his dull knife penetrated the breast feathers and wishbone and lodged in the heart, the goose managed to bite Keeyaw's nose. It honked and flapped and walked about Keeyaw's feet with the knife protruding from its bloody white breast before it collapsed, its webbed feet paddling the sodden forest floor.

Keeyaw muttered to himself.

Then he hung the creatures one by one—the fish, the bird, and the other bird—from a strand of twine attached to the branch above him. His smoking heap was already too soaked to catch flame. But he cupped his hands over his mouth and blew into the smoldering. He searched but could find nothing more in his mule's pack to add to this strange arrangement.

Then God appeared.

At the time I didn't know It was God. I lacked the experience or knowledge needed to understand my wonder. It flew in so silently, no one saw It or where It had come from except me. Like all crows, It could fly in between the branches and land just above the human without his knowing. While giving all of Its attention to Keeyaw, the mighty God Crow craned Its magnificent head to the side and studied the branch just above It. It scraped and sharpened Its bill, both sides, on the branch It clung to.

Keeyaw looked wearily at the three creatures turning from the twine above the smoke. He moaned.

"You can hardly call it a burnt offering if it won't burn."

With the God Crow above him, Keeyaw's words came to me as clearly as my own. Still, he seemed unaware of God and complained to the trees, to the dampness, to the three sorry creatures that turned in the air above the hissing hovel of smoke all around.

"I know these are not much, as far as offerings go," he said. "I know you prefer the creature with hooves, the creature with hooves and horns. But I wasn't planning on the flood starting so soon. This is the best I can do, on such short notice."

With his dull knife, Keeyaw sawed away at the string above the carp, and with a thud, the fish disappeared into the damp cushion of smoke. The God Crow turned Its back completely on Keeyaw, then stretched a wing to the side and scratched Itself with Its claws. But It was intently fixed on Keeyaw. This was the way not only of God but of all crows. You can watch creatures better if they think they're not being watched. So God turned Its back.

"There," said Keeyaw. "Happy now?"

Then Keeyaw stood, arms open, as skinny as a tool handle, his wet robes matted to his bones like his hair and his beard, and the blood of the birds still awash on his clothes. Keeyaw's own blood shone brightly from the wound on his nose where the goose had bitten him. The wash of blood ran down him like the rain.

"What else can I do?" said Keeyaw. "You're flooding the world before the ark is finished. It can't even float. I never asked to save anything in the first place." And Keeyaw collapsed in a gray puddle on the forest floor and sat, rubbing the heel of his palms hard against his eyes. "After all, it was *You* who asked me. What did You expect? Am I more worthy? Is it too late to pick someone else? Or maybe a few others, nearly as worthy, to help out?"

Keeyaw trod off again, hacking away at the bushes in search of his maul.

"And those strange black birds," he said. "Why do they mock me?"

But before he could find his tool, the rain evaporated. The great God Crow arose in the humid mist and left without notice from anyone, man or bird, except me, to whom It cawed out in a loud, ornery voice, *"You! You!"*

I shat my guts. Its dark wingspan grew ominous, and I thought this would be the end of me, that I'd be plucked away to the other realm along with My Other.

"Yes, you!" said the God Crow.

"Me?" I moved quickly along the branch to get back down into the filthy mulch of my own beginnings.

And It flew over me and beyond, just as silently as when It had appeared.

"Be ready when I call," It said, and was gone.

They may share the "cognitive capacities"
of many primates. . . . To date, all the
experimental results point in the same
direction—in various trials, corvids [the
crow family] have scored better than
chickens, quail, pigeons, rabbits, cats,
elephants, gibbons and rhesus monkeys.

—CANDACE SAVAGE, *Bird Brains: The*
Intelligence of Crows, Ravens,
Magpies, and Jays

9. *Wind of the Long Journeys*

God the Crow spoke to me, and no other bird seemed to know or care. Maybe Its Mightiness kept in constant contact with everyone in the same way that the wind washed over the woods and moved the trees. The morning's wind came in pure and steady and made the trees want to fly. They flapped their branches as best they could, wishing they were crows. And I had to *be ready,* as the God Crow had decreed. Everyone has a patron wind that guides his wings. I needed one to fly and forget, to go to a land beyond Keeyaw, where I was no longer the Misfortune, where no one would know my face.

But in the plentiful winds, everyone forgot about me anyway.

Alone in the nest, I had too much room to hop around and scratch the tufts of sooty feathers that grew from my skin. I'd reach my claw toes over my head. I'd stand up straight and stretch my legs, pulling them to make them longer and working my wings, flapping and flapping so that the great beyond might take me to its promise. But just at the moment of release, I had the same anxiety I had when I looked out over the edge of the nest and saw nothing but the air and the leaves below, all turning and swaying above the endless underworld. It was a great fear in me. It was glandular, ancestral. It grew up from my skin like my new charcoal coat. All I could do was to grab hold of a branch, hold my wings out, and wag them slowly.

Over and over again, between feedings, at night, awake or asleep, I had the same dream.

I'd leap from our tree and keep rising until the world dropped out from beneath me. In the sky there was no forest and no valley and no human city burning on the horizon. I'd be lost in the clouds without perch and keep going. That, or I would fall and my legs would weigh me down like the bough of a tree and pull me under and smash my hollow bones across the face of the underworld.

My nightmare was upon me one day when the wind blew in brilliant and clear and pushed the clouds from the sky. The sunlight swarmed all around me in and out of the nest. Trees rocked on their stems and creaked until they loosened. This wasn't one wind but a treacherous force of many hidden currents and names. Under the conflicting furies, the world was coming apart. All except my family who rode the invisible waves as I'd never seen them before.

My elder siblings dropped from the sky, and the wind tore them from view. Their feathers splayed like wild leaves. Seagulls soared in outrageous circles; starlings shot past in agitation as if the wind might scatter their flock. Farther off, my mother and father looped around each other, rising until they disappeared like ashes into the sun. Surely this was a favorable wind of pure sources.

Keeyaw was able to negotiate these superior currents and make his way to Our Tree. But the dreadful blows against Our Giant had no force.

The wind took the grim *keeeyaaack* and sent it awash. He flailed as if he were underwater, swinging his implement through an unction heavier than air. And my family shot past. *"Fly,"* they cried, and were gone, behind the bending trees.

"Fly!"

I looked down from the heaving nest. The scrub and grasses all trembled, pointing in the same direction from fear. I stretched my legs out again, elongating the bones so I could see out over the edge, and the instant I lifted my wings, the wind ripped me away.

Before I even knew it, I was gone.

Was I flying?

Falling?

I rose and fell at the same time. I tumbled. My wings worked too fast for what little they did. I smacked up against other trees and branches and whacked into a tangle of twigs, where I tightened my talons and tore at the cones and needles, breaking the twigs free. But I managed to hang upside down, sideways, right-side up, until I edged my way to a thicker part of the branch and cried out. The wind engulfed my cries in the oblivion of its sad siren.

The elder siblings, when I saw them, kept playing in the violent currents. They were joined by strangers and dove in groups, in pairs, in singles. Crows swarmed in ragged formation, more crows than I'd ever seen, diving, rolling, lifting into the caterwaul. Some of the strangers' caws I'd heard before. Some were entirely strange to me.

Seeing my brothers or sisters, I called back. But to no avail. Like shooting stars, the minute I saw them, they were gone.

And though I heard him through the trees, Keeyaw seemed much smaller now, his threat like the trailing off of the wind.

I called and called.

But the wind ate my caws.

"Where?" Our Many called back. *"You are, aren't you?"*

"I am!"

"You are!"

Like a black fireball, the welcome Mother of Many lit beside me, her feathers rattling. She clipped at my eyebrows and neck. *"You are, of course. You flew, didn't you?"*

"I did?"

"Such a strong flier," she said, covering me with crow kisses and the exaggerations of a mother. *"In such a strong wind, the Wind of Long Journeys. So——"* she took me in with a proud, wide-blinking love, *"that must be your wind."*

"I'm hungry," I cried, and she bit me hard near my eye.

"Not so loud. You're not in the nest anymore. And you can't fly——not well enough. So you must be silent. You must. Wait here. Not a sound."

But where could I go? I could barely hang on. And she flew to a split in our tree, where she withdrew a long and drooping head with a spine attached. *"Here. In celebration,"* she said. *"Your first meal as a crow."* I pecked at the catfish brains, all mealy-good with rot. She watched me with pure love, following every movement of my clippers. *"I thought I was going to have to coax you up from the underworld, which would have been hard to do today in this wind, your wind. Look how far you flew. But listen,"* she said. *"There is the hawk. If you cry out, he'll pluck your feathers and you'll watch as he eats your throat."*

"The hawk?"

"And the owl."

"The owl?"

"At night you must be absolutely still. And quiet."

She gave me the last bit of catfish. Even bone——hard nubs from the prickly spine.

"Owl?" I said.

"Listen. Do you remember the raven?"

I nearly coughed up the sharp, scraping bone.

"These are just as bad. No, worse. They're waiting for the time you're like this."

Just a few trees away, I could still see Keeyaw, but his anger looked foreign to me, foreign and mute, just as it had sounded when I'd first come from the egg.

10. Lone Crow

In clearer weather I was still stranded, but managed to make a safe and comfortable home out of the tree where the wind had taken me. For rest I found a cleft between two branches, despite the tree rodent's disapproval. Up here I could hop up the ladder of perches and finally see the world. I saw the sky where the trees leaned and where the clouds wondered. I saw where the river slid to every day in a lazy way that said, Come follow. And up here branches always wavered, bristling with danger. Songbirds never stopped prattling in their sweet, mindless anxiety, and large birds saw too much.

Up here I actually liked to watch Keeyaw fell trees. So did other crows— strange, meandering onlookers from foreign woods, here to take note of the changing geography of the trees. A loose, shifting daytime roost had gathered just beyond Keeyaw's attack on the Giants. Then, right beside me, a stealthy presence made the branch dip.

At first it pleased me because I thought one of my siblings had come with food. But the more I looked, the more worried I became. I knew it wasn't a raven, being too small and nasty and full of ragged feathers. Its dull, matted coat lacked the luster of my family's, and there was a sleepy, greedy, half-opened look to the eyes. When the strange crow who'd been swinging his head in all directions finally looked at me, I had the sinking feeling it wanted to eat me.

"Hungry, are you, I Am?" He cawed my name with mocking derision.

"How do you know my name?"

The strange bird gave no answer but bobbed and shrugged nervously.

I said, *"Keep to yourself. Unless you're the Old Bone. Then I have business with you, for I Am the Misfortune."*

"Oh. I see. I thought it took seasons beyond counting for the Misfortune to appear." The bird laughed to himself, or coughed, or gurgled, I couldn't tell. *"Great dangers, feats of daring. A little egg like you?"* The bird's laugh was a strange, derelict wheeze that seemed idle and corrupt. If this bird couldn't learn the sounds of a crow, then how could it ever imitate nature? *"But, your worship-fulness, your eyes are still blue. You can't even fly——"* the bird leered wickedly, *"——or so it seems. And that wispy bit of fuzz on your face——"*

"How do you know all of this?" I asked. *"Are you the Old Bone?"*

"Me? Oh, no, not me."

The strange bird bobbed and pecked at the bark for no reason. It cringed. It pecked its own claws. Its eyes spun, then crossed. It shivered, startled by nothing.

"Then watch how you treat me," I said. *"For I bring bad tidings."*

"You're better off watching yourself. A Misfortune only brings bad tidings upon itself."

"Why should I believe you? Do you know of the Old Bone?"

"Keeyaw! Keeyaw!" the strange bird called out, as if his wits had flown off. *"Keeyaw is the one to watch out for. A bird's curse is nothing next to his."*

I perched there silently, listening to the far-off chopping of Keeyaw, hoping the bird would leave me, or at least be silent, too.

"Of course. Every crow knows of the Old Bone," he said. *"But few know him."*

"Have you seen him?"

"All birds see the Old One, flapping around, flap, flap. But few see him."

Just then Plum Black sounded distantly in the woods.

"Aawwwk." The strange crow tried to sing like my family, but from him, it

was disgusting and embarrassed me. I'd heard the mockery before while I was in the nest and always wondered where it came from. Maybe the bad part of a dream.

Then Fly Home's rage warp sounded from the trees.

And the Lone Crow took off when my father shot past in a wheeling attack and followed him through the branches.

Directly afterward, my sister Plum Black lit beside me. *"You didn't eat anything from him, did you?"*

"No."

"He wanted to feed you. He watches where we hide food and steals it."

"If he steals, why would he give it back?"

"He wants to be like your Plum Black and live in Our Mother of Many's song."

"Why?"

"He is lost, a Lone Crow, without family or song."

"How could he ever join our family, born from another nest?"

"I am from another nest."

"And from another song?"

"Yes. But I learned your mother's song well enough that hers became my own. And in her old motherhood, she thought I was one of hers. First setting eyes on me, she called me Plum Black, and I've been Plum Black ever since. When it came time to feed you, your father did not chase me off either. But I grow too old to feed another's. Soon I will be chased off. I will become the Lone Crow."

"How will it end?"

"With the season of my own nest, I hope."

"I will come to feed your nestlings," I said.

"You say that now."

And Plum Black, the Beauty of our aerie, lifted easily into the air.

"C'mon," she said. *"Hurry. The winds won't wait."*

She flew off.

In the distance, my father continued his complaint, warning all Lone Crows and those of other songs to be wary.

*crow's nest: 1. A small lookout platform with
a high protective railing and wind screen,
located near the top of a ship's mast. 2. Any
similar lookout platform located ashore.*
—The American Heritage Dictio-
nary of the English Language.

11. Tree

Our Giant was about to fall.

Keeyaw had that nervous excitement about him in the way he drove him-self at Our Giant's pulpy wound. It was there in the sound of his chopping. He'd spend all of his time there, until the end.

Night Time and Plum Black made giddy, savage dives at Keeyaw. They perched on the branch just above him, where they hacked away at the bark and sent tree dust and chips falling down on his mane. But Keeyaw kept swinging. His brainless attack on the tree weakened the spell of Our Many's troubled song, so when she came to the part about My Other, the Promise of Pure Flight, *who could see things just before they happened,* he did not return. No bird dared light on our tree, and when Our Mother of Many sang out my name, I grew fierce and hissed at the strange beast below. But did he hear it?

It could have been his own head he sent against the trunk. He was far too lost in his manic need to fell things and haul them off to oblivion—lost, but still too great a force. I've seen the awe before in my father, how he can wait out a long storm and how his drenched feathers stick to their pins, showing the bluish-white color of his skin—skin under our own feathers just as ugly and strange to me as the face of that—no, there was nothing in that beast of the underworld anything like a bird. My father lit near and watched with his calm, fatalistic detachment.

Night Time wheeled above Keeyaw and let loose a long stream of excreta that landed across that man's lifeless, colorless beard. But did Keeyaw see it? Or slow from his tireless pace? He cackled to himself and wheezed in anticipation. He took pulpy hardwood wedges and sent them deep into the incision he cut. He swung the frayed, pulverized head of his maul with all his clumsy might, and our tree quaked like bubbling doom.

Then Our Giant began to creak.

It whined like a wolf puppy.

The whole world began to tilt.

Keeyaw scampered off into the bushes. He had a clumsy gait, with his head hunkered down, as if Our Giant were headed right for him, and he hid behind other trees. All of us watched as my father watched, with rapt attention at Our Own Giant's doom. Just then, when I thought it was going to fall, like water slipping through my ribs, like my worst dreams when my wings won't work, it stopped.

I was waiting for the tremendous noises, the groundswell of thunder, the rumble, the aftershock, the echo from the hills.

But they never came.

Our tree leaned over now, slightly, hung up by the shoulders on another tree almost as large.

Everyone in my family, and crows I'd never seen before, looked on silently, expecting our tree to fall as if struck by a bolt from the sky. Instead the breeze rustled the needles and cones the same as always. The lone twine of a spider web shivered, suspended between the limbs of a tree half-severed from its roots. Only a small section of the trunk was cut up, like the mangled mane of a horse.

Keeyaw walked openmouthed back beneath our tree and studied it. He ran his hand over the shattered trunk as strange sounds came from beneath his beard, and he looked to the sky, dragging his tool, squinting upward. He began pounding the giant's wound until the wedges fell out. He kept hammering away, looking spooked as if the injured giant might take sudden revenge and fall on top of him. Instead our tree remained upright in the embrace of the neighboring tree, as if the leafy neighbor were a lover and the two supported each other in grief.

As if I'd been flying all my life, I raised my wings and lifted in an easy, thick flapping motion. I flew like heavy liquid through and around the branches of our aerie and landed on a low branch of Our Giant right above Keeyaw. I lifted my claws, one claw at a time, and made sure they had a good hold of the branch. Then I held out my wings as if ready to fly again.

"*Now,*" I said to Keeyaw, "*be gone! How many times must Our Giant beat you?*"

I kept guarding Our Giant with my wings outstretched.

Keeyaw stepped back and looked up at me. He walked backward, wide-eyed and suspicious. Then he joined his mule and petted it as he reached deep into his knapsack and began other preparations.

*"The birds, the fish, the snakes, the wild
things. They never plot and scheme. One day
of life to them is as a thousand."*

—ROBERT GRAVES, *King Jesus*

12. Burning Creatures of the Sea

Everyone was there to watch me chase Keeyaw off again, including the
rude, gawking foreigners from other lands. Except this time Keeyaw wasn't
packing up his mule and disappearing into the trees. Instead the sad creature
had a strange, preoccupied walk as if freshly awake from bad dreams as he
reached inside the knapsack and began searching its contents.

Perched above him in our fierce Giant, I was sure I'd scare him off again.

Silently my father lit near me and studied Keeyaw, first with sidelong
glances, then counterbalancing himself with his wings, then facing the other
way, then idly cleaning his beak against the bark. It was a manner of watching that I'd first learned from him, though I'd seen it in the gods and other
crows. If you intentionally watch a creature, it is more likely to take note of
you, for better or worse, and act differently either way.

Using twine, Keeyaw hung three strange, eelish creatures from the low-
est branch of our tree. Below them, he gathered firewood and took out his
special rocks and struck them together, summoning the specks of lightning.
He blew into the smoldering, and his breath added to the fire. His whiskers
rose and fell as he huffed. With the fire going, he lowered the three eels, dry
and wrinkled with their fins stuck to their sides, just above the flames. I
found the creatures, with their webbed fins and flecked scales and dried-
open eyes, slippery and exotic, suggestive of flight.

At just that moment, the God Crow appeared again and perched far
above us. There in our severed tree, I saw It, the Bird, Its head craned to the

side, looking far into the mysteries of the mute green cedar palms, then turning Its back, flipping Its tail and wing feathers out in quick, random motions, like eye batting. Yes, It was watching me, I was sure, watching me and Keeyaw, yet turning the other way as the beastman spoke to It in Its supreme grace and indifference.

"Hey, You with all the names, You must remember this—my special tree! Your favored Ennouch, my grandfather, labored long and taught me to plant it. Just as he did with the tree You gave away to the Nephalem. Long have I labored, and now *this* tree is denied me, too. What have I done that is wrong?"

Keeyaw waited for an answer.

The God Crow was pecking away under one of Its wings.

When none came, Keeyaw continued.

"I offer You my favorite, eels." Keeyaw gave a sidelong glance at his mule. "I know how You like the creature of hooves, hooves and horns. I ask only that I might be Your servant, and to do so, I turn to this tree."

The eels spun idly on their strings. Their oils dripped into the flames and sputtered. Their lowermost fins turned black and crispy. Keeyaw threw more kindling and pine needles onto the fire, and they burst out in bright, metallic colors.

"Okay," Keeyaw muttered to his mule, but mostly to himself. "He doesn't want me to have it?" He scratched his head. "The whole thing's off, then, I hope."

Without a sound, the good God Crow flew away, while our severed tree held fast against its mate. Keeyaw cursed into his thick mane and kept cursing as he disappeared into the bushes, every once in a while poking his head back out through the vegetation, making a face at his eels and his fire, and then disappearing again.

But he couldn't stand it. Looking around guiltily, Keeyaw clipped one of the eels down from its string and chewed sullenly on its belly, afterward restoring it half-eaten to its string. Then, with a grunt, he gathered up his defeated tools and led his mule away with him into the tangled secrets of the hollow.

II.

Fledgling

600 years, less than 600 years, passed.

The country became too wide, the people too numerous.

He grew restless at their noise.

Sleep could not overtake him because of their racket.

Ellil organized his assembly,

Addressed the gods his sons,

'The noise of mankind has become too much.

I have become restless at their noise."

—Atrahasis, Mesopotamian flood myth.

And God looked upon the earth,

and, behold, it was corrupt; for all flesh

had corrupted his way upon earth.

And God said unto Noah, The

end of all flesh is come before me; for the

earth is filled with violence through

them; and, behold, I will destroy them

with the earth.

—GENESIS, 6:13

In the beginning, God was a perfectionist.

—BLU GREENBERG, *GENESIS: A LIVING CONVERSATION.*

1. *Triumph of the Tree*

Deep of night.

When the greatest fear was the fear of owls, the tree below us shuddered. It creaked with a massive lurch. The lovers' grip failed, and our own Giant fell forward. The whole world tilted. I was thrown.

"*Get!*" Fly Home yelled.

I jumped into a confusion of wingbeats in the rolling dark. The thunder of falling was like the dark Apocrypha of Keeyaw, as if sound could rattle everything, everything, and turn it to dust and leave us flapping through a greater dark. I heard the caving in of other Giants. And the splitting of branches. And smaller trees. When Our Giant finally hit ground, I flew out as fast as I could—to where I couldn't see—but I kept going, into the rumbling hills. The Giant bounced three times, each time raising tremendous clouds of smoke and dust, and I crouched under some growth in the dust-filled dark.

Then, nothing.

In the sudden hush was an eerie stirring. Wolves bellowed bewildered questions. A fleet-footed creature *whished* enormously through the brush above me, barely touching ground. I thought a shadowy creature was behind me in the bushes. But I kept quiet as I had been told to do at night. Among the calls here and there, I heard muffled squawks from my family, but they were too scattered to bring any comfort.

Down in the tangled growth of the underworld, I remembered how Fly Home had told Our Many that our tree was strong now. He said the augurs alive in the leaves were full of power and he no longer needed to consult the Old Bone, even if he could find him, because I was not the Misfortune and we would not have to take refuge elsewhere in the woods, all because our tree had beaten Keeyaw and sent him away.

Down in darkest depths, I waited for morning.

As the gray mist rose, so did our songs.

"*Night Time*," called Night Time.

It turned out I hadn't flown as far as I'd thought, because I was still in the rubble of our tree.

"*I Am*," I called, and found Night Time perched on a branch sticking up from the felled Giant.

Plum Black lit, too, and called out.

But, "*EEEeiiyaawhhh!*" Fly Home hollered, deep from the splitting stones of his gut. He was perched on the tangled ruin of branches directly above our nest, which was smashed along with the underside of the tree, all a mangle now of splinters, shards, and broken spears. Blood and bones and flattened feathers, trapped beneath the lopsided nest was Our Mother of Many, her wings twisted and pinned by the wreckage. She, too, was a mangle and didn't move.

"*Who did this?*" yelled my father. "*Who?*"

Who would come by in the night and knock our tree down a second time while the world had its eyes shut? Perhaps the demons that lived in the wind. Or an owl. Or the raccoon.

We cried out in grief and disbelief and tried to fly over Our Many, disfigured by the tree of life and lost within the broken web of sticks.

But when we approached, our father chased us off.

"Fly Home!"

He guarded our sweet mother's black feathers, crushed below the nest I came from.

Yet, until shown otherwise, we can assume
that the same powerful mechanisms driving
behavior in one species apply in another.

—BERND HEINRICH,
Mind of the Raven

2. Lost Songs

"Fly Home!!"

Our father wailed as he swooped above the flattened bed of feather and bone that was Our Many. Landing, he cried out, then dove above her again, and if we ever wanted to get close to her we had to shriek and dive past her in the same way or else get chased off, our father broad-browed and open-beaked, diving over her and diving back. He landed on the ground near Our Many and approached as if afraid, sneaking up beside her, afraid of Our Giant. He acted as if the branches were going to reach out and pin him to the ground, too. He tried to feed her, opening his pouch up to her mangled beak and dropping food inside it. But his offering dropped to the ground.

Then he flew to the highest point of the fallen Giant.

And from his horn came a sound I'd never heard him make before. I was stunned that he'd ever paid enough attention in his life to make it. My father sang the Mother of Many's song in a high, raspy falsetto, with perfect pitches and eerie sadness, though he got the order of the names wrong and sang names I'd never heard before. Perhaps his memory was better than or at least different from Our Many's. Rest her feathers somewhere on the ground of the underworld. Already flies were beginning to wheel in the air above her thinning, stiffened wings.

My father called out, *"Fly Home,"* to my mother. Or he called her name and *"Fly Home"* afterward.

Soon other crows flew to our woods, crows that I'd never heard call before, and they perched and waited in trees just beyond view. When my mother's song, sung by my father, hit a certain chord, a bird in the near trees would chime back again, again, flying nearer, hooded and proud-shouldered, extending her feathers, keeping her distance.

"Too Blue!" called my father.

And *"Too Blue!"* called the woods.

"Guided by Voices!"

"Blood of Mary!"

"Why Be Me?"

The woods answered back.

And these were the elder siblings of songs long gone, old birds, most likely older than my father, with a great ongoing curve to their beaks that they could barely keep trimmed and long, gnarly talons with many superfluous angles, curving blades, out-grown points. And these elder siblings lit in the distant, respectful wood. Such was the scope of Our Mother of Many's song.

Lone Crow hung with his hooked posture nearby and made his pitiful mockeries that made no sense until he was idly chased away by Plum Black, who landed then beside me and preened me. Her eyes were cloudy with that awful weather that had afflicted Our Mother of Many.

Now and then a sojourner crow called out, *"Many, of Many,"* from the trees.

Then a crow called out its alarm. A few birds scattered, but all took note. The idle, excited squabble of foreigners ceased, and the silence of the woods announced a single rustling coming up the hill.

On a pathway rarely traveled by humans, Keeyaw appeared, moaning to himself, eyes downcast, in a fight against the reins of his mule. His animal, stupid enough to allow himself to be the beast of another, could not bear to look at the fallen tree. But there it was, and the mule knew it, and knew what he'd soon be forced to do. Keeyaw came upon the fallen Giant and tied the unhappy beast to it. Looking over the trunk's size and girth, he pulled at his long, sad, lion-like beard and made sounds of strange moaning rapture.

Meanwhile, the gathering of foreign crows dispersed in a beguiling way, escaping through and around the branches of the forest without making a noise, and none of them passing before the vision of the man who probably wouldn't have noticed them anyway.

"Keeyaw," one hissed. *"The pale beast, friend of the pale bird."*

Keeyaw took out a jawbone sickle and began to strike away at the branches that had once been the shoulders of my world. From different perches, my father called out. Not angry, not grieving, he was more than that, or less. His wits had flown completely away. *"Fly here,"* he called. *". . . here . . ."* then *". . . there . . ."* It unnerved me when he landed beside me. I found myself crying out as he did, the woe grinding away, making a bruise of my heart where the hot blood spilled out. Plum Black flew near and told me to follow. We flew off to a safe distance, where she arranged the feathers searing my face and told me to be brave, that soon I would have to find my own way. Her eyes clouded over again with that same faraway weather. How could she not be one from Our Many's song? Plum Black snipped delicately around my eyes. She said soon everything would be different. Then she flew off to one of her caches in a crook of the fallen tree. Keeyaw stopped chopping and looked at her with something akin to wonder but continued his hacking away as she flew back to me with a scrap of gut gone dry and hard to swallow. The grainy offal was like grief stuck in my throat.

When Keeyaw had enough branches stacked and tied together, he reined the mule to the bundle. At first the mule feigned ignorance, grazing on a lump of grass. But Keeyaw hit him with a switch from our tree, and slowly, off they trudged, beast pushing beast, my old home in a tangle of sticks, snags, and horns, dragged across the face of the underworld.

．　．　．

Keeyaw returned with four mules and three sons. The sons were all lank and groveling, following along the dirty embankments of the underworld. But unlike Keeyaw, their manes were wildly dark. Keeyaw barked and instructed them as if they were his to yell at, like his mule. And like his mule, his sons seemed resentful and unwilling to the point that they were all dulled by their submission, asleep and dreaming of elsewhere. They even moved like sullen beasts, necks heavy in their yokes and traces and no means to rebel. All except the youngest, the beastchild, who ignored the rest and ran back and forth in the Field of the Dead, waving a fan of cedar leaf over his head.

Looking over the fallen Giant, the sons joined their father in uttering strange moans of ecstasy. The dead tree pleased them greatly, and they took to truncating the rest of the branches without noticing our mangled Mother of Many or the nest below. That was when the God Crow appeared in a nearby tree again without notice from anyone, man or bird, except me. Eyeing Keeyaw, It blinked Its bone-colored eyelids and held Its majestic horn half-open and kept it that way, tilting Its head sideways as if about to form a question.

One of Keeyaw's sons spoke, the one named Ham, whose voice rose and fell in such wild syllables that I could almost understand him even when the God Crow was nowhere near.

Ham said, "I believe this is a sign."

"Of course. They're all signs," said the oldest son, picking up the nest and tossing it onto a pile of hacked limbs.

"This is no sign," said the youngest, who picked up Our Mother of Many by the claws and carried her upside down to Keeyaw's mule, where he threw her into the knapsack. "It is soup."

"No. Listen——" said Ham. He looked about the woods, troubled and spooked, as if trying to remember something, as if he knew the wind's meanings. He said, "We are being watched."

"Watched?"

"Yes. By those black birds back in the trees."

"Put your eyes to good use," said Keeyaw, who held up a jawbone sickle for his son. "And your back, too. It is because we have destroyed their nest that they're watching. If there is a sign, Japeth is right. It is everywhere. The God of Adam does not need to work through birds. He is a righteous God, and a straightforward one, too."

"Is that why He asks you to build a boat so far from water?"

"Oh, Lord!" Keeyaw shook his jawbone to the sky. "What good is a man if his own sons doubt him?"

And he struck the tree near the God Crow, Who flew off with a burst and a great clapping of wings.

"*The tree, the tree,*" It said, unruffled and remote, in Its vast, steady *whooshing.* "*Follow her there.*"

. . . and he knew that beyond reality

Was the other passion of mythology,

That myths were sensual as tears or dreams,

—RICHARD EBERHART, "KAIRE"

3. Funeral

Strange crows flew in and out of our songscape without a worry, and my father let them. Once the sons of Keeyaw put Our Many into their mule sack and dragged her away, my father stopped flying altogether. His sunken body seemed like nothing more than the curved, hollow instrument of his wailing.

"Come fly!" he called.

"Fly somewhere."

Seeming to act on a single pair of eyes, all the vagrant crows flew off again at dusk, secretly, to their own secret places. I would fly through the traditional pathways and stick my claws out in the dark, only to remember that our tree was no longer there. Home was nothing more than a trail of leaves and debris and sticks too small for Keeyaw's purposes. Through the clearing I could see out to the ends of our aerie, where the mangled stumps of other fallen Giants had gathered in the fields of the dead below the moon.

The nighttime whippoorwill's comic repetitions seemed somehow louder, as if the absence of the tree only amplified the night. Stars that were once the warm glow of a fabric behind our tree's limbs and needles were now as bright to me as the naked knowing of eyes. But whose eyes? Without the urgent, seeing quality of an iris, yet with a calm otherliness about them, as if they could commune slowly back and forth across the silvery dark. They trailed across the sky, and as they approached the morning, they disappeared. It was hard to sleep with all the dreams that kept landing beside me. I thought they were the elder siblings, none of whom were as beautiful to me as Plum Black, who had been lured away by the foul croakings of Lone Crow. The visitors that circled in the sky turned out to be vultures, but vultures with black, crow-sized bodies. One of them landed beside me with its naked, burnt-red face, and the vulture said, *"While you are alive, I will love you."*

"And when I am dead?" I asked. *"What of then?"*

"Then I will become you." And the face, scorched hideously from years and years of soaring far above the earth's shadows, living directly near the sun, gave me crow kisses upon my forehead and brow and took a sharp nip at my neck with that one long, curved tooth of her beak and drew blood. Then we flew off together, and it was Plum Black, now a vulture, and she spoke: *"Come with me to the Tree of the Dead; at the Tree, we will find her."*

"Many . . . of Many . . ." I awoke to the sound of a crow moving like a herald across the sky.

At first came the respectful. But now the curious, and worse, and they lurked in every tree. They gurgled back and forth in their foul gibberish. Why weren't we off following Keeyaw to the Tree of the Dead? Hadn't my father or the others heard the call? The loose murder of younger birds, perhaps a year or two older than Night Time, eyed me in a sidelong manner.

That's him, their silence seemed to say.

An arrogant crow would land on the perch my father had just abandoned. Two or three belligerents would land in my father's view. But only one at a time would challenge him there at the ends of the aerie. The grief floating across his brow wasn't ready for the savage assault on his home. My father seemed foggy-eyed and off balance, but he flew ready to die. You could hear it in his cries. Somewhere flew my father's growling attack, and the young bird cowered away, and my father kept at it, screeching between the trees.

Calls and black feathers flew at the strike of beak against wing, midair. But it was too great a force for the broad birds of youth, who weren't ready to die. All morning my father stood off the challenges to his aerie with a raucous, bubbling squawk. *Out,* his feathers would go, *out,* with each blustery call, ready to give any newcomer chase.

My father cawed and bobbed and shot like a ragged bolt at whatever straggler was left, but not everyone he harassed was a crow. Far above the trees, a red-tailed hawk kettled, wings out, unmoving except for his windy tilting side to side, adjusting his flight to the slightest degree over the thermals. Our father met him so far above us it seemed like a slow drift. *"Fly Home!"* And the red-tail lazily flapped away with my father in excited pursuit. *"Fly Home!"* He dove like a mad thing at squirrels. He chased jays, starlings, even sparrows, little birds.

Seeing me, my father usually called out, *"Come follow."* But now he just glared and struck the branch below him with his horn.

"I Am!" I cried out.

"Quiet," called Squall.

"Pale bird!" said our father. *"Will you burden this new nest, too?"*

But my father avoided me and tore after Squall, who flew away into the woods, and that was the last I ever saw of him.

Night Time flew by me, too, squawking.

"Shut up."

Then he flew away before our father could return.

"I Am!" I cried. *"I Am!"*

But my father seemed too spooked to chase me. Plum Black escaped by circling the various trees of our songscape, trying to land back on a tree no longer there. Finally she grew weary of landing on nothing only to get hollered at and harassed and pecked. So she hurried beyond the boundaries of the sky, to places I'd never flown before. I had no other choice; I followed. The last I saw of my father, he was humped over and grotesque, perched on the uppermost tree of our home, hollering threats at us as we fled.

When the blackbird flew out of sight,
It marked the edge
Of one of many circles.
—WALLACE STEVENS, "Thirteen Ways
of Looking at a Blackbird"

4. *Vanquished*

Plum Black was a speedy flier.

My wings ached, and I fell behind.

Out here Night Time dove in front of her now that our father no longer badgered us with his sudden lunacy. I wondered if it was too late for her to become a Pure Flier. Perhaps she loved the fallen nest too much. Without a break in her flight, she dodged Night Time and left him behind as if he were a mere afterthought of a speeding wind. Meanwhile, I felt as if my own wings were clipped. Unable to keep pace with the siblings who disappeared behind a row of trees, I grew frantic in a fight with the air.

All at once the trees fell out from underneath me. Below was nothing but a great, gray expanse of water, and bits of the sun and sky leapt up out of it, and I didn't know that such a thing existed, though I'd heard of one before. With no place anywhere to land, my bowels gave way. All was the same, just one watery wave after wave across the great body of water. Plum Black worked steadily far ahead, almost to the far shore.

I called after her.

Instead of actually seeing her, I saw a silvery, mirror-like flashing far off in the sky. Night Time looked clumsy, cawing in her trail.

"*I Am!*"

"*Hurry!*" she called, her voice diminished by the span of the lake and the swiftness of her flight, which made her wings work faster.

Far above the cloudbanks, a thick hawk soared, and there was no tree cover until we reached the far shore.

In the woods across the water, I imagined we drew closer to our sweet Mother of Many and the Most Merciful Tree, but I lost track of where I was and called out again and again, searching strange trees far and wide, flying circles I could never hope to repeat. Here beyond the lake, even my Plum Black had forsaken me, and despite her warning, I called her until I felt utterly exposed. Without a single reply, I kept flying—to where, who knew?—above the shores of unnamed trees and grasses and valleys without end.

From far off, I heard the calls of Plum Black and Night Time, but their calls disappeared in the impossible woods. There was the land of small trees and boulders, and the landslip that had sunk below the green, lurid waters. All that poked its head out of the filthy bog were trees and tufts of greenish grass. I called out the Song of Our Trees. But neither Plum Black nor Night Time answered. Mostly I flew through woods that seemed no different from any other woods, though I knew I was far from home and that was gone, too.

I flew to a clearing where a river fell off the edge of the earth and figured this was as good a place as any to die. The river made a strange, loud, lovely song as it spilled over the edge. So I found a tree and sang the song of my family the way my Mother of Many had sung it before the great tree had fallen on her head. That was the proper way to go, bringing your songscape with you. I had the odd sensation that our song was singing back to me, but it was just my own dying madness and the strange chasms of underwater music falling over the cliff and onto the rocks below. Then it grew hard to sing, being so hungry, which was how I figured I'd die. I was only a crow, but I did know how to poke around in the decaying leaves for potato bugs and grubs and the like. So I flew down and began turning over leaves, quieting my death song long enough to catch those wiggly nudgers and grubbers by surprise. They tasted so good now that I caught my own catch, so bloody and succulent, exploding in my mouth, not all soaked and deflated in somebody else's throat pouch, halfway dissolved in some other hot esophagus.

Then I had the sun and the stars knocked out of my head, and I was pinned onto the deadened leaves. I looked up and saw a goshawk above me with his wings spread out wide, guarding me from any other hungry bird that might want to take a bite of me before his sharp hook was finished plucking me right down to the nub of my heart. I was nothing more than a severed head and two wings held together by a wishbone. I called out at the hawk that angered me.

"Who are you? Is the Great Mother of Many in you? What of the Tree of the Dead? Can you take me there? Or must I fly to where the beastman took her myself?"

But that magnificent arrowhead of terror no longer saw me as anything other than that day's morsel to pluck, pinned below him, begging for the quick law of the woods. More than a crow, less than a crow, the hunter of birds became nothing but the sharp-boned instrument that would deliver me to the death I'd sung for. It lacked any of those special powers that might allow it to become me and glorify me as the being it had consumed. But what the hawk knew, it did know, there in the herky-jerky doom of its ever-open eyes.

Before the hawk could finish scanning all around itself, a whirl of black beating wings fell over us. The hawk flew off in a confused screech. It was Night Time. Plum Black was with him, too, and they cried, *"Get!"*

"What? Are you going to lie there until he comes back!?"

We flew off to a tree covered by denser trees, and Plum Black preened the drops of blood off my neck.

"I thought you were already nothing but song," she said, *"after I heard you sing the Parting from This Earth. Then I saw the hawk. Look."* And she pulled some loose hawk down from the corners of my beak. *"You must have bitten him once or twice."*

"*Yes,*" I said. "*I bite hawks.*"

"*I thought I was hearing our great Mother of Many's ghost,*" said Night Time, himself the luminary of mimicry. His eyes blazed bright like polished coals from the fight with the hawk and the stirrings of our song.

"*C'mon,*" they cawed.

"*Hurry!*"

"*But I'm so hungry I could eat my own wings.*"

"*Don't argue.*"

And I didn't.

"*And don't linger this time either,*" said Plum Black as I took off, nearly blind now from my own ignorance of the world, having to follow Night Time again, since Plum Black had already flown far ahead of us beyond sight.

The oldest known American Crow in the wild lived until its 29th year. The next oldest, however, lived only to 14 and a half.

5. *The Old Bone*

Wanderers of the sky.

Without welcome.

No far shore. None near.

There was a hypnotic denial pushing our wings along. The Brave West Winds would protect us for as long as we rode them—zephyr, borealis, terra nimbus, aerial plateau. The farther we flew, the less our father could deny us a place in the trees, and the more I could believe that Our Giant had fallen and taken Our Many with it. Meanwhile, our wings took us far above the pull of the old earthly winds, where I could peer down at my own grief as though it still squawked there within the overgrown acres of vegetable life below. We three became the endless otherness of the sky. We passed like ghosts over the wreck of our old injured selves. Up here, the tranquility of the dust clouds covered everything at the horizon and blotted out survival's harsh, repetitive drama.

All was wind, sun-chilled and steady.

It didn't matter what was below—savanna, foothills, greenbelt, river gorge—the earth had no bearing on the winds we took. If we did skim the treetops, it was to dip below them and graze on the crunchy wee creatures that lived there. But I was afraid, deathly afraid, of the underworld and the slow behemoths that toiled there. Huge creatures of horn and beard and stretched, veiny teats chewed slowly and moved even more slowly, with a gentle, mindless nibbling across the face of the leafy earth.

"Hunger is the best teacher."

Plum Black hopped down among their hilly bullocks and flipped over a cow patty, pecking at the dung dust for beetles. She swallowed them whole with a quick throw of her head, neglecting me in my begging.

In one field, Night Time called, *"Get!"* from his high perch, and we scattered.

It was only a dog, but one of Keeyaw's, one I'd seen following around the Terrible, sniffing and lifting his leg at the roots of the Giants. The dog came out of the bushes and loped among the livestock as if she were a creature of singular importance due to her doggish ability to chase things. Without uttering a sound except the chuff of her breath, she lorded over those slow, mammoth creatures, much larger than herself.

"That dog," I said to Plum Black.

"I know," she said, with the faraway weather affecting her eyes. *"I know."* She scanned the woods beyond the field, as if the lank, sinister Keeyaw would come out of the woods at any moment, bearing one of his gruesome implements.

"Keeyaw!" Night Time mocked us.

He grabbed hold of a branch and flapped as if in a fight with the tree. I thought his wits had flown off, that he and the branch had been seized by demons. He kept whacking at the air and riding the branch, getting it to bounce. He flapped and aphids fell to the ground. Tree frogs fell to us. Beetles, hoppers, crawlers, manna, giblets, kabob, all of it fell when Night Time flapped. Plum Black and I hopped to the ground and craned our heads to the sky, waiting in the rain of food. It felt as though Night Time were shaking the very Tree of Wonder.

There was the game of shaking branches, of balancing on flimsy limbs, of flying off with leaves in your mouth, of hiding them, of picking up stones.

In King of the Hill, we fought and lunged for a stick at the top of a dung pile when I saw the most gnarled, untrimmed hooks I'd ever seen at the end of a crow's legs glomming on to our thin trophy. The strength in those ancient, goitered knees, thick of bone, mocked the audacious waste of energy and optimism found in youth, all wrapped up in that pitiful little stick we fought over. The hooks didn't move. They clutched so unconsciously tight to the stick that moisture dripped from the loam in his claws. It was a huge old bull of a crow, standing above those awful hooks, heavy with years and bumpy like ancient tree roots or land swells beneath his feathers. Like his hooks, the horns of his face were long, wild mandibles he must have stopped trimming ages ago. He looked at all of us with a crow's one-eyed stare. Then, when he turned his head the other way, it was eerie in the way the God Crow was eerie, for the other eye was entirely scarred over. Even the scar had scars, as if the blown-out eye socket had bled and healed, then opened up to bleed all over again. The wound was like looking right into the empty space of his head, where his own death lived. It was like looking into his stubborn unwillingness to die despite its probability any day now.

When the old bird flew off with the stick, we saw something else just as ghastly as that one sunken hole in his head and all the gory emptiness behind it. He grasped the stick with just one set of claws, and where the other foot should have been hung a single sharp bone, severed below the knee. None of us followed, stunned by the ghostliness in his head and now the sharp bone swinging below him.

But, "Come on," he yelled with a weary patience, not turning around. "Come and get your stick."

It was strange to follow that old crow through the woods, staring at that one splintered bone that he dragged through the sky. It was a crooked bone that had obviously come to some violent end and, with most of the old crow's tail feathers missing, was all too visible. I nearly smacked up into some branches from watching him. He had a knowledge that lived solely in the actions of his black feathers, and if he ever stopped flapping he would surely fall, having lost too many feathers to glide. He descended slowly, wagging those stiff tree-branch arms, until he lit on a tree leaning over a stream.

And there we saw him, Doom of the Woods himself, Keeyaw, standing upright in the stream, so strange and tree-like, as wet as he was, with his gray weeping tendrils soaked to his head. It seemed as though Keeyaw might also be a creature of water, for he stood half-submerged in the soft current that sparkled with daylight. Through his stiff, wet beard, he spoke, but to whom or to what I couldn't tell, as if he were addressing the woods and the sky.

"Look at this place, so gorgeous and peaceful. Like paradise, isn't it?"

Keeyaw reached into a satchel dripping wet around his shoulders and took out a tool. He had three tools, each with a handle, and he threw them into the stream.

"Take these back."

Two sank and one floated, moving downstream like a long-necked waterfowl. Back on the banks, he moved more easily. He sat down and began lashing a good-sized rock to his ankle, using woven vine. As he tangled the vine ropes around his legs, the one-eyed crow spoke.

"I was hoping Keeyaw was going to feed his dog. But that doesn't look like it's going to happen. Look who's here."

Above in a clearing, the God Crow circled and lowered Itself until It landed all the way down on the banks directly beside Keeyaw. The Bird had a supernatural splendor. The sheen of Its coat alone was a purple-black corona of light. But did Keeyaw see It, or turn his head away from the lashings around his leg? No. The God Crow took a few double hops, folded Its mighty wings, and began pecking away at the far end of the vines, weakening them all at one spot. Keeyaw kept his attention on his ankles, unaware of the Goodly Bird. Finishing Its work, the God Crow flapped off, fully luminescent in Its black, crow-blue way, and lit in a tree far above us. Its tail feathers twitched in a motion much like an eye batting, and though It glanced now here and there, It was intent on the scene below.

"*Although God is everywhere*," said the old crow, "*sometimes It is at one place more than the others. That's called focus.*"

The old bird squinted with his scarred-over eye as if seeing particularly through that.

Keeyaw of the weeping tendrils seemed even more tree-like once he was upright again. He bent low to pick up the rock lashed to his foot, and the rock made him clumsier as he struggled back into the stream, using both of his arms to cradle the weight before his chest. He sloshed out to the middle and spoke again, but this time to himself.

"I sacrificed everything. Everything I could think of. Chickens, lamb, oxen, even fishes—though they are not domesticated. Either to save the world. Or drown it—right now. Just get it over with."

"*Impatience!*" God's imminent Caw fell over the far reaches of the woods, so that afterward all the singing of the birds and insects was magnified. "*The world will not be cured through impatience.*"

"*And drowning it will?*" said the old crow as an aside. He shivered as if ridding his feathers of some unpleasant dust but then resigned himself with a shrug and scanned all around him, trying, it seemed, to hide his thoughts from the Goodly Bird.

Below, the strange tree-like beast of the two elements heard neither of them but kept muttering to himself.

"I did wait until my sons were old enough—old enough to fend for themselves and their mother—before I offered myself up, so that the world might be saved—*this* world."

The beast looked up into the sky, squinted, and closed his eyes tight.

"To save the world."

And he heaved the rock before his chest out into the watery element. The rock splashed, his lashings disappeared, and . . . "*Ahh . . . Ahh*," he uttered in shock and fear, until he, too, disappeared, pulled under the waves.

Soon the woods all around us were calm and in their natural state, as if the stream had opened up and engulfed all of the earlier agitation.

The one-footed, one-eyed crow flew over to a fallen log and hopped his one-footed hop until he was directly above the calm of a pool, looking down. And so was I. The water was as clear to me as a memory, where I felt I could just reach down and pluck up a pebble. But the pool was deep enough, too, for the beast to have drifted there, bobbing below the current, attached to his rock. He undulated calmly, his gray hair fanning out like eel grass, his arms out at his sides.

I looked down at the strange, soaking beast with unutterable dread. How were we ever going to get back to Our Many and the most merciful Tree with him drowned?

"You're not worried about them." The old crow looked right through me, as if his scar could see past my eyes and down my throat, into my guts. *"You're worried about all that stuff Keeyaw's throwing back into the water. Rocks, tools, himself. What else is he going to throw into the drink? That's what you're worried about."*

"I Am?"

"Kee-Yawwww!" the old crow cawed. *"Kee-Yaw!"*

Keeyaw looked up through his watery whiskers and began flailing and kicking until the water above him erupted in bubbles. Then the beast himself burst through the surface, gasping and crying out. He lunged for our log, and we flew to safety. When we landed, Keeyaw was already hunched over on the banks, vomiting water.

"I couldn't—" he retched up small amounts. "I lacked—I couldn't— Forgive me."

"Good man, Noah," God called back in Its commanding, reedy caw, then spread Its mighty span and took to the air.

The half-blind crow flew after It into the woods, and they were gone.

This Noah—why had God the Crow called him *Noah?*—picked up the frayed ends of the vines lashed to his feet, severed now where the great God Crow had worked Its magic, and the creature spoke again to the air: "But . . . *everyone?* The innocent, animals, children, everyone? Then me, why not me? Surely there must be some other way. Cannibals, sure, drown the cannibals. I'll even help. But *everyone?*" The beast Noah began yanking on the vines. "Oh, sleep, sweet sleep, why have you forsaken me?"

He kept moaning, but it all became gibberish as he hung his head in anguish with his legs still bound.

The old bird reappeared again a few days later, as if he knew what was happening all throughout the woods, including where we were and how to direct us to his advantage so he could steal a dog's meal, or an egret's.

"Do you know who I am?" he asked me from the scarred, doomy, blind side of his head. He stood like an old bull crow, proud but dim-witted, unable to realize that his aerie had long ago been taken from him.

I said, *"Yes."*

"Do you?"

"You're the one-eyed bird who keeps showing up in the woods."

"But you. I hear the Mother of Many in your song."

"You know her?"

"Now, be a good bird. And come along."

And slowly he took off, humping and flapping with big heavy heaves, the frayed branches of his wings barely lifting him up.

"You know of Our Many?"

The thick old crow gave the impression of having heard me but also of following some faint, long-vanished wind that had a constant pull on his arthritic wings. To follow him was like abiding some dark change in the weather.

"*I have a taste in my beak for the dead things!*" he yelled. The Old Half-Bird shouted as if everybody else did, too. He had bad ears and leaned down toward my beak, then yelled, "*But I don't know how to kill them! That never stopped me, now, did it?*"

Then he hurried ahead of me, heaving and flapping as always. He was not a fast flier but was steady and never slowed or took rests—which for him probably wouldn't have been rests at all, having only one leg to rest on. At first I thought his wits had flown off without him. He led me to the long, watery expanse known as the sea. We flew past the edge of the woods, and the pastures of rock and sand until he was calling out over the great crashing noises. "*There,*" said the old bird, perhaps the only word he'd spoken all day. From the sea came beautiful swirling currents of air like a field you could glide on. It was here under the green ocean swell that I noticed other birds that swam like the old bird. Fat little offshore birds dove underwater and just raced below the waves for fish, unable to glide but flapping and pushing their heads against the salty ocean element. The Old Half-Bird was not as fast as these, as he pushed his head against the air, but he could go longer than any bird I knew. And if I squawked at him to stop, he only grinned back at me with that gory wound of an eye seeing me more clearly than any normal eye. That, or he just wouldn't hear me, heaving and humping in a fight with the air.

Crow roosts on the outskirts of large cities
have been estimated to be of a million birds
or more.

6. The Phenomenon of Crow Leaves

No matter how far the Old Bone led me, the winds from the setting sun always led to the Nighttime Roost. We'd look and see a small band of crows, and we'd rise to become them. We'd find another murder of birds in the trees and circle down to them, or we'd just meet the others in the sky. Whatever bountiful and mysterious number it is beyond seven—that was how many birds we were, all flying in the same direction. As our numbers grew, so did our voices.

Soon we were a whirring cloud of black wings, filling the valleys and canyons of the sky. The far-off ends of our flock moved like a dark smoke over the treetops and the hills. The clouds of us joined other darkening clouds, and we descended, circling, flying back into ourselves. The trees below us called out, and their branches exploded into a confusion of crow wings that took off when we landed. When would we ever be done calling and bickering and preening and greeting and turning over leaves and ripping small twigs from their branches and filling the trees with crows? Long after we descended on the marsh of the roost, the clouds of bird wings kept coming, not in one straight descent on the Tree of the Roost but landing like a swarm of locusts on the outlying woods. On our own tree, the flock seemed to part, and many would avoid the same branch as mine.

"Do we have to be around all these birds?"

"Stay with me!" yelled Plum Black through the flapping and drifting of wings. *"Don't worry about them. We're staying. You made it, you did!"*

"Well, not the *Roost, precisely,*" said Night Time, imitating our father's love of the Lofty and Gathered Knowledge both Cryptic and Commonly Understood. "*But the Late Summertime Roost, frequented by vagrants and thugs. But you'll make it to the Great Roost. In time, in time.*"

Night Time nodded to me from his branch like a bird full of musty old crow-lore and peppy things to say.

As darkness fell, the last few birds lit over the swamp. They flew in sad circles trying to find a spot, crying out, where the trees already dropped, heavy with crows, and no branch hung unattended, and there under the full force of the moonlight over the water did our hoarse, needy, happy, sour voices finally calm to a murmur, and the lake water lapping the shores made a quiet rhythmic sound like the close breathing in and out of a mother as she combs and cleans the feathers around your eyes and face, one by one, even the pale ones, folding them into place, where they belong.

"Shhh. Go back to sleep," said Plum Black. "*Time for rest now. Time for sleep.*"

Winter came, and it delivered the deep, tranquil sleep known as the Phenomenon of Crow Leaves.

The phenomenon occurs when the leaves of fall abandon their branches. Then the bare winter trees foliate at night with crows. Only then can we assume the lofty attics of the Giants' psyche. Trees learn what it is like to travel far and wide and gather bright, useful knowledge of the world. And crows experience once again what is second nature to them, to lean quietly into the sky with a gentle, enormous repose, to spread their wings, this time not to fly but to gather those who can. Yes, trees love their green summer leaves, but in winter, without their Crow Leaves, they become lonely and depressed.

Also, we came to the Roost to gain a hook-hold into the vast knowledge of the world and to bicker over the arcane principles that held it in place. Here in the clash of nasal calls, I learned to decipher the many trills and squabblings of foreign dialects. At the Roost we learned of who had died, who was now oldest, who had braved a journey to the Tree of the Dead. We learned how to pluck an eagle midair, how to begin a storm at sea (by dropping a pebble from a specific cypress into the bay), what animal of the underworld looked most like a crow (the elephant), and what animal was spiritually most like a crow (the elephant). As dusk darkened to night, I sat in the branches heavy with crows and listened to all the stories that wove the world up into its illimitable fabric. And if you shimmied your way onto the Tree of Science, there all voices were hushed in the presence of those most venerated and learned birds whose knowledge was inexhaustible on any subject imaginable: that, for instance, of fish—fish that had a pebble in their heads, fish that hid in winter, and fish that felt the influence of the stars.

And it was here that I heard the story of how the affliction of the white feather had turned the Old Bone into a Misfortunate of hardship and woe. As I listened to the ritual singing of history, I hid the afflicted side of my own head, despite the night's shroud of darkness.

"Before the terrible blight of Keeyaw cursed the earth . . ."

I couldn't see the Bard in the darkness. There were too many other birds in the trees around her. But she sounded thin and trembling, a mere filigree of plumage—". . . *A crow named Yamah did fly . . .*" She sang in the old style. "*. . . From tree to tree, and across the waters, Yamah flew with the goodly God Crow, and watched over all creatures, all that flew across the sky, and all that crept upon the underworld, as the God Crow had instructed them to do. Now Yamah watched over a particular beastman, a Shepherd who slept every night by his fire. Knowing that if Yamah did try to eat thereof, peril would come unto him, and trap him forever in the viscera of the beast, God did speak to the Goodly Crow. 'Yamah,' It did say, 'first, eat you a hole in the stomach of the beast, and thus ensure you an escape route, lest you yourself be eaten.'*

"And Yamah did this thing. He plucked a hole in the flesh of the beastman, and from the ribs of the sleeping beast, out flew the generations of the perished. And many were the Perished, who covered the sky in black, and who did smile upon the might of their son Yamah and bid him, 'Take wing in Our blessing.' But the wrath of the beast-man was great; and a leg of Yamah was smitten, and rendered free; and with the talons of that leg, Yamah was blinded on one side. As Yamah yet took wing to flee, the beastman did reach out for tail feathers, and lo, much harm was done. Still, to this day, does Yamah fly in the blessings of the ancients, who protect him in his broken-down state, now the Old Bone of Misfortune, unto the ends of the wind. Amen."

It wasn't until here, at the end of the story, that I realized the song was about the old, injured bird who had shown me the sea. My soul seemed to levitate, and the top of my head felt ripped wide open—so wide that any-thing could have fallen in. Such is the rapture of inspiration in youth. I had stolen fish with a Holy Bird.

The Old Bone . . . Random cries rose up around us. The Old One . . . Nearby, the old bird shivered, lifting a few nape feathers, as if the story of his own affliction was a draft, affecting him while he slept. ". . . May he see with the Everlasting's special powers of sight . . ."

". . . Yes, the God Crow is a merry joyful mightiness, and if you get eaten, the God Crow wants you to be happy just the same . . ."

I awoke like a bolt from my dreaming but calmed quickly as all the crows around me were asleep—rustling occasionally or flapping, but mostly asleep as the leaves of the trees we'd become.

The Norse God, Odin, kept two ravens
perched on his shoulders, one named
Thought and the other Memory, that flew
the world by day and returned by nightfall.

7. Mob

It was neither morning nor night but the gray passage between the two. Below us, the lakewater barely stirred the small trees and bushes that overgrew its banks. Occasionally, there was a fluttering in the branches as our restlessness grew, and a caw here or there. It was still too early to fly, but too late for sleep, and we perched on a new rumor of plentiful foraging. Soon, somewhere in the approaching day, we'd land on a feast of so much burnt flesh that the beasthuman couldn't possibly eat it all. Not to mention all the cakes and breads and all manner of delectables left to soak in narcotic potions.

"Where?" muttered the Old Bone, Holy Bird of Misfortune and Woe, with all the special powers of sight given to him by the God Crow. He must have been seeing through his scar because his good eye was fast asleep.

We always assumed that the first to fly would know where the feast was. But to take off first without knowing anything only invited too many followers, who themselves knew nothing.

Before the morning's first rays, we heard the *whack* of bird wings. Then we flew from the greater roost with all the stealth we could muster. In a fumbling wave, we lifted with heavy wingbeats, whole branches of us at a time, bumping into each other and fighting for a space in the sky. A bird up ahead called out that he had seen which way the others had flown.

Where? Where?

The bunch of us flew in distraction, and soon we were mobbing an eagle's nest precariously close to the roost. We dove and squawked with the mock bravery of numbers, and the eagle ducked and flew off.

"*Eagle!*" we cried. "*Eagle!*" which is the same as imitating its screech.

"*That's an eagle all right,*" said the Old Bone, who flew right beside me with all the special faculties of observation given to him by the God Crow. "*Keep an eye out for the young ones.*"

Filled with courage, we lost track of trying to find any feast, and the elder birds kept up the seasonal task of pointing out potential enemies to yearlings such as myself. We swooped on the aerie of a suspicious hawk. We attacked a tree known to be the daytime roost of an owl, even though there was no owl in sight. Still, we made our nasal owl sounds and mobbed his tree.

"*Owl,*" said the Old Bone. He didn't bother with the imitations. His voice no longer carried. "*Watch your back at night.*" And he hummed a little screech to himself and dove over the tree empty of owl.

Then we flew over a clearing and happened upon an abysmal creature, a lone beastman. We spied the long, bony animal sitting on a log before an open flame, surrounded by what looked like his own aerie. He just sat there roasting a large animal with no skin and no bowels and no head.

None of us knew what sound to make for this creature. We flew over his campsite silently, like burnt ashes in the wind, and circled beyond the ridge of trees where we couldn't be seen. We whispered.

"*He doesn't even think he's a creature.*"

"*He burns the blood right out of it.*"

"*Disgusting.*"

"*Idiot.*"

"*Now, this one,*" said the Old Bone. "*This is the one you have to look out for.*"

The closer we flew, the more my guts crawled, and I bristled with familiar dread.

"*Because,*" the Old Bone went on, "*when you see a cow, you know a cow. You see an elephant, that's an elephant. You see an eagle, after a time, you know an eagle.*"

And so on. But this one, I still don't know what to make of him. Except, of course, for his wars. With his wars, he's too generous. I get hungry just thinking about it."

"That's Keeyaw," I whispered, seized with fear, Keeyaw of the lank figure and the mournful locks, the one whom the God Crow had given a name. But what? What name? I searched his aerie for Our Giant and the Tree of the Dead and the Lost Love of Our Many.

"What do you mean, what? He's not going to give us any of that. That's one tasty morsel. But it's useless. Let's get out of here."

But I lit on a tree just above the beast.

"Noah!" I called.

I called the beast, *"Noah!"* who in his admiration of the burning, headless creature had neither heard nor seen us.

crow's foot: a carpenter's mark of
measurement.

8. The Fires of Keeyaw

"No birds land here," said the Old Bone.

"Why not?"

"Because they land somewhere else. Something wrong with your eyes?"

While my own eyes watered from the smoke twisting through the trees, the Old Bone saw the way God sees and stood on his one good bone. He cleaned his beak back and forth on the other bone just hanging there all gory like a pestilence. Above the trees I watched the last of our little mur-der of friends flap off to the adventures of a new day, and the Old Bone was aware of them as well as aware of the one called Noah, though the old bird did nothing but study the stillness of the clouds beyond the hills.

For the longest while, the Old Bone and I just sat there and watched the beastman roast the open animal. Behind him was a huge pile of severed trees as skinless, bowelless, and hoofless as the beast above the flames. As truncated as they were, I could still pick out our old nest tree among the fallen Giants. Noah was burning their hacked limbs, and I wondered if he was going to feed our old home into the flames. I recalled all the life that had once spread out and landed there, held up in the breeze by those thin, leafy limbs. I could hear Our Mother of Many and her varied, wavering song from the uppermost part of the tree now just a twisted, tortured shape among other nightmares sprawled out in the daylight across the worn-out earth. My fledgling days were burning right before my eyes, and perhaps the mysterious whereabouts of the Mother with them. And Noah did this with his wits flown completely out of his head, his eyes wetted and withdrawn into their sockets but still fixed on their smoking source of discomfort. Even his bones didn't move, stretched-out, simian, and bulbous at the joints. He sat arrested by the flames.

"*This is his nest, you know,*" said the Old Bone.

"*Whose nest?*"

"*The beastman's.*"

"*Where?*"

Crow conversations can be short, with very long pauses between remarks. As the Old Bone watched, his feathers twitched, a motion much like eye batting. But since he had no tail, he had no counterbalance, and his twitch was more like a lurch that threw him off balance, especially on that one leg.

"*Right here,*" he said, catching himself. "*You're perched on it.*"

What I thought was a hill was really a mass of shorn trees all heaped together and cinched in place by enormous fibers made stiff and shining with black, tarry bitumen. It was a steep hillock of trees, dripping and pooled up with the black, tarry stuff.

"*This?*"

"*Something wrong with your ears, too? It is and has always been. In the time before I was born, a time long before your great Mother of Many, Keeyaw was already building it, collecting the forest, restacking it. Already it was enormous.*"

"*But what about the time before Keeyaw, when you freed the ancients perished within the ribs of man?*"

"*What? There has never been a time before Keeyaw. No bird remembers it. Keeyaw has always been.*"

"*What about the ancients trapped within the ribs of man?*" I asked, thinking of Our Mother of Many within him now. "*Can't they ever be freed?*"

"*How'd they get there in the first place?*"

"*Weren't you ever called* Yamah?" I asked.

"*Crows used to call me that.*"

And the world became flat and empty to me. I was overwhelmed, yet I despised the knowledge of the Old Bone. All the sacred notions of the roost skittered away like water bugs escaping a surfacing frog when he spoke. I had the urge to leave him and fly down into the beastman's nest, because I thought that there in the tangle of dead trees I might find the one Tree of the Dead and clues to the whereabouts of Our Many's ghost. But I didn't want to tell the Old Bone a thing because whatever hunch I had would vanish when he opened his beak.

"*Look,*" he said. "*Birds don't land here, and birds don't go down inside. They don't go poking around in the beastman's nest. What good can come of it?*"

I wanted him to fly off to his infested swamp. I didn't need any Old Bone to chop down what was growing of my hopes. Besides, once, the God Crow had spoken to me, or at least I thought It had.

"*Oh, It did, did It? What did the Endless Eternal say?*"

I despised the Old Bone even further for knowing just what I was thinking. Finally, grudgingly, I spoke: "*It told me to be ready.*"

"*Ready for what?*"

I looked down at the tangled hill of shorn Giants below us.

"*Well, don't let me stop you.*"

So I readied myself.

The one-eyed, one-footed, tailless crow would not go down with me into Keeyaw's mountain of dead Giants.

"*I'll call, though,*" he said, "*if the beasts do anything funny.*"

I flew in alone through a large, branch-woven opening at the uppermost part of the nest.

Going down inside was like filling my wings with wind for the first time, but a wind of foreboding awe. Below I found dark, fathomless spaces, which I had to wade through until my eyes could adjust and I was covered with dusty cobwebs pocked full of hollowed bugs. Occasionally, seams of light shone in between the trunks, but in most compartments was utter darkness, and I avoided these. I found myself drifting closer and closer to the opening where Noah and his family often walked in and out and where the daylight poured throughout and seeped gloomily into the compartments. The gangways were flanked by strange latticework, like those of the pens where the beastman kept his animals. And there at the bottom of the nest, more like an island of dead trees, the weevils and worms had worked their way up the wooden dunnage and scaffolding to the bottommost trees of his home. Some of the limbs of the hull had already spliced back into the earth with roots. Why should any creature need such a mountainous home? Yet I was drawn to its wood-cave coziness and felt that the large, inert power of it was dormant. This landmass of trees was awaiting some otherness too large to comprehend that involved chaos and terror and motion. The limitless hulk of it was doomed and unfit for this world and waited there out of time, and out of place, saddened by the burden of itself. There was a stratum of carpenter ants and beetles, and the mildewy world of the mosses had foisted their way up into the gopher-wood construction. And there, where the sun shone deep into the catacombs of the vessel, tiny spears of grass and mustard weed grew up through the hull and had actually taken root on the bottommost ribs and beams. And following some mice there, I found the most spectacular thing of all, huge stores of grain, whole hillsides of it, compartments and compartments, foodstuff enough to swim in, like a small, hapless fish on the ocean floor.

This was where I belonged.

9. *Kindness of the Beast*

When I emerged from the mountain of hewn Giants, the sudden sunlight burned my eyes as if they'd been rubbed in salt, and I couldn't make out a tree to land on with all the sun spots wandering beneath my eyelids. All I could do was yell out from my own blindness midair.

"Food! Mountains of food!"

It was difficult flying, wondering where to light.

"Of course there is."

Hearing the Old Bone, I found his branch and landed. *"But you don't know how—"*

"There's food in all of their nests," he said. *"They're stuffed with it."*

"Are they?"

"Yes. That's the way the beastman is."

"All just like Keeyaw?"

"How much food does he have?"

"You can't see it all, there's so much."

"And so it is with all beastmen," said the Old Bone. *"And they can't hide it all that well either, or don't bother to, anyway."*

"Let's go in and try some," I said.

"Oh, no. Couldn't do that."

"Why not?"

"Crows don't do that."

"Why not?"

"You must be wary of all that creepeth and crawleth, and all that, until you know them and know you're in no danger. With the beastman, you can be sure of only one thing: there is danger. That's what I've been trying to tell you."

And we flew away from Noah's rookery with its foul smoke and its sprawling nest, clumsy and misplaced, looming like a mountainous mistake, filled naively with stores enough to feed every crow in the world for a lifetime.

All night at the roost, I wanted to sing out the song of the food I had found. My dreams were consumed by vast glacial drifts of food spilling out of their wooden caves and valleys and engulfing me whole. I was carried off in a slow tide of grains and figs and cakes and all manner of foods eaten by the beastman, some of it on fire, whole piles still smoking and some sopped with narcotic potions. The birds who tell other birds of the great food bonanzas, they are the favored birds, courted and doted on, revered, inspiring fear and affection, sung of in lore, copied in song. But what if the bonanza buried in Noah's mountain of Giants brought only harm? What if his legend-sized cache brought death, to even a few, or just one? What would my song be then?

Perhaps another day.

I'd wait until I learned more about his nest.

Besides, word had spread of a beastman's army approaching, and though I'd fed before from the feasts of the Long Jubilation, I had yet to see the kindness of the beast firsthand. On the eve of the Offering, it was hard to sleep, especially with all the strange theories concerning the beasthuman and the dangers of eating too much of this humanity.

. . .

Before dawn, we flew through a gray forest that was eerily too quiet. From the distance came a crow's incessant call.

"Here."

He called, *"Here."*

And we flew here.

Then, *"There."*

And there, under the trees, there was nothing.

We moved swiftly below the treetops and through the deathly silence. In the dull mist, I could make out the hulking shapes of beasts moving quickly away from the direction we flew, a pheasant beating the air, a boar grunting his escape, a deer disappearing with her fawn. Even the snake flinched and gave its presence away.

Then, there was a loud, shrill call.

Other crows shot up from their hiding places and joined us.

The drums of the beastman spurred us on, and we flew even faster below the treetops to a clearing of denser smoke and noise.

Below us spread a vast valley of armies. The beastman filled the land.

Vaster fields of them stood along the edges and waited, while those in the lowlands converged in the shallows of a river that ran red. They brandished spears with stone points, arrows, sticks, shields, ropes, wagons pulled by bulls. They employed flames, drums, banners, horses, elephants, camels, hooded falcons on their wrists. The battle between the humans moved slowly, like a tide, a mass convergence to oblivion in the middle. In a strange way, it was distant and unspectacular. Mostly what we saw from the trees was the yelling mass of beasts and the columns of smoke. The sun was a pale orb barely able to show through it all.

By nightfall, the Great Offering had yet to begin.

We neglected the usual winds to the Roost, and by firelight, we watched the heated celebration. Humans danced, and drank, and mounted and en-

slaved one another. They twanged harps, thumped drums, blew horns, yo-
deled, and clapped.

The Old Bone stood beside me as though he could stand forever on his
one good leg and watch the beastly happenings with the scarred-over, cadaverous cavern that used to be an eye. With his one good eye, he looked at
me and blinked. I was not looking at him, yet I could do nothing to keep my
attention away from him and his mutilated stare, judging me, looking at me,
seeing only half of me, seeing the way only the Old Bone sees.

"So. This is the Long Jubilation," I said, trying to make conversation with the
beam of scrutiny coming from the Old Bone's scar, even though it was not
turned my way.

But the Old One only shuddered and blinked with his one good eye, as if
blinking wakefulness back into his brain. He grunted. *"What? Did you say
something?"*

"Were you awake?"

"No," he said, without a visible change in his eye. *"But I could have sworn
someone spoke to me."* He preened and scratched himself with his stick of a leg.
"Maybe it was God again."

"What did It say?"

"The Ever Eternal wants to know when the eating begins."

"So do I," I said. *"When is that?"*

"When the living abandon the dead."

"When is that?"

The Old One didn't answer. He only stared at me with his eerie open eye
falling asleep, and his other scarred-over cadaverous eye watching the humans leap around by firelight.

10. *Slumgullion*

I awoke with my head pounding to the disturbance of dreams, the sky torn apart, all trees vanished, and the dead floating upon the dead, which gave me a strange queasiness and hunger. I was utterly alone, with my mouth open to the sky and the very clouds filling me until I disappeared into a turbulence of vapors. Waking, I kept spotting crows perched on the lookouts above the Great Offering, waiting along with the vultures and ravens.

Then I saw him again.

The Man Called Noah.

As always, he was wary, staying on the outskirts of the woods, peering through the tangle of bushes and his own hairy head. Noah pulled his mule past the edge of the mercenaries' encampment, where he seemed even more lost than he did in his mania to fell trees. And as always his mule packed around his tools, all except his jawbone ax, which he had slung over his shoulder, making him appear all the more like the dark harbinger he was.

In the dregs of the celebration, only a few last beastmen groveled across their heaps of blankets and skins. Everyone else slept in gangly derangement. At one point Noah looked at them as if he was about ready to speak, but walked away instead, puzzled, angered, pensive, and stoop-shouldered from the weight of his endeavor.

"*That's what it's like,*" said the Old Bone—I had forgotten he was still perched beside me—"*when you keep all the food for yourself.*"

Slowly Noah led his mule past the encampment to the field of the dead, and I took to the air and followed, and the Old Bone did too, asking, *"Now what are you doing?"*

"Why do you keep watch over me?"

We lit on a tree, and the Old Bone said nothing.

Noah stood and beheld the scene below, the endless sprawl of corpses, the looters who picked them over, the mourners who wept for their fate. The wizened Noah squinted up into the sky for a long while and then left the lush field for the thick of the woods.

With the coming of morning's light, the looters fled the field. Mourners wandered off, too, but in a lost, aimless way, as though they had nowhere else to go. Perhaps it was too dangerous for them to stay after the soldiers awoke.

Yes, we were only crows and got only the gristle and sinew from God's great bone heap. But today there was too much to attend to, and one had only to land, anywhere, everywhere. The kindness of the beast was endless. So why were we still in the trees above the Offering? From their perches, even the ravens waited, or especially them, majestic, cautious, sphinx-like, almost God Crow–like, three times our size. They watched and waited and occasionally croaked a clacking sound way back in their throats, an evil taunting sound, like a mockery.

Not yet, their silence seemed to say, while we crows eventually swooped down from the trees and joined the vultures and jackals. The Old Bone and I fell upon a dead soldier who had two large, furrowed wounds, big enough to get some real work done.

Maybe the ravens were waiting to see if we'd be ambushed, or if we grew sick from the poisons in the beastman's blood. The flesh still had the sharp, metallic tinge of adrenaline to it, and that put me even further on edge. It was unnerving to be in the watchful gaze of the large birds. *When?* The ravens called to each other over surprising distances, in good numbers, with only a few in view.

"Fly Home!"

My father's call spread across the sky.

By reflex I lifted my wings to follow, but stopped and watched my father arch over the valley and away.

How did he know I was down here knee-deep in humanity? The Old Bone was up past his bone in the wound of humankind, too, and he looked up, startled, not at my father's yawp but at my reaction. All the other birds, vultures included, had flinched and flown away when I raised my wings, all except the Old Bone, whose face dribbled as he turned his one good eye on me and the fibrous gut he yanked on snapped. Perched in the pit of the wound, he looked like a normal enough crow. You couldn't see the severed leg or the missing tail or the cadaverous eye, all covered up and sticky as it was.

"What?" he said.

"My father just flew over. He called a call I haven't heard since I was in the nest."

"Perhaps you should follow."

"Should I?"

"Only you would know."

"But there is so much goodness here," I said.

"And so there is."

The Old Bone sank his face back into the bloody furrows, and I took a moment to look over our meal.

The soldier's eyes were gone, and he lay staring with his smeared sockets at the sky in a very tranquil sleep, one arm cleaving to his sharpened stick, which surely must have been a beloved thing. As we ate, I felt the welcome release the fallen beast must have felt at leaving his dead body and entering the form of a crow, as did all creatures. When consumed, they soon enter a state of excitement to fly. Crows are especially famous and envied for their flying abilities.

"*If you don't leave now,*" said the Old Bone without poking his head up from the beast, "*you'll never catch up.*"

"*I wonder what he wants.*"

But the Old Bone didn't hear or didn't care, tugging at the fresh, wiggly flesh. Taking a last bite, I flew away from the ample goodness and searched the open sky.

11. Hookbill the Haunted, the Curse

I heard his powerful *eeiiyaawck* in the sky but couldn't figure out where he was headed. I mean, I knew what direction. But to where? To what end? The old aerie was back the other way. He flew over the gray swamplands and across the great body of water where on the far shore goshawks jump on your heart and pin your wings to the ground. Fly Home was a fast and fearsome flyer. I had forgotten how fast. Each pull of his wings shot him far ahead of me into the wind. True, lately I had been flying with the Old Bone, who had to fight his way through the sky, but my father could pick up speed while bucking the wind in a glide. It was a great beauty to catch up to him and hear his feathers rattle in the headwinds. He seemed to see me without turning from the direction he flew and pumped and rose high into the air and into a field of cloud. Then we were completely covered by clouds, and the clouds dissolved everything from view. I thought we'd left the earth.

Though every once in a while the slope of a mountainside peeked up through the cloud cover, and we rose to avoid it.

Finally we dropped below the clouds and lit on the back of the mountain. It was a barren, craggy mountain full of rock and scree and the occasional shoot of stubborn weed life that had somehow found enough mineral moisture to take root in this inhospitable land. We were far, far above the tree line, yet Fly Home managed to find some trees, or trunks of trees, that seemed to have stopped growing ages ago and stood petrified in communal lament.

There my father perched.

From a distance, I saw an old, dilapidated nest falling apart yet fixed in its unraveled state, and next to the rickety ladder of twigs a bird not at first noticeable, mostly because I couldn't believe a bird that odd and ancient could exist. It looked like a corpse of burnt twigs, stiff and frail. I thought she was some tumorous growth in the crook of the tree. But when my father lit beside her, she moved, not suddenly but with a long deliberation, as though the bird had just emerged from a deep and demented dreamscape. She was a withery old hunchback. She had an enormous overgrowth for a beak, a deformity so large and ill-shaped that my father had to duck in order to place his offering anywhere near her. Turning sideways, he coughed up the round, perfect, bloody-red eyeball of a human and placed it on the branch below the twisted horn protruding from the hell hag's face. The withered bird could only give the eyeball a slight push with that warped deformity, until the eye lay in her talons. She began to roll it back and forth along the branch. Every once in a while she pecked at it in an idle manner, looking all around her between pecks. The size of her beak affected her ability to look around.

The two of them mewed and rattled back and forth, and my father preened her delicately around the eyes. They sat there in silence, occasionally fluttering in the petrified trees, and they seemed content. This was not his new mate or even the Ghost of the Many, because I would surely have recognized her faint song, as I did sometimes at the nighttime roost, when her long, winding tune came humming just above or below the cacophony.

Then the two of them spotted me.

But was sight really the faculty she used to take me in with those cloudy orbs in her head? She saw me in the way the suddenly blind stumble and fall upon things. I felt her frail, cracked-feather weight all over me. The cobwebs of her scrutiny made me itch.

"One of your own?" she asked, knowing the answer. When she spoke, her vulgar horns parted but hardly moved.

"My latest," he said. *"Fledges are such hard work."*

"Most die."

Fly Home glanced all around him in silent agreement. *"This is the only one left from his nest, the one of the Pale Feathers."*

"I know."

"Sorry."

All three of us perched, staring at each other for a while.

"Does he even belong here?" asked my father.

And I felt my quills tighten in anger. Why wouldn't he ever admit I had a place anywhere?

"The answer lies before you."

My father looked at her, then he glared even more fiercely at me.

"Fly Home!"

He racked the air with his alarm and bobbed and flapped himself large.

He dove down from the tree until he was a sharp shadow just above me, beak open and wings pointed like a great open mouth—*"keei-waaahh!"* he cawed. *"And clean all that human off your wings. Maybe you could keep up with me then."*

He was gone.

. . .

The ancient one kept rolling the eyeball as before, aware of me yet not looking at me, strangely toying with me all the while.

Slowly I approached.

She grew annoyed. Only because the eye had lodged itself on one of her long, untrimmed hooks.

"Preen me," she hissed in a hoarse, whiskery voice.

Because of her deformity, she could not preen the feathers on her back, which were a tangle of brambles and weeds. Feathers long dead and shriveled had wound themselves around other feathers trying to escape. She groaned as I worked the dull feathers free.

"Who—" I wanted to ask her who she was and why my father had fed her. But I barely had time to utter a sound when her song crept forth, a weak and murmuring slather of words sung from behind a thin gap she could barely open.

"I Am Hookbill the Haunted, the Seer, the Curse, but a curse to no one but myself, sibling to your father, Fly Home, so far back in his line he can never reach that part of his song, so many have come afterward. I can see farther than any bird or other living thing. The future to me is like looking into the next tree over."

"I Am—" I was about to enter into my song, but, *"Stop,"* she hacked and hissed. *"I know everything already, I have always known you would come. You are I Am, the last of Your Mother of Many, gone to the realm of song. I know what will be."*

"What?"

"Feed me."

She wheezed.

I went to peck at the eye snarled in her claws.

"No," she said. *"There is food already in my bill. Push it down my throat."*

I scraped at the gelatinous glob in her beak and pushed it down into the cavern of her face. She opened her obscene mandible as wide as she could. The breath from her ribbed esophagus seethed in and out, *yes* and *no,* as she sucked me down into her gullet. *"More,"* she said, *"more."* Trembling, since I feared I'd be eaten, I pushed the tissue down into her beak again, and down

I went, far into the seething in and out, the yes and the no again, and the wailing of winds that dissolved my sight. As I moved within the hissing vapors, she breathed the curse of the deluge into my ears. *"Fish shall swim in the sky,"* she wheezed. *"And birds shall fly in the sea. Upon the face of the dead, you will float, whereupon all flesh on earth will lose its breath below the waters. You will be among those safe in Keeyaw's nest. But you won't be of them. You alone will return to the flood. Now hurry, please, feed me."* And I felt my claws lifted from my perch as I fell into a venting of powerful forces that surrounded me and pulled me under, all my feathers soaked in the slurry. I circled downward. But the more I fed, the more I felt the curse go away. And perhaps I did feed her enough and she lifted the curse, or I'd altered it, because when I awoke, I was in the sunset again the same as always, flying with the regular sky of crows to the nighttime roost.

Just as I would on any other night.

I called.

And the sky answered back.

III.

Deluge

By 5,600 B.C. the ocean had risen to a height where it stood poised to invade the Bosporus valley, and plunge to the Black Sea Lake five hundred feet below. Driven by the wind and tide, the waters must have repeatedly washed up onto the top of the divide to fall back, leaving damp patches on the soil, until a final surge began to flow continuously across and down the slope toward the lake, finding old gullies and dried streambeds in the rough ground between the trees and around the litter of boulders. . . .

Someone escaping the onslaught of the rising tide on this shelf would have had to travel, on the average, a quarter mile per day to keep up with the inundation. If fleeing up the very flat river valleys, they would have had to move half a mile to a mile per day . . . .

Ten cubic miles of water poured through each day, two hundred times what flows over Niagara falls, enough to cover Manhattan Island each day to a depth of over a half mile.

—WILLIAM RYAN AND WALTER PITMAN, *NOAH'S FLOOD: THE NEW SCIENTIFIC DISCOVERIES ABOUT THE EVENT THAT CHANGED HISTORY,* 1998

*Some observers believe that crows have a
language of their own, consisting of the
variations of their caws, wailing cries, and
other sounds.*

—OLIVE L. EARLE, *Birds of the
Crow Family*

1. Fleece of the Hills

Green season.

And in the trees, the furled buds waited for the next shower, when they would burst and the flowering streamers would hang from the maple heavy with lore. All the clamor of the woods convinced me that no other bird, beast, or green growing thing knew at all about the floating of Noah's nest across the waters of the dead that would soon smother all living things. I hoped that they knew better than I did. But what did I care? In the happiness of spring, I was spring's absence. I was the dark bird with no color but winter on my face. Even my own kind avoided me. Everywhere the green season kept busy with itself. Dragonflies flew, one stuck to the other. Two sparrows circled, each with the same spear of grass in its bill. The flower seduced the whole kingdom of honey-gatherers. And in the full heat of the noon, the hills were on fire with their green growing green. On the steppes where little grew, the farmer's cow incited the bull. Cut loose from the rope, the bull charged across the desert, his eager member wobbling like a palm frond in the blue, beads of discharge bubbling off it into the wind. What was this restless urge in the hot oven of anatomy? Soon the water would put an end to all this.

Perhaps the Old Hagbill was wrong, or I would prove her wrong, or the ignorance of the mad season had already proved her wrong. If only I could feed her enough, which was the only remedy she offered to her prophecy and the only possible escape. I flew to her far-off copse of trees, nearly dead, choked by vines and tufts of tawny weed life. Every day I flew to the Old Hookbill's mountain, doubting her prophecy, and lit beside her, hoping to divine the source and reliability of her predictions.

"They say that your body was caught by vermin and eaten while your soul was off elsewhere, flying."

"You see what is before you." She whispered with long, trembling interruptions. *"I cannot say what happens to me while I'm gone."*

"When you fly into the future, have your reports ever been wrong?"

"Many of my glimpses of what will be have yet to come about. Perhaps they never will. Yet we still have more future before us, do we not? Or some of us do, anyway. There is still time."

Usually the visions of Hookbill the Haunted brought a crow hope and awe, but her consoling was of no help and left me ill-at-ease. I was too afraid to learn more. Perhaps her predictions were more than just early-warning signals that could be avoided. I scraped the last morsel down into her horrid beak and took off.

When I emerged from my thoughts, my wings had already taken me far out over the endless expanses, to the distant places where the wind ended and where it began. But even this cave, breathing in and out like the hot bellows of the earth, would be snuffed out by the flood. I searched the foreign woods for my old songscape and a tree that had long ago fallen to the underworld to become a stick in the doom of Noah's nest, soon to float upon the face of the dead. I had to get back to that tree and that time, to feed in the way I'd fed Old Hookbill the Sagacious, the Woeful, the Wasted, trying to push food down that old hissing horn and into her ancient enveloping esophagus, red and convulsing, needy like a spider's web. If I could only feed her, or any bird, fast enough, with juicy amounts large enough, perhaps I could avoid the oblivion in whatever form it might come. Maybe the flood wasn't for years and years, or next season, or never, I flew hoping my wings might know more than I did.

I flew through the drying season, and my wings grew dry. My feathers lost their luster, the purple cast of our family, and the black of my feathers turned coal-colored with dust. Rain did not fill the swamps, streams trickled away with themselves, and though the land remembered, water did not return to the cracked beds of its memory. The earth's eggs grew afraid and did not leave the womb, clamped shut and dry. Dark pasture lands, green hillsides, and the tangle below the trees, all bleached. Only thistles and last season's hollow husks cowered in the hot wind. Everywhere, all the broad world bred alkali, and the beasts who lived there came to the crow for help.

The buffalo, with bones like blades, wandered to us from the field. *"Crow,"* it said, *"you who imitates nature. Imitate the wind, so that it can bring clouds, and the clouds bring rain."* If the buffalo did say that, how would I know?—its lips discharging only the rime of famine. But I perched on its back and ate the mites there. Hogs came to us, unable to wash their hide, and laid themselves down. In the dust, one pig asked me to rid it of the ticks and lice assailing its raw wounds. I flew down upon its flanks and helped myself, eating what afflicted it. When I pecked at its festering scabs, it grunted and lifted itself, and I remembered the hog wasn't dead yet as it let out an insulted grunt and waddled away on dainty hooves, kicking up dust.

Even the catfish came to the crow for help. In the night, the walking catfish lost their way, and we found them in the morning on their sides, their skin cracked, their fins shriveled. They lay across the rocky lakebeds that held water now only in the fishes' memory. There, we helped them on their way to the waters of the dead. And as the waters of the great lake retreated, we speared sticklebacks and minnows in the evaporating puddles of mud.

Sparrows bent low to the packed-hard earth and fluttered their wings, bathing themselves in dust.

"What if I see them during the morning?"

"You won't see them in the morning!"

"But crows fly all day."

"Not your emissaries, you fool!"

—CARLOS CASTANEDA,

The Teachings of Don Juan

2. Sleep of the Bloody Potions

Only in Noah's nest did I find abundance.

I found the Old Bone there, too, perched in the trees as if asleep. Even his good eye was asleep. When I showed up, though, it opened.

"I've been waiting," he said.

"Waiting?"

"For the Winds That Bring Spring Floods. I don't know why they don't come."

"Spring was so long ago," I said.

I wanted to tell him it was because I worked to drive away the floodwaters of Hookbill the Haunted's prophecy by feeding her. But I chose not to say a thing, because the Old Bone would disperse the spell, or my belief in it anyway.

"Perhaps you're overdoing it," he said. *"Sure, keep the floodwaters back. But let a little through."*

"How?"

"Spare me," he said. *"I suppose you're going into Keeyaw's nest."*

"Why don't you come along?"

"It's unnatural for a bird to go below the ground," said the Old Bone. *"A bird needs the sky above; that's the place to hide from the beast."*

"But there's so much food there."

"Only a fool would crawl in after it. Still, I suppose I'll watch over things and call out if anything strange happens."

"It never does."

"Never—see, the word of a fool."

Still, we sat for days in silence above Noah's busy rookery. The ark was a land formation unto itself, while the beastmen inhabited only one small cave of it just behind their crude opening. The rest of their home was dark and empty, except for a few cramped stalls where they housed their animals and all the food stores below. All day the Old Bone and I watched Noah and his family walking in and walking out of their ark, walking out and disappearing into the woods. The fields of their rookery were penned in with rough fences holding their huge land animals. Every evening the animals were herded up and kept inside the ark, and every morning they were brought back outside again. But the animals brought in at midday never made it back out. The fires the beastman loved so much burned constantly within, or at least thin ribbons of smoke escaped here and there between gaps in the logs.

Once I saw Noah come up to the ark with a freshly fallen tree, pulled by his large land animals. After he had dragged it where he wanted it, Noah sat beside it all afternoon, very contented in the presence of the enormous trunk, where he petted his dog. The more they sat, the more they began to look like one another, he and his dog, happy and hairy and panting in the sun next to their immense treasure. After a while it seemed it didn't matter what they did or where they went; I knew I could go in and out of the ark without any of the beastmen knowing.

"I'm going in," I said.

I left the noonday sun for the strange aquatic light under the roof of the crater-sized nest. Flying down below the woods and into the cave of the ark was always against my instincts, as if Noah's underworld nest was filled with an element heavier than air. I was afraid to breathe it in but could no longer hold my breath. Down in the pitch of the oil-colored light, I watched the small window to the sky grow smaller and dimmer and disappear altogether. The light that filtered through into the lower rungs of dead trees was silty, like a thicker air that smelled of mulch and bark. The branches Noah used to furnish his hell house still had wild twigs on them, curled up and flecked with dead leaves. The leaves fell into the dark as I passed. My eyes and wings were scratchy from collecting cobwebs.

Down in the lower compartments, it was like landing on top of beaches, dunes, and hills of seed.

I ate.

I stuffed myself so full, I couldn't lift myself into the air if I wanted. I would need a strong wind. Then I remembered the need to take an offering to Old Hookbill the Haunted. So I filled my pouch until I could barely waddle to the next compartment, where I found the headless, sewn-shut skins of animals, used as bladders to hold Noah's bloody potion. One of them leaked, only a trickle. I would take just a nip and replenish myself until I felt well enough to fly again.

Instead, I gorged myself on the narcotic juices stewing at the bottom of his stores and was absolutely weighed down, with rocks for wings and stars for eyes and the stars whirled round my head. I hobbled through the wooden caverns dripping with bloody opiate that begged me to drink more. I fell asleep across the fallen timbers and heard the noises that all the trees made when they were alive, the whole forest, lifting their knobby arms to the sun with leaves that spoke of greenery. I could hear the creaking noises the trees made while they grew and leaned into the wind and leaned back. I heard the turning of the worm in their severed trunks. I would sink right here into the rot of the ark, where the roots of the dead things would grow round my heart and strangle it. And I had dreams in which I was being thrown across the darkness by voices. My eyes leaked so badly that my feathers stuck together and I couldn't fly.

At some point, the strange singsong of a human voice carried me up and laid me back down. I kept waking up to the warm languor of being back in the nest again, but a warmer, darker nest full of sumptuous sleep and dried naked bones to keep me snug.

Still in a stupor, I managed to stand up and pick my claws over the corpses of birds yet to be plucked and eviscerated. I hopped onto a set of goat horns on the table and, looking down, realized there was no body attached to the goat's neck. In the room's source of fire and steam, a plump beastwoman stopped her singing. She shrieked. Her face was surrounded by red, sweaty hair, and her mouth lined with nubby teeth. She turned on me and might have caught me, except her plump, whitish arms were petting a chicken, both of them bathed in the steam of a soup. At that instant, I caught a glimpse of the fiery ovens in the next room over. There was a dark, thin girl on her haunches with a mortar and pestle between her legs, grinding down bones, and next to her one of the long-haired sons of Noah, the largest and oldest, wearing an apron and applying concoctions to a large flayed skin. All around me were the excruciating tools of the butcher—the bonesmith, hornsmith, lapidary, and tanner. I flew off into the darkness and searched for an opening in the dark, realizing only afterward how lucky I was that I hadn't been injured or bound.

When I returned to the sky, I called out for the Old Bone and lit on his tree. From his perch, the Old Holy One spoke.

"I was sure you'd ended up in Keeyaw's pantry. You've been gone for three days."

"Three?"

"Let me take a look at you." The horrible scar on his head trembled, as if he were bubbling up inside the ancient eye socket. "Well, okay, for now. Then again, you got Old Hookbill the Blind to look after you, and she can only see three crows any-more, that I know of. You, your papa, and me. But me, I'm fading. I'm growing too faint for her. You know what that means, don't you? When a blind one stops seeing you?"

"No," I said. "I don't."

"It means you're no longer under her protection. It means, soon I'll just sing my song, and fall from the tree."

3. Hookbill the Haunting

To feed the Old Hookbill took courage.

More and more I found her melting back into the scabby tree she came from. She seemed nothing more than a heap of cracked feathers and a rubbery skeleton, all curled up among the glittering objects she stole from the beastman and carried through the sky. She had more of the glittering trinkets down in the stick pile of her nest. She'd lined the bowl of it with a mat of decomposing feathers that I thought were hers but that turned out to be the pale feathers of all of the Misfortunes who had ever come under her protection. I looked for my own down there, brought by Fly Home seasons ago. *"Oh, they're there, all right,"* according to Hookbill My Benefactor. I left my offering on a branch below her cankerous horn.

"No," she said. *"Preen me. Preen me, then feed me."*

She opened her beak, just barely, as if asleep. I felt uneasy about pushing the food down into her papery thin horn. She could barely lift her beak, and I felt she would suffocate from the food I left there. As I nudged her, I felt her give way, and she fell from the branch as a leaf falls, swaying, twirling upon the breeze as if floating downstream. But she landed like a dried-out cow patty, ready to break apart into chunky flakes.

I flew down beside her.

"*You?*" she said. "*Is that you?*"

"*I Am.*"

"*For now. Follow if you can.*"

"*Follow?*"

Her words were as feeble as the weak rasp of her breath.

"*Where I am carried,*" she said, "*follow me there. But I can't let you in, where I'm going. You'll have to find your own way.*"

The offering of grain I had brought from Noah's nest lay scattered in the dirt. I thought of gathering it up, as her last meal. But when I turned around, there was Noah's dog, huffing and chuffing and all too eager, its mangy beard slick with spittle and dust. It woofed Old Hookbill up in its jaws.

I flew up to spear the dog, needling it with my call.

"*Bite harder,*" said the old bird in her scaly voice.

As the dog lunged and bit, Hookbill's feathers cracked more loudly than her bones, and that was the last sound she made. With the old rack of a bird in its mouth, the dog jawed on her a few more times, and then dropped the mess of feathers at its paws, panting. From the trees, I knew right away that old Hookbill was happy to be released from the suffering of her bird's body. Her solace burned bright in the eyes of the beast that had changed, as the dog blinked at me, full of Hookbill the Erie's weird, sagacious ways. With its nose, the dog rolled old Hookbill's charcoal-stiff body across the dirt. It licked at the feathers of the dead crow a few times, then stooped down and lightly carried the withered carcass in its jaws.

The dog turned and trotted down a path through the woods.

I followed.

It's too easy to follow the beasts that toil across the earth on all four legs, or two, having to slog along step by step. With them, you're stealthy without even trying. The dull, shaggy animal didn't even know I was following. But old Hookbill the Heady would look up at me, using the dog's eyes— eyes she inhabited now as the animal loped through the thicket, unaware.

Once upon a time the gods were closer to this
earth; once they walked among us and sat at
our tables. But that was long ago.

—LEWIS HYDE,

Trickster Makes This World

4. The Many Faces of Crow

The shaggy mongrel carried Hookbill the Hollow, or what was left of her flattened corpse, back to the foot of Noah, where the beastman and his family were busy preparing their nest. In the trees above their rookery, I saw Plum Black. She, too, was following the dog's trail, swooping silently from branch to branch. Also in the woods laced with smoke from the beastmen's preparations, I saw the Old Bone and my father.

Seeing me, the Old Bone spoke quietly, or what was quiet for him.

"It was on a day like today that they brought the Mother of Many here."

Much of the nest was shrouded in smoke from the beastman's fires. Above the flames hung large vats of molten pitch that burped and fizzled, making the sound of an evil brook spewing its bluish, blackened smoke that spread out above us and blocked the sun. In the funnel of smoke, the tree branches shivered and bristled, as if trying to fly away. Below were cauldrons of bitumen, pitch, and oil. Noah waved the smoke from his face to see what was in the dog's mouth. He made a face at the mongrel and then turned his attention back to his work. He dipped a straw implement, somewhat like a broom of fern leaves, already dripping with the black ooze, into a vat and slip-slapped it across the bottom of his nest. All of his sons did the same, turning the naked trees of the ark to the glistening, oily color of night. When the afternoon's light broke through clearings in the smoke, it was magnificent. The logs showed through with a cast beneath the black glaze, now the color of shallow swamp water, then of copper's polished glint.

The youngest of Noah's sons, who was rarely any help in Noah's activities, moped in the bushes beyond the smoke. Then even he noticed something in the dog's mouth. He watched as the dog placed the crow corpse down on the dirt and studied it—Hookbill the Demented, studying her old demented self. On a childish whim, the son picked up the corpse and dipped it into the molten concoction. Then he held her up over his head, thick with pitch. He made the strange whinnying sounds of his kind as he climbed the scaffolding to the ark and used her as a paintbrush. Feathers stuck to the logs. One of the other sons protested, and the two argued. Old Hookbill's carcass became so plastered to their nest that the young boy just left her there—embossed, wings out, enraged, her beak opened in a screech, melting into a wing.

Then Noah himself walked near to see what the commotion was about.

"Now look what you've done."

I searched for the God Crow, wondering why I could suddenly understand the strange sounds of human speech. But I saw only the Hookbill in the eyes of the hound and she barked up at me.

"What?" said the boy, who seemed embarrassed now by his attempt to ridicule the crow corpse.

He tried prying the old bird body from the bulwarks, only to have the tips of her bones come loose while the feathers stayed. Frustrated, he mashed all of her back into the pitch.

"I thought things might have gone faster," he said.

"That was thinking?" said Noah. The old man squinted round at the shrubs, and the treetops, and the clouds, then the prow of his nest, where the dead crow was stuck for good. "At least someone was thinking."

· · ·

In a copse of trees, without a noise, appeared the God Crow. It was the God Crow to me anyway. But each of us saw something different, each according to his or her own story. The Old Bone saw what looked like one of Noah's own kind, also old, wearing a long white beard. This God rode in on a donkey and had a rooster on his arm. Plum Black said she'd noticed a break in the weather that distilled the smoke until it disappeared. Noah climbed down from his scaffolding and talked to a tree. At first I thought Noah was just muttering to himself. But as he spoke, a tiger appeared from the underbrush and sat in a bank of tall grass, swishing his tail just beyond Noah's sight. Another tiger neared, and the two of them disappeared as if of one mind back into the thicket. A camel raised its head above the hedge and studied the human family busy at work. An owl landed, as did its mate. Strange birds never before seen flew in quick circles through the waning smoke, and a hyena laughed its lonely, hideous laugh somewhere far away. At one point my father thought he'd seen the Bird: God appeared to him, in size about halfway between a human and a crow. It had the body of a crow, crusty-winged and crow-blue, but the face of the beastman, dull, naked, and slow-moving like the human, drawn to either what was entirely obvious or entirely obscure. Then again the waves of heat and smoke altered in the air, dulling my father's sight.

But I saw neither the Half-Bird nor the creatures. For me, the God Crow watched in much the same way Our Mother of Many did. You felt the presence of the mother, but also felt she wasn't watching. Then, just when you forgot she was there, she would reproduce the long, low hum you were humming, matching you note for note, and the feathers on the back of your neck would stand. All my attention fell upon It when It landed on a log next to one of Noah's many fires. The old man walked over and sat down beside It, and the two spoke.

"It's been far too long," said Noah. "I build in darkness."

The God Crow pecked at the bark of Its perch, ruffling and unruffling Its feathers.

"Okay, okay," said Noah. "What do you want?"

"Let's have tea," said God.

They did.

Noah put the tea down in front of the God Crow, Who was busy watching a fly wheel through the air, but for only a second. Then the Bird began preening Its feathers.

Finally, It spoke.

"Noah, do you believe in me?"

"I build the ark."

"Still, you doubt me?"

"Must all drown?"

"Yes," said the God Crow. *"The fallen ones, the giant corrupters, everyone."*

"Even beasts? Even children?"

"Stop," said the Lord. *"Already, I mourn. My creation has always saddened me. But soon, even more."*

"Oh, Great God of Adam, for fifty-two years now I build your ark in the hope of delaying your vengeance. But also with hopes that humankind might rid itself of at least some of its evils."

"Fifty-two years?"

"Well, it takes time," said Noah. "To find the right trees, invent the right tools."

"It took you fifty-two years just to get started."

"The trees had to grow."

"And what did you do until then?"

"Oh—" Noah picked at a wild strand from his beard gone stiff and black with bitumen. "Same thing I'd been doing the last four hundred years."

"Did you think I was not?" asked the God Crow. *"Not serious, or not truthful?"*

"I thought it was . . . well, I thought you were . . . testing."

"Testing whom?"

"All of earth's flesh," said Noah, trying to get the answer right. "So that the violence might calm down a bit, and purity come to dwell again in human hearts. It could happen."

"It seems you've been delaying the ark much longer than you say."

"Yes, perhaps it has been too long in the making, yet—"

"You doubt me."

"Forgive me. How can the world be destroyed with water when it is so dry?"

"Would it help if I shot my great lightning bolt across the sky?"

"I need more time," said the beastman called Noah. "People need more time. What am I saying? I don't believe you can do it."

"Three days hence, I will shoot my bolt. That will be the onset."

"I will need more time," said Noah, "to build another ark, so that the fearful might repent upon seeing the floodwaters and find haven in your most merciful boat."

"What you've done here is enough."

"But even that's not finished. If you drown them now, then I'll go with them."

Then the one known as Noah looked with anguish at his three strong sons at rest at the far end of the ark. They laughed and joked with one another, unable to wash the pitch from their arms and robes as their mother brought them their supper.

As if moving in a weary slumber, Noah began chopping.

"Leave me now, please," he said to the God Crow. "I can't bear the thought of it."

And he swung down with his implement into the pulp of a fallen Giant.

5. *The Garment*

I followed after the God Crow, who flew beyond the rookery, but lost sight of the Endless All-Knowing in the thick of the woods. Below, on the beast-man's path, I saw a man with a walking stick. He was heading back toward Noah's inferno. Old Hookbill, who lived in the dog's eye now, lumbered over with the clumsy gait of a dog to greet the traveler. She barked up into the trees at me, and I followed them back to Noah's nest. Perhaps this was the god the Old Bone had spoken of, because this one had a long white beard like Noah's and walked slowly and deliberately like him, using the walking stick. But then, this god had no donkey and no rooster on his shoulders. His face bore crying whiskers; his crying whiskers hung in billowy clouds.

Upon seeing the traveler, Noah once again dropped his brush of pitch and stood before the stranger. The two smiled long at each other and did not speak. They stood face to face and placed their hands one upon the other's shoulders until the words came from their beards.

"Uriel, my friend, how is paradise?"

"As lonely as always. But use your own eyes. You could see Eden from here, if it weren't for all the smoke."

"Shall we have tea?"

They sat down on the same log that Noah had sat upon with the God Crow. The traveler squinted uneasily at the cloud drifts of smoke above Noah's home.

Instead of tea, Noah came back from the ark with one of his animal-skin bottles.

"Here, friend," he said and sat again on the log.

The traveler held the large bladder-like body up over his shoulder and the red liquid poured from the open neck.

Soon the talk of the two humans became strange gibberish to me again as Hookbill the Mongrel scraped her toes across the dirt and walked up to the feet of Noah's sons. There she begged for scraps from their plates that they readily threw down to her. Old Hookbill seemed happy to be an inhabitant of the dog's eyes, one blue and the other brown, so the ancient sorcerer could inhabit only one eye at a time, and keep not only her identity but a crow's one-eyed stare. She could perform feats of the will without the dog ever knowing. Such were the powers of Old Hookbill—the intermediary between beast and crow. What did the sons talk about? Back and forth, over and over, babble, chitchat—until the one known as Ham threw his plate down in a fit.

"Why don't we just plaster all of God's creatures up there?" he said.

"Relax. Father and his guest are beginning to take note. Besides, up there, this bird will be our benefactor."

"Blaspheme your own home," said Ham.

"Oh-ho, always so serious," said another, as Ham stood in a fit and stomped into the ark. Hookbill the Dog Now followed.

Throughout the nest, all up and down its long passages, the dog barked. But it was the Hookbill Within who showed me the secret accesses into the vessel. These openings were often up high, where the logs of the hull and the main deck met. Some were large enough for the dog's entire head to fit through, where Hookbill would look out at me with one happy, surprised eye. Other openings were so small that only one paw fit through, and Hookbill would do this for me, scratching the wood with her nails to get my attention and getting pitch all the way up to her dewclaw. In this way, I learned all the entrances into the ark that the beastman never used or even knew about. The holes were too large for the pitch to plug up. Now I could enter and leave their nest whenever I wished in even further secrecy.

But hunger returned to the hound as it brought Hookbill back to the log, where Noah and the traveler sat. Once again, I could understand the discussion between them. As he spoke, Noah worked his strange, spider-like clutches through the Hookbill's dusty old mange.

The stranger coughed from the thick fumes in the air, and spoke.

"And to think you were the source of such laughter, Noah. Seeing your fantastic ship now, they'd really have a howl."

"Would they, Uriel? Have I turned my back on everyone? Have I turned my back on you?"

"It's the will of God. Why?" The stranger shrugged. "Who can say? Still, you won't believe me. Look. Three magnificent sons. You have much to be happy about."

Noah walked into his ark and returned with an eel. He removed one of the cauldrons of black stewing tar and held the eel up on a stick above the flames. Where had Noah possibly gotten this tender morsel? It had been months—since the drought began—since we'd seen a creature of water. The extremes of the fish, the eyes, the mouth, the fins, all began to curl back in a skeletal shrivel.

The Old Bone and I watched from our perch.

The Hookbill walked near, attentive, already begging.

"This offering," said the one known as Noah, "is not for my God. It goes out to your daughter. How old is she now?"

"She grows so fast," said the man through his weepy tendrils. "Eleven years now."

"Then I will dance at her wedding."

The two nodded their heads, and sipped from the severed neck of the hide, then held their heads in silence.

"Noah," said the traveler, "every day now, a mysterious rumbling sounds from the ground. A rumbling that grows closer, each hour, it seems. Each night now I hear it rumble up through the ground, to my bed, and my pillow. It sounds up from beneath my sleeping wife. The side of my head grows weary with it. In the lowlands, twice a day now, the raging tidewaters flood the land, unearthing the dead from their graves and sending them awash. The sky rips open. It howls. Rivers run backward."

"Uriel, go to your home. Return quickly with your family. We have all that you will need here. Hurry."

The traveler spoke. "The people with boats," he said, "they have already fled. And the people of the lowlands, who know of your great ship, already they make progress on the journey here. Noah, safeguard yourself."

"But you. You can find refuge inside with us."

"No. I am only a messenger. I've been sent to give you my message, and that is all."

"All?"

"One last thing."

"What?" Noah placed his eel on a stick against the log, the fleshy flanks blackened and the fishy juices gone. "You haven't been listening to me," he said. "You can be saved."

The traveler reached into his knapsack and pulled out the garment of a very small, newborn beastchild.

"See that it is worn again, Noah." The traveler rose to his feet. "You have my blessing. Now I must go. I haven't much time."

And the traveler walked away through the clearing, moving much like the smoke that clouded the air. Noah held the small garment up before him. He could open all of the material across his fingertips. With just one knobbed, paddle-like hand, he spread it out, and he studied every inch and stitch of the child's dress.

The eel was too tasty to me and the Old Bone and to Hookbill the Dog Now, too, who left most of it for us. Afterward, I flew into one of my new openings to the ark to have my fill there as well.

And it came to pass at the end of forty days,
that Noah opened the window of the ark
which he had made:
And he sent forth a raven, which went forth
to and fro, until the waters were dried up
from off the earth.

—GENESIS, 8:6

6. Butterfly Net

Dead of night.

Almost day.

The noise came from far off, like the echo of a whole forest of falling trees. All else was silence. No songbird sang the joy of the day to come, no beast slumped the forest floor, and no crow sang, *Come follow*. But the thunder was constant and low and traveled beneath the ground. The earth trembled with it, even the uppermost leaves, and above the hills, the sky exploded from within. Thunderheads flashed in the ominous dark, then receded back to darkness as the lesser bolts continued to twist and disappear. The lightning was like a school of trapped fish that flashed and wrangled against the walls of the mushroom cloud that spread out above the lake that had no other shore. The apparition of the world's end was a horrific monster, spreading its monstrous wings out in a magnitude that would be too fearful to look upon if it weren't also awesome and spellbinding above the reddening horizon.

"I've got to see what that's all about," I said.

"You don't know?" asked the Old Bone from the next tree over.

"That's why I want to see it."

"Lightning," said the Old One, flapping after me. "If a bolt doesn't get you, the thunder will. It gives little crows like you a heart attack."

Many a crow met its end that way, even if the lightning struck nowhere near.

We flew down to the lake that had no far shore, and now it had no near shore either. What once was swampland was now a dirty sargasso tide that spread out in all directions, and at the horizon, the sky was the same earthy gray-brown color where the tops of the hills dissolved into the cloud cover. The floodwater, flat and dull, broke out into large effluvial rips that frothed and roiled full of the flotsam of the land, and dead fish, and animals. The top halves of all the trees of the forest rocked in the underwater currents and eddies spilling up around them. Small mammals clung to the branches of the surrounded trees and stared with round saucer eyes at the water assailing them from below.

"The beastman," said the Old Bone in a whisper as we flew. "The beast." Though to me it was the God Crow who had perpetrated such a madness as to make the rivers run backward. We flew on in the direction of the city of humans. In the river's ravine, the tides buoyed up the waves of corpses. Pale bodies spun and bobbed, more fishes, rows of them, fowl, animals caught unaware. A stag sloshed against the rocky embankment, cut hugely from the violence and pushed by a flotsam of uprooted trees, rotten vegetation, insects, fungus, spores, seeds, pollen, all mixed with algae and the brackish swill of lake weed water. From the air, even a crow could smell the stench. The Old Bone and I flew on.

A thick mist, made sharp by saltwater, hung before us and grew into a violent, rainy fog. It made the flying hard, and I wanted to leave it right away, but I wasn't sure if we could, or which way to fly. At the human roost, surrounded by water, the inhabitants broke apart their homes on the village earth mounds. They used the larger trunks and beams to build makeshift rafts and tentatively pushed themselves off into the flowing streets and the slurry beyond the city walls. Some sent themselves directly into the onslaught, where their rafts broke apart or spun out of control and disappeared into the abyss. Others pushed themselves off as best they could to shores where the flood had not yet reached and were still swept off by unseen forces. On the hillsides, small herds of them moved toward Noah's nest. They moved there from all directions, heading uphill.

"*A Great Offering,*" said the Old Bone. "*A Jubilation, perhaps.*"

And though I was already engorged and groggy from the stewed carrion at the rim of the flood, we followed the herds of beastmen out of an uncontrollable excitement from the thought that a strange Jubilation might take place. We flew from tree to tree as they slogged along at their cumbersome pace, and there was less reason than normal for us to sneak above the poor-hearing creatures. The opening of the sluiceway from the mountain filled the sky with a rumbling, and the beastmen wailed one to the other, or to the woods, or to no one.

The humans trudged uphill above the clouds and into the sunlight. The first waves of them found Noah in a field far from his rookery, holding a small net and watching a pair of smart butterfly wings bandied in the breeze above the meadow. One from the herd quieted the others, and he alone approached. As he walked through the field, he waved his arms to get Noah's attention. But Noah kept his perplexed stare on his little net.

Without looking up, he spoke: "You scared him away."

"Him?"

"The butterfly, orange with black markings along the wings. The he of that kind. I already have a she-butterfly of that color. I thought I'd caught a he, but I injured him with the net, and he did not survive my attack."

"Noah, we repent. We heed your God's warnings."

"Of course, now——"

"We must board your boat."

"No. First the small. First the very, very small, so I can place them in all of the out-of-the way places. That way I'll have room for the rest."

"The rest?"

"Of the earth's creatures."

"Animals? For food? We will help you. Noah, do not turn your back on your own kind. We must go in now. The water rises daily. It follows our path. You have no choice. Look at our numbers. We're going in."

"Oh?" Noah seemed relieved. "Very well, then."

And the herd of his kind started in an orderly procession up to his home, where they hoped to outwit the rising floodwaters. The man called Noah sat down in the field and watched them in speculation. He muttered to himself. "It will take them a forever going that way." He picked up the reed cage and watched the butterfly batter the delicate dust off its wings against the wickets. Once all of his kind were gone, Noah cried out, "God of Adam! How am I ever to do this thing?"

Then the God Crow flew near. Or maybe It had been there all along. In a tree just above Noah, the God Crow watched unannounced and left Noah to speak unknowingly to the air.

"So far, I have just the she and he of the honeybee, the locust, and some other creeping-crawling kind. But of what kind I can't say, nor can I tell for sure if they are the she and he, since to me they are all alike. And tell me this, before the ark is swamped and we all perish. Is not the thinking of the people more than the silence of a grub, or a whole snorting, bellowing forest of baboonery?"

To that the God Crow flapped magnificently, puffing Its proud feathers, when from a clearing came a giraffe raising and lowering its great, broad neck as it neared. Noah stood, readying himself before the great spotted beast could trample him. But the giraffe stopped just short of Noah and also stood, as tall as a tree, knock-kneed, flicking its ears and looking down. Then the God Crow Itself flew down on top of the giraffe's head, between the fuzzy horns, and spoke.

"Noah, today your goodly grandfather, Methuselah, has died, mentor to you in the useful sciences of horticulture, metallurgy, apothecary, alchemy, astrology, religion, healing, animal husbandry, truths of heaven and earth, moralistic tales, and the art of growing trees. At the age of nine hundred and sixty-nine years, he has died. It is the time of grace and mourning."

"Of course it is," said Noah. "Must you kill everyone?"

"Enough. Worry not about the gathering of the earth's creatures. Go now and sit beside the door of your ark and observe each creature as it comes to you. Waste no time, Noah. I know you won't."

And the majestic God Crow receded, riding the crown of the giraffe, whose neck and haunches surged smoothly with each loping stride back into the woods.

The one known as Noah went forth as the God Crow had bidden him. And the Old Bone and I flew as if the Mighty Bird had instructed us as well.

All throughout the forest, strange sights passed before our eyes. Mist from the pounding flood grew as thick as rain, and gray shadows like ghosts ran through it. Two humped shadows big and buffalo-like swept through a clearing, then disappeared back into the thickening gloom. It was hard to make out the shapes. For a time, I even lost track of the Old Bone. But we called to each other. I thought I saw him, but it was a pair of strange birds I'd never seen before, resting from the heavy air and waiting on the branches. With strange amazement, Noah noticed them, too, all the many creatures, especially the larger ones, scared, lumpish shapes that moved with a weary patience.

Noah knew the forest pathways much better than his fellow creatures and took a shortcut. I followed above him. Back at his home, Noah sat on a stump below the ramp to the ark as he had been instructed, and waited.

Then a small herd of massive, hulking beasts hoofed their way through the mist of his rookery. These were the horses, their manes flattened wet against their necks and their arched necks steaming as their hoofs came down.

"Oh, my," said Noah, "a piebald, two draft horses, an Arabian for speed—"

His eyes twinkled, and he wiggled his fingers. He made a mugging face at his mule. "You see that?"

And then seven—because they were considered clean—seven clean, fine horses clumped up the gang ramp and rang through the decks, and they knew just where to go, into the stalls where Noah's family had thrown down fresh hay. And so it went. Seven each of the clean kind, and two of those unclean, found their way past Noah into the cages and stalls and compartments awaiting them. At first the chosen beasts would wait at the outskirts of Noah's rookery. Then they would creep before the ark as if they were shy, or in the wrong place.

But when the Old Bone and I cast our eyes downhill, the approaching of the beasts had turned into a long procession of animal life, great and small, with no end to all the wide heads, tall horns, houses of fleece, time-heavy tails. You couldn't imagine so many forms of fur, feather, or scale. Most of the creatures arrived in pairs, but some in sevens, while others arrived sopped-skinny and alone, as if the storm and the chaotic migration had singled them out. A furry, ferretish creature—but with webbed feet—climbed somehow down from a tree and watched the procession for a while before rushing in under the plodding of the hooves and disappearing into the ark. An anxious doe splashed in the puddles alongside the throng and then bounded up the ramp. Needing no paths, the birds swarmed in from all directions, like bursts of wind. Flurries of the mixed flock descended, then nothing, then a few scattered birds, and then a whirlwind all over again. They fought against the gales to enter the ark.

"*Aren't you going in?*" asked the Old Bone.

"*Me?*" I thought of the hot ovens that burned deep in the hold, and the disemboweled corpses, and the piles of feather. "*No. I'll take my chances out here.*"

"*I thought you liked it inside Keeyaw's nest.*"

Then the dark angel of doom himself, the raven, came down. Instead of flying straight in, the raven sat in a tree beyond the ark, as large as the God Crow Itself, where he could observe all the comings and goings. He flapped and bobbed as he called out to the one they called Noah, "*Who? Who? Who are you?*"

Noah gave no answer but only lifted his eyebrows in scrutiny.

"*Very well, I know who you are, anyway,*" said the raven.

And instead of entering, the raven shot his sharp glances all around.

He lifted his throat and from his great horn came sounds faint and familiar to me, made even stranger because the raven couldn't possibly have known what he was saying. There were calls deep from his gut, where hungry brother My Other still lived. Somehow my sibling was able to pipe his little song through the raven's throat. He sang songs from his time as My Other, and even from his season down in the yolk. "*I Am! Pale bird! Fear not,*" he called. "*I will always watch over you.*" He called out to the bubbles and the last creatures of creation, still flailing in the headwaters, or climbing higher into the trees. When the raven turned his eyes my way, there he was, My Other, in the raven's stare, except he was all raven now. He bid me to beware and laughed at the same time and then entered the ark.

"*Fear not.*"

Owing to a heavy swell right on shore, the
Vessel struck and was lost: the Loss of this
Ship had been foretold . . . In the Spring of
the Year, a Flight of Crows were fighting in
the Air, and making a dreadful noise. One
of them was killed by the rest, and fell upon
the Deck of this Ship; the whole Swarm
immediately descended, and entirely
devoured the vanquished Bird, leaving no
other Vestiges than the Feathers behind.

—THOMAS DAVISON, *Rural Sports*

7. The Unclean

The passage of time from day to night blurred in the sky, until there was
neither. In the limbo of God's wrath, the last animals on earth plodded the
paths uphill, one behind the other, slouched heavily at the neck, unable to
hide their faces from the onslaught. Between the lowering of the sky and
the rising of the waters, the inhabitable plain shrank to a thin nimbus lit
from below as if the powerful sea drifts, held at bay by the land walls of
the valley, could throw out their own light by their movement. The vast
whirlpools of gray-green light moved as the flood moved, surfacing like the
afterthought of some infinitely large indifference. In its slow path, hillsides
gave way, sprawling forests disappeared, uprooted trees twirled in the rips.
The clouds were dark from the flood headwaters having turned whole hillsides to pumice and sending it up into the air. The droplets spun in confused
circles without falling, so that the cattle and sheep could not figure which

way to hide their heads. The gray, wet air hung like smoke and left its film on everything.

It was in this earthen smoke that the herds of humans arrived as if sleep-walking, feeling their way uphill, their garments wet and plastered like their hair to their white, sickly skin. Again one from the herd stood before Noah, who still sat beside the door to his ark, as he had been instructed.

She was a righteous woman, carrying a large child in her arms, and two girls walked behind her, shivering.

"You must——" the woman gasped. "No, you must," she said again. "Not all of us have God to tell us what to do." Water flew from her face with the blow of each word. "Many of us were swallowed on the way here. Parts of the path collapsed under our feet. The water rushed up behind us."

Noah hung his head. He said, "The ark is so full. I have not enough food and space for those already inside."

"Who? Who is inside?"

Noah did not speak.

The crowd began yelling threats about the beasts on board, and how the ark had filled with vermin when Noah wasn't looking, and how they'd fix that.

But the one they call Noah spoke. "You are too many for me to fight back, even if I wanted. But also, you are too many for the ark. It will not survive your numbers."

And the full herd of humans moved—slowly at first, then with much shoving and incidents of flying fists, and individuals flung down, and many trodden underfoot. There was a great panic to reach the ramp before the others. Seeing the throng, Noah turned his face to the sky.

"You see how it is?" he asked. "The ark will be swamped."

Pushed by the advancing waters, many of the earth's last beasts had gathered on the outskirts of Noah's rookery, including the largest of God's creation. As if on command, these hippos and buffaloes stepped between the ark and the mob of hysterical beastmen. The great brown bear, destined to be ravaged by the flood and sucked into the bubbles, stood before the entrance of salvation and roared. An enormous tiger leapt up into the throng, affixed his teeth into the skull of a human, and dragged the fresh corpse into the thicket. Wolves and lions tore the fleeing humans to pieces, and dispersed the rest. Elk, boar, and bull ran through the crowd, goring men and women and hurling them aside, and the human herds broke out into a mass scurrying. Soon the field before Noah's ark became empty again, except for a low, guttural, rumbling underground, which was the flood drawing near.

Then the awful creatures came to the ark—leeches, ticks, naked mole rats, monsters, creatures of the dark that live only by moonlight or deep under the earth, and it pained them to be out in the darkened afternoon—shrews and water rats and creatures too loathsome for Adam ever to see, let alone name, virus, pestilence, plague, the unseen and evil to everything but their own kind. These, it seemed, were not led here by the wings of the God Crow but came of their own accord, in unregulated numbers far exceeding the rest.

"Lord!" Noah's voice rose in anguish. "Lord! How are we to survive? We are so few! And now these cancers of creation wish to enter back into the world."

But no sign came from the Crow. No act.

And when Noah stooped to keep one such creature from entering, they all scattered. Like drops of mercury, they shot up the ramp and deep into the recesses of the ark, where they lurked unseen and expectant, outside the cages, beyond Noah's law.

The Fifth Day

On the same day with the fishes, the birds
were created, for these two kinds of animals
are closely related to each other. Fish are
fashioned out of water, and birds out of
marshy ground saturated with water . . .
mammals were formed out of solid earth.

— WILLIS BARNSTONE, HAGGADAH
(JEWISH LEGEND), *The Other Bible*

8. *The Door*

The field below the ark pooled with muddy wallow seeping up from underground. Soon Noah's rookery was inundated. A river without banks ran through the wash, and what should have been rapid whitewater was the same gray-brown churn, roaring until the waves grew constant. The frothing headwaters lapped against the dunnage below the ark and spilled around the trees. Still Noah stood outside, waiting for God's will to change, and the waters to abate.

All at once the ark lurched. One end of it bucked the hillside as the land below caved and gave way. With the animal mass inside and the water forces pushing from without, the untested hull threatened to burst. The blackened timbers, stacked in place for more than a lifetime, creaked and complained. From outside, Noah turned all about himself and did nothing, except for more of his watching and wading through the roiling slack water for a sign. He listened, mouth open, to the siren's long lament above the ending of the world. Wringing-wet animals and humans cried out and took refuge in the trees as the earth sank from sight. But most of the animals floated by, their gray, wet heads above the flood, dog-paddling as best they could as they were carried off. On one branch, a large, ferocious cat snarled, sopped to the bone like a water rat, unable to move or let any other creature near. On another tree, a man handed a small child up to a higher branch where the mother waited. There the woman sat, cradling the child's head as if it were an egg.

Noah looked at the last vestige of the world's beauty, being swept from sight. He looked at the tangled mess of his ark, unshorn branches reaching out from house and hull, hardly finished, black, shriveled leaves held in place by pitch.

"How can you choose *this* over the wonders of your own handiwork?" he asked of the air. Meanwhile, the floodwaters rushed at his knees, then his waist. In the tide he looked like nothing more than a thin, bent tree; his robes and mane hung like streamers of moss, flailing in the storm.

From inside the ark, a beastwoman cried out, "Noah. Come inside! You'll be swept off!"

Finally he waded back toward the ramp, but fell and was carried a small ways off.

"No. It's time to die," he said, half-swimming. He was calmed by his motion in the water and studied an eddy from his hand. "For me, it's time. Now, you—you are just. You save the world. Our children are on the ark. That's enough."

"Fine!" she yelled, and disappeared within.

From the ark's ramp came a chair, flying into the drink. It was a huge chair hewn from heavy wood, and it floated down current, toward Noah.

"Woman! What are you doing? That is my chair."

"I thought you might need it," came the answer from within.

Noah tried to drag it back through the onslaught, but made no progress and let the chair go. He neared the vessel almost in a swim now, when a riptide threw him back into the ark. As if by an invisible hand, the ramp to the door swung closed and tumbled Noah deep within the darkness of his own handiwork.

Then the door to the ark was latched shut behind him.

The God Crow—I could barely make out Its silhouette in the grayish-green light that seemed to rise up from the sloshing waves—flew down and perched Itself above the bolted door, where It preened and stretched out Its feathers. Below the Great Bird, the chaos once quelled by Its Mightiness and the light once parted from the darkness all rolled into one glistening gloom and reclaimed itself.

The passage from day to night, or the difference between the two, was obliterated, and the sky gave no answer. Not even lightning could break through the thickening sky. And the banks of stinging, salty fog grew into an ether neither water nor air but hovering between the two.

"What now?" I asked.

Before the wind had calmed, it pinned the Old Bone up against a tree trunk, so that he could stand propped up on his one good foot.

"I had a pretty good life," he said. *"Now I will sing my song, and go. And I will sing for you, too; for what I sing, you sing. We sing from the same songscape."*

And he sang of all the Mothers of Many who filled the woods with song, and who helped him trick an egret or two out of catfish, and of the young jack crows who taunted the beastman's dog away from his beastman's food, good crows, too, every one of them, wherever they flew to. *"But it doesn't matter now, does it? And what about my very own sibling, your sweet Mother of Many, dragged under by her own nest? She must have seen it coming, though, because she asked me to watch over you—"*

"She what?"

The Old Bone stopped singing.

The flooding below us grew constant, after the saltwater wash had claimed all of the land, and had nowhere to go but up. The Old Bone and I waited in the trees. All the creatures waited there for days it seemed as the huge riptides rolled by, and you could see the pattern the drizzle made on the flood's surface. Occasionally an animal swam by through the canals between the treetops, a set of antlers, or a small, dark head above a pumping body. The filling up of the world with water would take a while. And all the creatures I saw, clinging to the treetops or floating by on a raft of debris, had a calm, shocked patience, as though this whole miserable affair would all go away soon, if they could only wait long enough.

I asked the Old Bone about his song again. *"My mother came to you?"* I asked.

"Yeah, well. Not really. She just called my name."

"And what did she say?"

"She said, 'Old Bone!'"

"I mean what did she say when she saw you?"

"She said we Misfortunes should stick together."

"Where are your white feathers?"

"Keeyaw got to them when he chopped off my tail. I had one or two back there, at one time."

"Our Mother of Many," I whispered slowly, amazed once again at the reach of her song.

"Who can say where she is now?" sang the Old Bone, a little impatient to continue his song. *"Not like old Hookbill the Haunted, stuck by the feathers to Keeyaw's nest, and her soul singing somewhere inside that mutt of man's. What wonders she will see in the next world. Hear me now, the song of Old Bone the Tailless, as I sing my tailless song, short and simple, like my one good foot. And I sing for I Am, too, a pretty good bird in his own right. I know. I've seen it, with my one good eye. Why, I tried to show him the ark of Keeyaw, but when the time came, he wouldn't go in. Good for him. May he hear this song, so he can sing on and on about our most beautiful aerie, our songscape, amen."*

And the Old Bone blinked his one good eye against the salty spume. Even the death in his scarred-over eye blinked.

"*C'mon. Let's go see if your old aerie's still there,*" he said. "*That's as good a place as any to die.*"

So up we flew, for the last time, to the home of my old song.

But the wind took us completely. All was floodwater and waves and clouds that engulfed us. We were in the hurly-burly of chaos, like an angry cloud of bird wings, large wings, small ones, and raggedy-feathered ones that could no longer beat against the wind, and the birds smacked into us and flew past knocking into more birds.

Then the sky calmed, and we found a clearing where we flew through the eye of the hurricane over the ark. There a bird could hold steady over the flood that had engulfed all things, all hillsides and mountains. All was water. Already nearly every surface of the ark was covered with birds, like a crowded nesting colony of every color, shape, and size. The ark listed perilously from the weight. The Old Bone and I searched for a place to land. But there was none. How long could we flap in the clearing above the ark?

Because the Old Bone had no tail, he could not glide at all but kept flapping and flapping, going down despite himself. All around us, birds were dropping from the skies, making hardly a splash in the momentous seas.

The Old Bone said, "*Do you see a spot to land?*"

"No. I don't."

"*My wings,*" he said. "*I'm setting down anyway. Farewell, my friend.*"

He let himself drop in among the birds on the ark, and I kept in flight just behind him, watching the seagulls and other large floating birds, well rested as they were, peck at the one-eyed crow for a brief time until he splashed into a wave crashing against the hull and disappeared without a trace to the foaming seas.

When Flok, a famous Norwegian Navigator,
was going to set out from Shetland for
Iceland, then called Gardarsholm, he took on
board some Crows, because the Mariner's
Compass was not yet in Use.

—THOMAS DAVISON, *Rural Sports*

9. Trespass

The ark listed horribly from the staggering weight of all the earth's birds, and the skies were full of more. A funnel of birds like a wobbling twister followed the ark, where the birds fought and died for a place to land. On one side, the bulwarks dipped below the boiling seas. The bow stem and stern would alternate, each sinking below the waves while the other thrust itself up, until finally there were so many birds, the ark could no longer lift its nose from the seas. It lay like an injured whale beginning to turn its belly to the sky. A wave would spill over the ark and wash a broad flank of birds into the sea, only to be replaced immediately by more that dropped from the sky. Birds fell and smacked up against me on their way down to the hissing waves, where, faintly, I saw God's face move upon the waters.

The Great Beak opened and blew.

From the mouth of the seas came a furious blast that swept all the birds from the ark and blew them away, and just as I was sweeping past the vessel, it righted itself and I hit up against its sides. Pinned by the wind against the dead trees, I looked and saw that I'd landed beside the sickly husk of Hookbill the Haunted, beak open, embossed on the hull. And I remembered the secret entrances she had shown me. Flopping down to one, I entered easily.

．．．

Inside, the ark was a place now of rank and humid darkness, desperate and dangerous to trip through, and too dark for flying. The distant, fiery antlers of the beastman would temporarily cast their dim light from somewhere within the ark's tangled structure. And just as quickly as the torches appeared, they vanished, but not before revealing cage after cage of spooked, cowering creatures, subdued and staring out with passive eyes or curled up asleep in pools of their own bile. The turbulence of the flood dulled them as though they were soused in the beastman's bloody, narcotic potions.

And the ark rolled, not like a single vessel but like a float of logs loosely tied together, like the long spine of a sea monster, riding along the crests and troughs of the sea. The howling outside was still the sad siren of devastation, and the clacking, creaking, twisting sound of the ark was a faint, lost complaint beneath it.

Once, when one of Noah's sons passed by with the fiery antler, I saw the cages of creatures in the orb's smoky glow. I realized that I was of no pair, no part of the seven clean beasts, and no part of the two-by-two entry of the unclean either. I was not supposed to be on the ark. I was not to be saved. But hadn't the God Crow told me to be ready when the time came? Or was Everlasting All-Knowing talking to Plum Black, or Night Time, or my father, when I'd mistaken it as a message to me? Perhaps my place was in the flood, to drown, or to see what was beyond it. Perhaps the birds were faring better out there.

I stuck my head out from between two logs and into the stinging air. I saw nothing but the wings of God that shot like arrows across the waves. The long lines of wind had no end and no beginning except that of darkness, and like a strange, aggrieved outlaw, I ducked back inside and stayed where I was.

IV.

The Ark

Dismantle your house, build a boat.

Leave possessions, search out living things.

Reject chattels and save lives!

Put aboard the seed of all living things, into the boat.

The boat that you are to build

Shall have her dimensions in proportion,

Her width and length shall be in harmony,

—EPIC OF GILGAMESH, TABLET XI

In the end the ship fell far short of the necessities, and to this day the world still suffers for it.

Noah built the Ark. He built it the best he could, but left out most of the essentials. It had no rudder, it had no sails, it had no compass, it had no pumps, it had no charts, no lead-lines, no anchors, no log, no light, no ventilation; and as for cargo-room—which was the main thing—the less said about that the better. It was to be at sea eleven months, and would need fresh water enough to fill two Arks of its size—yet the additional Ark was not provided.

—MARK TWAIN, LETTERS FROM THE EARTH

Berrossus, the Babylonian high priest from the temple Bel Mar Duk, states that in his time around 300 BC, remains of the ark could still be seen and some get pitch from the ship by scraping it off and use it for amulets. . . .

In 380 AD, Epiphanus, Bishop of Salamis, visited the land of the Kurds and stated that he was shown wood from Noah's ark. . . .

At 11:15 on July 31st 1969, [Fernand] Navarra and the SEARCH team struck pay dirt: five pieces of wood resembling planking, with the longest piece nearly 17 inches long. This new additional find confirmed Navarra's discovery, and for many scientists proved conclusively that Noah had indeed stepped forth onto dry land here on Mount Ararat.

—*IN SEARCH OF NOAH'S ARK*, SUN CLASSIC PICTURES

All animals, even insects, were human size in
the Garden, walked upright, and spoke. At
least they appeared human size to Adam.

—DAVID ROSENBURG, *The Lost Book*
of Paradise: Adam and Eve
in the Garden of Eden

1. Book of Sapphires

The ark creaked and moaned.

The blackened timbers begged for the mercy to bust apart and be sent adrift from the will of the beastman that held them fast. There they could die a fitting tree-like death and have their spirits released, too, pulverized by the endless words of the wind and the sea if that's all there was ever going to be. Every once in a while a mournful whining as if from a living creature traveled past in the wind. But mostly it was a barren, awful howling. Even the *yes* and *no* of God was gone, leaving nothing but the heaving anger, now beyond anger, until it was nothing, just nothing mashing on itself.

The ark was stifling with the soggy animal air, and seasickness, and the smells of wetted sawdust and pitch where it leaked down from the hull. The farther down you went, the thicker the stench became. Many animals swampish and cold-blooded escaped to the sumpwater at the bottom of the ark. Crocodiles, long-tailed dragons, and water snakes slithered around in the sloshing swill that grew as the ark rolled and leaned under the forces of the flood. The hippopotami were down there, and all manner of watery creatures pushed and ate their way from their cages to live down in the dark, bubbling cesspool. Elephants reached into the rank water with their trunks but did not drink. They only sprayed the salty element onto their backs and each other, bringing a humid animal mist into the already vapory compartments.

And seven. Seven elephants. Why them? So mindful. Such gentle natures. So slow and deliberate. Like the flow of a river that has long ago made up its mind, one of the elephants lowered itself one limb at a time down into the water. In sagacity and faithfulness so like a crow. Perhaps the elephants' size alone distinguished them from us.

I kept expecting to stumble upon the cage or compartment containing the seven crows. Most of the clean beasts of seven were from the farm, and these animals slept in the compartments with the beastman, providing comfort and warmth for all. Man and cow slept curled up with one another in the hay of Noah's compartments. Dog, duck, and goat slept nearby. And chickens. Even the dim-witted, ground-hugging chicken was considered clean and allowed to wander in and out of the beastman's quarters at will. What is a bird that can't fly? Seven horses, seven cattle, six hens and one rooster, three geese and four ganders, three sheep and four rams, one of them not paired off, one alone and useless in the continuance of things, all of them beasts of Noah, bleating, squawking, mooing to be fed when the beastman walked near, sharpening his knives, one against the other.

Here, in the compartments of Noah's family, both light and food were plentiful. And being one of my original raiding sites, the lay of the beams was familiar to me, making this an easy, interesting place to hide.

"Papa, shall we make haste to prepare a burnt offering?"

"No, Ham. We have no place for a fire large enough."

"What about a small creature? Like the rabbit?"

"No. When we have arrived by God's hand, then we shall make an offering."

"Offerings," said this son of Noah, and his eyes bubbled over, greasy and fish-like. Long and skinny, like his father, the one known as Ham spoke through large, crooked teeth. His hair was the wildest of all the beastmen, growing from him with the abandon of shrubbery. "Why do we offer up the fat of our efforts, anyway? Does Yahweh ever eat any of it?"

"We've been making offerings of our favored beasts," said Noah, "ever since our great ancestor, Abel, made the first one, so many generations ago."

"And look what happened to him." Ham leaned forward now with a fist clenched over the handle of his supper tool.

"We make offerings to show our reverence," said Noah, "and to appease the Great God of Adam."

"Just look. Is He appeased now?"

Ham pointed with his thumb back over his shoulder, out beyond the beams of the galley and the logs of the hull. There was a silence in the ark's house, except for the rocking, creaking noises, back and forth, and the howling from without.

Noah's face flushed red with exasperation as he fought within himself. "Are you trying to increase His wrath?" But the one known as Noah calmed himself as he neared the torchlight of the dinner table. There, he took his seat importantly. And the mammal ate. He shoved the food into his glistening, gut-colored mouth and worked his jaws. Then from the beast's lung-colored lips came the strange sounds of human speech.

"My son, my son, my son. Ham, and others, too, listen to me. For the generations depend upon your ability to re-create the stories I am about to tell you, and have been telling you all along. Why should we make offerings? Well . . ."

And as Noah launched into the drone that is history (for it is the same with bird as it is with beast), Ham and especially his wife, Nanniah, were the only ones listening. All others were passed out in their bunks of straw and animal hide from the rough ordeal of escaping the deluge, or from bouts of sickness with the sea. And though the seasickness did not allow some to sleep, it did dilute their attention.

There was the place known as Paradise, said Noah, and yes, all his family knew of it. But it was different, a lot different, way back when. Noah hoped that when they returned to the world, they could all return to the Garden as well and keep it as fresh and unspoiled as it had been before the terrible blight of knowledge had entered into the thoughts of humankind. Of course, their job would be a little easier this time around, now that Adam and Eve had already finished the naming of all of God's creatures. The supple, naked youths, Adam and Eve, slender and athletic and without a blemish anywhere, had little to do all day but adorn themselves with flowers and see to it that each and every creature on earth had a special word applying to that creature and that creature alone. The great monster leviathan bellowed above the seas, *What is my name?* It roared. And when Adam gave a name that pleased the whale, the majestic creature opened its spout and hissed its steamy breath in gratitude above the seas. *Pick me. Pick me next.* Throughout the garden, the different creatures followed the innocent lovers around. *What is my name?* Birds fell from the sky. Beautiful insects with willowy wings landed upon the shoulders of Eve. *What is my name? What's mine?* Indeed, the glories of the world were few and simple back then, but glorious nonetheless.

The stories of Noah's race were noxious and intolerable to a bird, but quaint enough that I began to feel the tender amusement one might find in listening to a child's humming, and the occasional magical misunderstanding that might pop out of that child's mouth.

But even by Noah's reckoning, the world had turned wicked almost overnight. Perhaps in the next world they would need extra safeguards against the abominable natures of humankind—a talisman to ward off fire eaters, piglet eaters, and all those with a gluttonous appetite; a way to put an end to the inventors of musical instruments, practitioners of perfume, those who steal secrets from heaven not meant for mortal heads, giants who crave the daughters of men, brothers who smite brothers, and so on, and on.

Noah stood from the table and reached into a large woven basket. He pulled out an object that gave him much pleasure. This book, he said, had been bestowed upon him by the archangel Raphael. Inside it was a sacred text containing the answer to all mysteries useful to humankind: the instructions needed to tame demons, herbs and practices in the art of healing, the many forces guiding the stars, and the plans used in building the ark. These were just a few of its useful instructions. According to Noah, all of the earth's wisdom could be stowed in one book and one head—one gaunt, sunken, Noah-like head. He held up the book, bound in sapphires, and when he opened it, a light shone from within that made plain and luminous his troubled features.

Across the table, Ham sat and listened. He listened as if paying attention no longer to his father's words but only to the queer sounds of human speech and the strange celestial glow coming from his father's book. He wore a look of quiet dismay, and beneath the table grabbed the hand of his wife, Nanniah, and the two of them rolled their eyes as the father spoke, not seeming to know or care that no one else was listening. When I saw the fall of Nanniah's thick black hair, a chill rushed through me that could be none other than the stirrings of Our Many. Her quick, moist, intelligent eyes peered all around her into the far shadows of the compartment. And I thought that if the others had partaken of the Great Mother, too, it made no difference; this was where her soul stayed. Nanniah kept tracing the slope of her stomach, as if bird wings beat within.

Beyond, in their berths, the rest of their family slept in heaps.

Along with the book's unearthly glow, a special pearl hanging from the timbers cast a kindly luminescence down upon Noah's family. By day, this pearl would dim, and in this way the human family was able to mark the passage of days, which to them was of extreme importance. By night, it burned intensely like a star, and I'd yearn for the beauty of our old songscape where at night points of the Milky Way shone through the trees. I spread my wings, and the pearl cast an enormous moving shadow across the walls.

"What is that?" cried one of the beastmen.

Wings, wondrous wings, I fanned them against the uneven beams. Now I was the monster.

The whole family was fearful.

"A creature out of its cage."

"How?"

I opened my beak and made my voice heard. *"How? Awk! Can't you see? The rats, they eat at the cages, they scurry into your food. Already mouse, shrew, and snake slosh happily with the larger creatures in the sumpwater above the keel. Insects fly and burrow themselves into the wood of the ark. And ducks, do you know where the ducks are? Wicker cages, wood cages, what are these to a creature that can digest hide and hair and man-sized mammal bones in its stomach? Only the sickness of the sea holds the lion at bay. It's the same with all of the stronger beasts, the wilder beasts. Not like those whimpering, begging beasts of burden you keep at your feet."*

One of them spoke.

"Oh, dark bird."

"Crow."

"Get him."

"And see that no other creatures are out of their cages."

"Did you not hear me? Oh, never mind," I said.

And the sons and daughters of Noah were helpless, watching me fly away.

2. Bird of Fodder

On and on the pearl brightened and dimmed as if in a dream without beginning or end or change. Just the drudgery of the ark rising and dropping in the swell, the moaning of the trees, the wailing of the empty wind. Whether the pearl was bright or dim, always the beastmen were busy carting food up and down the decks. It may have been Noah, or his wife, Namah, or any one of their sons or daughters. First the torchlight would appear from far off and always from the same direction. Then the bleatings and stirrings of the creatures would increase as the light from the torch neared their compartments. Even the animals in the sumpwater perked up. When they heard the cart and the falling of fodder down into their cages, they scampered up through the ark and back into the mockery of their kennels, even the pea-brained rodents, not by cunning or intelligence but by the mindless habits that their glands had set up for them. The human was no different. The beastmen moved through the half-darkness like blind nudgers hugging the fodder to their chests. Now and then one would fall asleep, cleaving to a bucket that rolled beneath him. Another would come by and kick the sleeping one awake, and the two would resume their feeding.

"Come. Come and eat." They bleated. "There you go."

And the sons of Noah flung fodder into the cages.

"Just look at us," said the one known as Ham. "And we won't even survive the trip."

The elder said, "And this gives you pleasure?"

"Feeding," said Ham, with a gap in his toothy smile, "pleases me not."

"Are you prepared for the alternative?"

Neither spoke in the tree-heavy ark, except for the chirps and grunts they used to instruct the animals to eat, as if the animals had forgotten how.

Just then Old Hookbill the Interpreter loped up behind Noah's sons, acting for the most part like a dog, sniffing their legs, the wheels of the cart, the base of the cages. And I knew why I could understand them. Aside from the human itself, their faithful dog was the only creature allowed to wander freely in and out of all the compartments and up and down the decks, made more faithful now that Hookbill, the old dream-giver, lived inside the dog's eyes, each of a different color, one blue and one brown. Sometimes Hookbill favored one eye over the other. As the humans moved their cart down the gangway, the dog briefly looked up at me with a crow's mirthful, one-eyed glance.

When the torch was far enough away, but still shedding light, I flew through the creaking, twisted branches of the ark to the compartments where the various fodders were stored. There wasn't much to do on the voyage but to stuff myself to the horn. Flying past the beastmen undetected was always easy. But I didn't take any chances. After they'd spot me or just barely hear me, they'd rattle the cages and curse and make threats, inspecting the various compartments for ways to escape. When the beastmen receded, I resumed the search for my kind, but I couldn't see anything in the hurling dark. The hooves of an occasional wanderer clamored across the decks, alone, like me. Voices were my only guide.

Once I heard the trilling and clucking of the beauty of our aerie. I realized Plum Black had infused her soul in the song of Our Many more than I'd ever imagined. Her calls gave me a sharp woe of memory that made my wings ache, and all at once I wished for a familiar clearing and the tops of the forest and a wind that had traveled far to gather all the many names and familiar birds in its kindly draft. My heart bruised against the stones of its longing, and I felt more than ever the skyless, sunless prison of our existence. But I wasn't alone. Hearing the sweet song of our Plum Black, other creatures tried to sing like the crow. All sorts of bellowings, bleatings, and chirpings filled the dark. And Plum Black, not only the beauty of the woods but also shy and modest and apt, rarely sang after that, not wanting to show up the other animals or cause a stir.

Once the sound of the feeding cart caught me by surprise.

I shuddered and landed as soon as I could and froze there. As always, the humans took a forever to be gone.

"*C'mon,*" whispered a voice, in the exact words of the beast but too close and with a nasal inflection that was far too sinister and crow-like. "*Come, eat up,*" said the voice. I looked all around me in fear and wonder. Beside me was a cage of enormous birds of prey. Their magnificent feathers jumped out of the darkness and threw their speckled light back at me, though all the hunters sat in shock, neither awake nor asleep in the slow, desperate languor of the crowded cage. "*Come,*" said the alert voice.

It was the raven, both the he and she of their kind, speaking not only in ways of the beast but in tones specific to the beastmen, looking right at me, as if instructing me in the ancient art of eating.

"*No. C'mon,*" said the ravens. "*Come.*" They blinked their bone-colored lids. "*Come and eat.*" And because I wanted to see if My Other was still inside them, I flew directly near the cage.

"*Oh. You again?*" said the magnificent bird of darkness. "*The other. At first I thought you were the God Raven. But you're too scrawny. Now, be a good crow and open our cage.*"

"The door?"

"Sure. It's easy. First fetch the beastman's fire in your beak, and fly with it the length of the ark. Then encircle our cage three times. Then sing to the primates. Then strike our cage from one end to the other with your beak. And lastly, you must pull one small twig attached to the door, and our cage will swing open. But you cannot reach the small twig from within. I can't do it myself."

"Are you sure?" I sat there suspicious of the enormous black bird with his glossy black feathers and elaborate claws.

Then the raven bent down close to me and spoke in confidence. "We didn't do a very good job of fleeing the plague of Keeyaw, now, did we?" The raven's eyes narrowed.

"Yeah. We flew right to him," I said.

"Especially you. You weren't even led here by an angel, were you?"

"How do you know?"

"I saw the birds fly through Noah's door. There was not a single albino feather in the lot. Now, I know you crows think there's something really special about that . . . aberration. But to everyone else, you're just fodder."

"Fodder?"

I wanted to tell him all about our ancient ancestor Hookbill the Sagacious riding like a patron muse on the bow rail of the ark, and how she now lived in the dog's eyes and had shown me the secret entrances to the ark, which only I used.

"You are not part of God's plan," said the raven.

"Yes. I am," I said.

"No. You're not."

"God talks to me, I Am."

"But you are without mate. You are not."

"I Am."

"You're fodder."

"Okay, so I'm fodder. To whom?"

"To my friends here. The eagle, and the owl."

These two, as well as the other large raptors and carrion birds, evil-looking, hook-necked vultures without feathers on their scaly pink faces, were all in the same cage as the raven who spoke.

"You see how they look at you. They know you are not with the Lord of the Universe, the God Raven's protection. You were not led here by the angel of your kind."

"Raven god?" I said.

"Look. I shall not argue the nature of the Endless All-Knowing with fodder. Did you, or did you not, see the hard time Keeyaw had feeding the chameleon? Until one day Keeyaw opened up a pomegranate, and out fell a worm, which the nearly starved chameleon devoured in an instant. Why would the almighty God Raven allow this to happen to worms? To be wiped out of existence forever? No, this worm was fodder. This worm was not led here by the worm angel. It was outside God's plan, like the flies you snap at, and the mice in the granaries, and the bugs that the chickens peck at, and like you. Look. Just look at the eagle. You make his eyes water and the walls of his stomach work together like two grinding stones. He has not had flesh to eat since . . . since the days beyond counting."

"What do I care what you think? You're in a cage. I can eat until I'm stuffed to the horn, and still, I'm free to fly wherever. You stay there in your god's plan. I like my own."

"You say that now. But listen," said the raven, "if you free me, I will assist and protect you."

"Protect me? From what?"

The raven narrowed his eyes to slits, then looked all around him.

"If I tell you," said the raven, "then why would you free me? We must strike a bargain."

"What do I have to fear from you?"

"Not from us," said the she raven, "but from God's plan. Remember. All were wiped out. All except those led here by the mysterious ways of Raven."

"Not all," I said.

"But for how long? Now, open the cage, and for our freedom, we will protect you."

Just then the glow of the beastman's torch shone directly from our gangway and the footsteps grew louder.

I flew to a nearby beam and waited.

When a creature ate an ancestor, you could very clearly see the bright burning of your song in that creature's eyes. Even the pithy song of My Other, the fledge, still played upon the eyes of the raven. And the shiver I got from the ravens grew as I considered our conversation back there in the dark.

And then there was the beastman called Noah, who'd not only dragged our Mother of Many asunder but who'd sat like a dull rock before the burning of the fallen trees, staring without blinking and no life in his limbs. Not Noah, nor any one of his sons, none of them showed any sign of her or her varied, mellifluous song. It just ended there in the pale, blunt brow. Slowly Noah took his forked instrument to gather the pig dung and heap it into his cart. Like his beard, the contents of his barrow slopped and steamed, and he pushed it along the gangway and wore a cross expression down at it and his soul was elsewhere.

After all were fed, after all the beastmen had fed throughout both day and night, and the cast from the holy pearl was a wan fog neither night nor day, Noah would crack the hatch to his window. He'd barely open it, just enough to lower a bucket of food outside the ark. After poking my head out of one of my secret portals, I beheld the recipient of this strange overboard offering. A giant followed behind the ark and kept his head above the whitecaps by clinging to a rope ladder. There, in the gray light of the water, the monster's gasping between the waves sounded like the hissing and escaping of vapors from a rotting corpse. But no, in the morning, there it was again, large, dumb, expressionless, and soaked pale, gaping up with that vacant, hungry look that always made Noah appear so guilty. And day after day, he remained there, the giant from that other world, sexless, alone, unable to continue his race, clinging to the rope and blowing the waves from his face so he could suck in more air.

Only the lion among wild animals shows
mercy to suppliants; it spares those bent
down before it, and, when angry, turns its
rage on men rather than on women, and only
attacks children when desperately hungry.
Juba believes that lions understand the
meaning of prayers.

—PLINY THE ELDER

3. Sign and Lament

Bears hibernated.

The great browns threw hay atop one another and formed a heaping mound that didn't quite cover their enormous hindquarters. Still, the weight of the hay and barley was enough to induce the deep sleep that they knew as winter. Frogs, turtles, and toads all buried themselves in the mulchy humus of fodder at the foot of the sumpwater as if it were the edge of a swamp, and they too slept their deep winter sleep. Caterpillars wove themselves into cocoons. All the creatures that could shut down, did. And the more voracious ones shut down against their will. The lion, constantly besieged by the feverish sweats of seasickness, was unable to prey on the creatures of God's plan. Instead the lions sustained themselves by eating grass like oxen, which made them troublesome and ill-tempered.

The long days of darkness turned into seasons.

When the beastmen weren't feeding, they were busy with the buckets of pitch, plugging up the constant leaks that weighed the ark down and threatened to roll it over so far that not even God could right it. Down in the swill, the water rolled in even waves from keel to stern, even though there was no forward or back to the ark, just God's will pushing it across the face of the flood. The animals in the heavy sumpwaters rolled, too, their calmly spooked eyes turned upward, sometimes having to dive below the surface to avoid a beam that threatened in a hurry. Ducks were especially adept at this.

One by one, I found all my secret accesses to the outside filled with a mix of pitch, sticks, and hay. So if I really was fodder, as the raven claimed, I was trapped now inside as one to be eaten.

The chameleon was starting to wear on Noah, who had to keep a ready supply of fresh worms for the lizard. He and his family kneaded shoots of camel-thorn into a cake and the worms were extracted from the pomegranate. Being mere fodder and outside God's plan, the worms were the only creatures in all of the ark allowed to procreate, there in the peat of the camel-thorn. Then they were fed to the chameleon, who was the envy of the ark. All the other animals complained. But how could the chameleon care, moving once every three days? My own hunger for the worm was tempered only by the knowledge that I was fodder myself and if I flew down to the wormy thorn cake, then perhaps I, too, would be discovered and offered up to some other hungry creature as finicky as the chameleon.

In his rounds, Noah would mumble to himself. He'd fall into such a foulness that whoever assisted him in pushing the cart would lag behind in order to preserve any hope of sanity. The physical rancor and disgust Noah held for his own kind always simmered just below the surface, ready to lash out at the animals in his charge.

"Oh, Great God of the Garden!" he cried. "I beg You for a sign. But no sign comes. Is there no way out of my prison? My life grows heavy with the smell of bulls, bears, and lions."

The Man Called Noah wailed this just as he neared the lion's stall.

Though it pained the lion even to open his eyes, the great cat raised his head from his sickly, curled-up sleep. He watched with contempt as Noah kicked the grass about his cage, and this was the lion's food. Still, the lion did nothing. But Noah, who noticed the lion's belligerent stare, turned around with equal anger and belligerence.

"What?" said the beastman. "I spend all my days feeding, and get *this* in return?"

The lion roared and swung his paw like an immense cleaver and sent Noah flying across the stall. The lion batted Noah's leg around a few times, then purred as it stood above the skinny creature with a forepaw on the mammal's throat and chest.

"Puny man. I am four times your size. My stomach can digest bone and hide much thicker than yours. What can you do?"

Noah was still lying down, straining his neck when he spoke.

"Why, I built this ark."

"I'd eat you right here if it would give me any pleasure. But I'm sick of eating, especially grass and your figgy bread. Leave me now. Before my anger returns."

And the lion released the beastman Noah, who hobbled away, bleeding heavily and guilt-ridden.

"You should have done me in," said Noah. "You do me a disfavor."

All of his family ceased what they were doing and gathered around the skinny, bearded beastman, who insisted no harm had been done to him. Though all of his family saw his shame and the bloodied flesh from fang and claw and how he limped. The clan of them was moving no faster than Noah himself, and this was my chance.

I flew steadily through the shadows and around the beams of the beastman's quarters and landed upon the camel-thorn cake that housed the worms. I pecked at them and slurped them up. I chopped them into tender pieces and cached them here and there in various hiding spots throughout the ark. I ate so many, so quickly, I could barely fly.

"*Oh, look at, look at here.*" It was the raven. "*Oh, Noah. Loose bird! There is a worm thief among us!*"

After all the raven's commotion, the clan of humans looked up and saw me.

"The dark bird," they cried.

"Check the cages."

"Keep sight of it."

I flew easily to the places where I knew the humans would be useless in catching me. But as I flew to my deeper, usual hideouts, a fanged creature jumped out at me and knocked a few feathers loose. Then a creature with claws lunged at me. And another. Armed ones, winged ones, spotted ones, predators with large, sharp eyes. I bounced against the ribs of the ark, avoiding their lunges, weighed down as I was with worms.

"*You see what you are,*" the raven called after me, with a wicked laugh, "*—fodder!*"

4. Island of Musical Instruments

I hid in the beams above Noah's floating barnyard. There the domesticated creatures were well fed, always sleeping or on the verge of it, and had no interest in eating me. Also the beastman was often absent, so it was easy to lurk there in the shadows above the precious worms in the camel-thorn cake.

Each day, the weather outside brightened, and this brightness leaked in through the fissures between the logs, as did the hissing of the sea and the gurgling of the slack water. The ark leaned into the trough of the waves. And the strange aquamarine light of the pearl began to mingle with the pale overcast from outside.

Old Hookbill's life as a dog allowed me to catch every word that the beast-people grunted to each other and the animals in their charge. But their meanings were lacking and sadly repetitious as they moved like sleepwalkers through the machinations of tossing hay down into the stalls, or herbs, or barley, or all kinds of mixed pulse, constantly administering to the needs of each species. They filled the tubs with soured water, emptied the cages, and kept the blood barely pumping beneath the hide of the earth's creatures that mostly slept and yawned and ate, then slept again in their own animal discharge. This was hardly the case, though, with the youngest, the beastchild,

Japeth, who would get a running start with the cart. Once it gained any speed, he jumped onto it and sailed it the entire length of the deck until it came to a standstill, and he rocked on its wheels slowly back and forth in the movement of the ark. When he found himself under the charge of one of the older members of his clan, he'd slink down in a submerged mean streak and throw the fodder at the animals as if hurling rocks. The stocks and grains fell like wisps of dust from his flailing arms.

But as the thin light from outside spilled into the ark and the angry face of God turned to a calm, passive sloshing, the animals began to stir.

When young Japeth went sailing by on his cart, his oldest brother's mate, a plump, red-haired beastwoman, jumped on with him and clung to him tightly, trying to hush her squealing. As the cart stopped, she rubbed Japeth's arms and squeezed him. With the cart still beneath them, the boy clouded over with confusion and hid deep within one of the pens, letting small primates and other creatures with clever hands sniff and paw his hair.

The flank of a camel shivered massively above him and its tail whipped at a fly. The lamb bleated. And the lap cat trembled and yawned and stood shoulders first, then hindquarters as it stretched and sank back down into its own idle dreaming. Old Hookbill the Dog was awake as usual, and she trotted through the humid stalls of the beastman, alert to all the stirrings and half-wakings and excited by it all, as if this were spring itself. She sniffed at the air and dreamt of rabbits and diving into the bush. Her dreams were purely a dog's now. Still, she communicated them to me and feared the angry hand of the beastman. The movement of the sheep nearly arrested her into an action she had no control over. Her authority in the barnyard stiffened her coat and pricked her ears to every sound. Below her ribs, her teats swung loosely, once suckled dry by mouths that had long since been filled with the stinging foam of the floodwaters but still with enough life in the gristled, hairy nipples to replenish the earth.

The warming animal compartments filled her lungs like sunlight falling over a meadow. And as she ran her rounds, she swung her hips and the juices in her blood seeped out in sharp scents from the rug of her hindquarters. She kept circling here and there, loosening her haunches, remembering the sun's lost rays and the mindless warmth of an afternoon a long, long time ago when she had lifted herself up to the heat. Soon an old hoary sheepdog was following her, sniffing at her tail so furiously that he pushed her forward. Then there was a growling behind that dog, and a fight ensued, for it was not yet established which dog would have her outright as he pleased and which dog would have to mount her in secret and finish quickly and slink away unseen. In the mongrel's eyes, even Old Hookbill the Sagacious smiled.

At night, when the pearl dimmed, the sleeping grew more constant. The creatures always slept, but the beastman never. One night, slowly, without the assistance of torchlight, one of the sons of Noah crept over to the horse stalls as if sneaking. There, he sat himself down, and pausing, looked up. When he saw me, I startled him, even spooked him, as if *I* had discovered *him*. At first the eyes seared through the darkness. Then they were like a pair of frog eyes that sink slightly beneath the surface, thinking this will make them safe. Ham lurked there with the horses and did nothing to draw attention to me but looked at me a long while, until soon his mate, Nanniah, crept into the horse stalls with him. It was true, the Mother of Many lived there, especially in her thick, glossy mane that shone wildly as if ready to fly. Ham huddled her into a corner and she sat with her arms crossed, looking inward.

Ham said, "I awoke this morning to the dream of an island."

"Shhh." Though her voice soothed him, her glance was sharp and shot quickly all around her, like a crow's. "Before we're discovered. Why did you call for me?"

"Not only an island, but the dream of our journey's end. An island of musical instruments."

"God drowns musicians."

"This music of my dreams, it rode up on the winds and dispelled the waters."

"Were these the same instruments invented by Genun the Canaanite, in the Land of the Slime Pits?"

"Oh, you are too much like Father," said Ham, "full of names, and who did what. Please, stop. It matters not."

"Of course, it matters not. Not to you. Your family didn't drown."

"Oh." Ham wrapped her in his wings. "Please. Forgive me."

She shuffled away.

"This music," he said, "in my dreams. It was unearthly. Yet it brought back the earth. On a wooded pathway, you danced and were lovely. This loveliness rang through my soul. My blood raced."

She kissed him shyly and said, "You mustn't talk this way."

"We mustn't talk."

And he succeeded in getting Nanniah in the embrace of his wings.

"Take care. We'll be discovered. Noah won't believe my child outside the ark is yours, whether we lie here now or not."

"But I told Father that the child was mine?"

"And look how he's treated. You shouldn't have lied."

"But *I* want to believe it. And if we give him a sister or a brother, he will feel more like our own. Then how can my father possibly deny him?"

She answered only with silence, and night after night, Ham would follow Nanniah around and try to bring her into the thick hay of the horse stalls. From their talk I learned the story of the creature who floated behind the ark. It was Nanniah's son, conceived during her life with the giants. When the world flooded, she had wept when Noah said he could not take this son, a giant, along on the voyage. Occasionally she still wept, and though Noah was persuaded to tow the large creature behind the ark, he could not be persuaded to bring the giant child aboard. In her falling hair and shoulders, I felt the pull of Our Many and her sad longing, and I wanted to sing the song of our aerie and call her back to me. Other times Nanniah and Ham would hold each other in the hay until I feared the sleeping horses would wander and trample them both. Sometimes Ham would try to mount her.

"What?" said Ham. "What is it?"

"Hush. Do you *want* to be discovered?"

"So be it. No. Watch this," he said. "I want to show you something."

The one known as Ham breathed strangely as he crept through the shadows cast by the glowing pearl, and returned from their pantry cradling a small, precious bundle in the folds of his robes and knelt back into the darkness of the horse stall. He undid the wrappings and plucked a morsel of food and held it up—an offering, for me. He acted as if he knew I'd be there, and had been all along. He made tick-tocking sounds with his tongue, a little crow-like, at least for a beast.

"Shhh," said Nanniah. "What are you doing?"

"We've been feeding all the other creatures, but not this fellow. He hides there in the beams."

"What's he doing out of his cage?"

"I don't know," said Ham. "But I think he's the one we keep seeing, lurking in the beams. He's clever."

Ham held the piece of cheesy breadstuff up for so long I feared we'd all be discovered. But I didn't like the figgy bread. No animal liked it, even though it was the beastman's favorite. I had free rein over all the foodstuffs left in creation, and now I had to eat the figgy bread. Why would any creature want to be the pet of a beastman? I waited as long as I could, until I felt compelled to hop down to their clumsy offering. But no. Still, I decided not to.

Nanniah's face hovered so close to mine in the dark that I would have hopped back if she weren't also carrying the well-traveled song of Our Many in her bones.

"Look at his face," she said. "Is there something wrong with him?"

"I wonder," said Ham. "His feathers mark him as if with an expression."

"Yes, that of crying," she said. Then she laid her hand on her belly. "Sometimes I can feel the child inside. It moves. I just felt it."

"I will treat your child outside as I will this one," said Ham.

"Don't," she said again, as he moved toward her. "We'll be discovered."

"When you grow large with child, we'll be uncovered anyway."

"But why hasten it? Perhaps we'll reach land first."

"Perhaps we will never reach land. How was it?" asked Ham. "With the giant?"

"Why do you ask now? You make me dizzy."

"Did you or did you not love him?"

"We were betrothed at birth. At night, he forced himself upon me. I did what I could to survive."

"Do you love me now?"

"Yes."

"The same?" said Ham. "In the same way?"

"To me, you are life itself."

"Is it because my father had the power to save you?"

"Shh. I hear someone coming."

"Just think," whispered Ham, under the sounds of the footsteps. "When we return to the world, it will be like paradise. It *will* be paradise. God will give Eden back to us, just as Father says. Except this time around, God won't tempt us. Except with beauty, which will be everywhere, and no longer a temptation. And when we find music, it will be because He invented music and He'll be proud of us or even moved by beauty and sing along."

"From where do these mad thoughts come?" she said. "My village had many fine musicians, and now they all are drowned."

They both fell silent, and I flapped up to the beams in the dark when the footsteps approached.

Night after night, I perched there and watched Noah limp past the sleeping bodies of Ham and Nanniah with an old man's walk. He saw neither his family nor the body of horses asleep next to the oxen and sheep, whose ribs rose and fell as the air wheezed from their nostrils and the ark creaked and groaned, complaining under the weight of its burden. In Noah it seemed that all the world had fixed itself into a single sleepwalking purpose upon his brow as he pushed the feeding cart with that gangly limp of his, now hardened into his bones.

And even animals were so corrupted with those
not of their species, horse with donkey and
donkey with horse and snake with bird, as it
says, "For all flesh had gone astray. . . . And
He destroyed all of creation which was on the
face of the earth, from man to beast."

—JAMES L. KUGEL AND MIDRASH
TANHUMA, "Noah 1 2,"
The Bible As It Was.

5. Greenhorn the Sailor

Beyond in the darkness of the rolling logs that was the ark, I heard a strange commotion of sharp voices, both beast and bird, and it drew closer.

"Let go of me."

It was the raven—the mocking, cunning bird—arguing with the beast-man Noah.

"This bird has disobeyed my decree."

"Decree? Who are you to decree?"

"I am Noah, God's servant, who guides through the storm, appointed captain from above, keeper of the knowledge of Enoch . . ." Noah thumped the gangway grotesquely and wheezed so heavily that his beard caught in his mouth and muzzled the imposing history he used to describe himself.

"You forgot apiarist," said the raven

"Enough."

Soon Noah had the raven in his quarters. He strangled the angry bird by the neck, the wings, then a single talon. All the while the raven bit and scratched at Noah and whacked at him with his wings and the beastman spoke through gnashed teeth.

"It has not only mated with its own kind; it has done the unnatural and approached the she-eagle."

Who's to say this is unnatural? Does not the horse lie down with the donkey? And the wolf with the dog? The bee with any flower it can? Nature is always seducing itself and expanding its own beauty in new and unimaginable forms. How can you blame any creature? I act only as I am."

"And I found it hiding behind the she-eagle's wing."

"I stood there only because you are so unreasonable and given to strange theories that make you abuse the rest of us and your own kind."

"Before the world is renewed, we must take no part in replenishing it."

"Look at me. I'm Noah," mocked the Raven, *"keeper of secrets, greenhorn the sailor, slave to hunger, servant to lizards and bugs, grumpy old gimp, a jealous old gimp."*

"Enough racket, bird. I should destroy your kind."

"Hah!" The raven blew out a contemptuous laugh. *"As you well know, I am a necessary ambassador to a most striking and original species. The last hope of my kind. I dare you to undo any of God's handiwork."* With that the wild bird grew calm and regal in the hands of Noah, who carried both the bird and a small cage over to the horse stalls.

"Here. Wake, son, please. No, that's okay. Good day, Nanniah. No. Don't bother to dress. Just keep a watch on your friend here, the raven."

And Noah stuffed the bird into a cage so small that when the raven protested, flapping his wings, he whacked them on either side against the slats.

Ham stood with his clothes bunched before him in his naked, already peeled state, and wanted to leave, but his father stood blocking the gangway.

"No," said Nanniah. "Don't. You don't need to hide, not from him, or anyone."

In the sharp points of anger in Nanniah the Beauty's eyes, I saw the Mother of Many still cawing at Noah. But the old man only grimaced and turned away with that injured walk of his, as if the walk alone proved his point and gave him an undisputed sovereignty over all moral matters.

"*Look at you,*" the raven called after him. "*A creature far beyond the springtime of his life. Of course it's easy for you to pass judgment, and pretend it's martial law. You no longer live under the sway of your passions.*"

"If there are new generations on the ark—" Noah thumped with much trouble down the long gangway, speaking with a God nowhere to be found, "—how will I possibly feed them?"

With the beastmen's quarters empty of their kind, the raven stood as proud as any God Crow. His tattered feathers glistened. His curved hooks were knobby like the growth of ancient tree roots, and his beak, as large as the femur bone of a mammal, stuck out of the cage when he spoke.

"*Hey, crow. The beasts are gone now. You can feed on the chameleon's worms.*"

The dark-feathered bird could even feign the omniscience of God. He spoke without turning my way but projected his voice as if he knew exactly where I was. I grew grim inside and felt the splay of my own nape feathers. I hadn't flinched since Noah had pulled the raven in by the hooks.

"*Really, you should eat. What was that I noticed on your face? A mange, or consumption of some sort, stealing your color? What? Are you sad? There are always the worms to cheer you. What are you waiting for?*"

"*I trust you not,*" I said.

But after a long silence, I flew back down to my normal feast anyway.

All the while the raven studied the way I swooped down and dug at the camel-thorn cake and extracted one worm and flew back to my sullen corner. But there was no joy in it for me anymore. "*Me, Me, I Am!*" said the raven with his usual jeer. "*I'm hungry! I Am!*"

I wasn't sure if he was mocking me, or if it was the simp sounds of My Other ushered up from his hollow bones. I flew warily over to his cage with an offering, but before I even landed, he lunged at me with his heavy clippers and bit and tugged at my wings. I tried to drop the offering as I jumped back, but the raven already had it when I jumped clear of his reach.

"*And now for the cage door,*" he said, chopping down on his morsel. "*I'm not sure which of the many remedies open the cage. Or in which order they should be performed. But try a few, and see what happens.*"

The raven had the soul of My Other in his stare, and though I wanted to free them, I couldn't trust him, and the raven sourly took note.

"*Very well. But you will wish you were my ally, after I'm free of this cage.*"

"My Child, what do you seek?"

"I seek my brothers, the seven crows," she
replied.

*The dwarf answered, "My Lord Crows are
not at home; but if you wish to wait their
return, come in and sit down."*

*. . . All at once she heard a whirring and
cawing in the air, and the dwarf said, "My
Lord Crows are now flying home."*

—The Seven Crows,
GRIMM'S FAIRY TALES

6. The Window

Above the table where the beastmen ate was a window. Back when the ark
was on dry land, this window, grown-over with dandelions and licorice
weed, was constantly open and a favorite entrance for me to raid their table
or the grain stores below. Now, as the brightness off the floodwaters grew,
Noah thought it safe enough to lift the heavy latch of the portal and leave it
propped open with a stick. But then the sea rushed in and its angry, salty
lashes soaked their bedding and clothes. These they tried to dry above their
small hearth and fire. But the animal reek of sweat and urine lifting with the
steam from the saltwater was putrid. Even a crow could smell it.

So the window remained shut.

Soon the daylight shone through between the logs of the hull in sharp
white stars, and the roll of the sea had calmed to a confused, sullen sloshing. The same tangle of driftwood gently knocked on the ark's side for days,
beckoning to its sad inhabitants. Though the holes were infinitesimal, you

could sense the green out there of the fair-weather sea, and the green of the bubbles in the cresting waves, and the haze in the air and how it turned white at the horizon.

Again, Noah tried the window.

The sky was clear, and Noah stuck his head out into it. An even wind lifted his whiskers and his raw, organ-colored lips smiled, until he was making the strange whinnying sounds of his kind. His whole family crowded near and gawked and gurgled in the same strange banter, but in such happy squeals that I forgot myself and my nasty suspicion of them. Even if it was for only a moment.

Noah was pleased.

And the family of beastmen went about the business of feeding with something akin to singing steaming up out of their heads. When the compartment was empty of them, I flew over to the window. The waves of the sea moved like a thousand clipped, tiny mouths snapping up at the air. The bright, briny bubbles, the cloudless haze of the sea. The steady wind pushed the ark along without raising the seas but was still strong enough to make the ark list.

I could not fight the urge to fly out into it all.

The blue was so welcoming.

I spread my wings and flew out over the open, airy sea.

It was like flying for the first time. Only better. There was none of the terror and struggle. It was how every bird wishes its first flight had been. The field of air was a solid cushion. I braced my pinions against it and rose above the green seawater pastures, hardly flapping, until the whitecaps below formed patterns like rolling fields of wheat. The sunlight sparkled off this watery welcome. The air cleaned my feathers and made them shine, and the wind purified my thoughts. Soon I landed on one of the uppermost branches of the ark. I could have kept flying as I had when Plum Black was a mirror-like flashing above the water that had no far shore. But now there was no shore anywhere. And if I did find land, would it have trees? Would there be crows? Who would show me the wonders of this new place? All I knew of beauty in the world was our old aerie and its everlasting song, and all of that was imprisoned down in the dark, foul, heavy stench below.

Fighting my urges, I made my way back inside the dismal portal, passing the body of my patron oracle, Old Hookbill of the Lost World, still laminated to the bulwarks, but broken up now by the storm and flecked like shale.

Why should I have returned?

My knowledge would not fit into theirs.

—W. S. MERWIN,

"Noah's Raven"

7. Ostrich-Egg Omelet

When Noah opened the window, he also let in spring, or a slight glimmer of it. Though this springtime was dim and nearly nonexistent in the lower decks, many of the she-birds still laid eggs, which were quickly swooped upon by the mother of Noah's children. Quietly, the one known as Momma, or Namah, had day by day assumed the overseeing of the creatures that her sons and daughters had done during the voyage. Noah himself increasingly exhausted his energies on what he considered the more remarkable creatures—the pachyderm, the panda bear, the penguin. Feeding them less and less, he lectured them instead, or admired them as if they were his to admire. Anything out of the ordinary would be noticed by Namah. She slipped hay under the heads of sleeping animals. She refreshed their cages, climbed onto their fresh hay beds, and hugged them to sleep. Confused, an otter tried to escape her, but Namah followed it, stooped over with open arms. "So cute, so cute, so cute."

Soon, from their pantry, came the sound of frying eggs. All the beastmen squealed with pleasure as Namah cracked open an enormous ostrich egg, which took some pounding from a cudgel. The ample yellow yolk of it slip-slopped back and forth in the pan, following the rocking of the ark.

Meanwhile, Old Hookbill the Dog Now stood before the open window, guarding the beastmen's stall. All day the sun burned away the milky cloud cover, and Hookbill stood as mute as ever, as if guarding the very sea. The

muscles on her face lifted her ears to different sounds and pulled her eyebrows back, but mostly she sat, unmoving like a lion statue at the gates,
squinting from the cloud's brightness. A human couldn't walk out of the
quarters, nor a rat scurry down a rafter, nor a dolphin plunge into the sea,
without first passing the watchful gaze of Hookbill. Hookbill the Hound
Now knew this and watched over the sleeping of the beastmen, or the
wheeling of their carts, all the while keeping her attention on more distant
matters.

That evening all of Noah's clan took the time to gather for supper below the
open window of the stars, and after the meal, Noah began to recite the history of his kind. He constantly feared that this story would die in its entirety
right there in his skull if he weren't always reciting it. And he wasn't much
of a poet either, swilling down extra portions of his narcotic juices as slippery bits of omelet slid to the ends of his beard and made it stick out, stiff
and shining. But also the fresh breeze and the returning stars spurred him
on, and now there was an absurd hilarity pushing the story of humankind
along. He lisped and made slithering movements with his neck when he
played the role of the serpent, talking with Eve. "'Oh, I'm afraid, I'm not
afraid,' says the mother of all of humankind. 'What? What do you want of
me?' 'Sit right here. By my tree, and I will show you.'"

Now, in the Garden, Adam had once lied to Eve, telling her that by just
touching the Tree, death would come unto the soul. And the Accursed One
knew of this lie. So he shook the tree and kept shaking it until the apples fell
down and landed upon Eve's lap. "'There,' said the Accursed One. 'You
didn't die from that, now, did you?'"—and so spoke Noah, holy-appointed
bard of bards, singer of songs, deliverer through darkness, planter of vines
and mighty trees, inventor of libations, seer of visions, knower of knowledge, offerer of offerings, and queller of the Almighty's passions. And here
Noah's posture drooped, as did his impromptu musical instrument, a bro-

ken antler he'd use to strike on the table, and he felt his forehead. He groped at it, reciting the disaster of Cain's first offering. "Why am I not dead?" he asked. "Or with a horn sprung from my own head with roots that strangle my brain? For I made offerings of web-footed creatures, and even of eels, and I ate thereof, biting into the juicy belly strip before the God of Adam could have His fill. And now the world is drowned."

Just then Namah approached and put her hand on Noah and spoke quietly above his madness.

"Perfection is God's alone," she said. "The giant corrupters were the ones who destroyed the world. You have worked hard to save it."

"Giant *corrupters?*" said Nanniah, Ham's mate. She glared. "You only call them that to demonize them. And because our cities were made of such large stones, out of jealousy you said only a giant could lift them."

"They tried to eat me once."

"What?" said Nanniah to the youngest of the clan. "Who did?"

"The giant corrupters. They wanted to eat me. I was on the highway when a band of ruffians captured me and soaked me in a huge tureen of marinade."

"We believe you, Japeth," said his mother.

"They did. I turned blue."

Shem's wife, Mona, laughed. "Wouldn't you taste good?"

"Silence," said Noah. "I can't bear the thought of it, not even in a joke."

"Please, go to rest," said Namah, urging Noah up from his chair. "We'll see to the creatures tonight."

"But—" Noah hobbled to the open window, still possessed. "There's more I could have done." He stuck his head out the window. "I could have saved someone besides my own."

Though Namah pulled on Noah by the shoulders, he broke free in a fit and stumbled up to the raven's cage.

"Evil one! I will send you to fetch news of the outside world. Be off with you, at once."

Noah made fluttering motions from the cage out to the window. But the raven spoke in a derisive innocence that passed Noah by.

"*My good bard, God's emissary, is it not nighttime? How will I navigate the darkness? Let alone find my way back?*"

Noah pulled on his filthy beard, trying to find the way through his cloudy thoughts.

"The stars!" Noah's eyes spun in their sockets, and he wore a strained expression as if trying to clear the way for both his own understanding and the raven's. "We could navigate by the stars—if only we could steer this barge, and there was somewhere to go."

The raven puffed out his furry throat feathers and stood with his trousers enlarged.

"*Though my mate and I are only two, and considered unclean, I don't think God, your master, hates us as much as you do. Have you forgotten his orders? To take seven of each clean beast and two of the rest? Just look at the doves—seven clean, fine, ripe-for-slaughter doves. If I should drop from the heat or the cold into the seas, your new world shall be longing for ravens.*"

Noah stood long, as though considering this fine argument as best he could.

"*Or,*" said the raven, "*is your lust for my mate so great that you wish her all to yourself?*"

Noah whirled around, as though he might throw all of his might upon the cage and crush it.

"*You don't dare harm me,*" said the raven. "*If the blood of any one of God's last creatures was on your hands, and yours alone, you would have failed Him yet again.*"

"*Agh,* these birds, especially this Evil One! Even my own wife is forbidden me while we are on this voyage. Tomorrow, with the morning's first light," said Noah, "I will send him off."

Then Namah and her sons pulled Noah away from the arrogant raven, who preened his shoulders and neck feathers and looked the other way.

. . .

While the beastman Noah slept and his clan busied themselves feeding the last of creation, I perched upon the ledge of the window and looked out over the nighttime sea.

The seas shimmered with an icy darkness—ghostly, and ongoing. The only light came from the stars and the dim light they cast upon the clipped, even whitecaps, like tiny open mouths that went on forever. It seemed an occasional mountain peak or iceberg stood above the sea, as if floating low in the sky, blotting out the glowing iciness of the horizon. Were they really the tops of mountains? I stared at them in the wishful silvery dark until they dissolved and reappeared and seemed to follow us before they disappeared again.

"Hey, crow——"

But I chose not to listen to the raven.

"Hey, fodder," he said, and my coat of feathers stood on end. *"Beautiful, isn't it——your home out there."*

I looked at a mountaintop following us and shuddered.

8. *Mountaintop*

The ark lurched and lifted with a shock. The mighty trees of the forest crashed their thunderous doom one more time. Broken-arked, bottomless, keelless, our island of dead trees seemed to wrap itself around the face of a mountaintop.

Noah arose from his drink-induced sleep with a fury.

"Why didn't you wake me?"

He yelled at his son Ham, of course, who watched the wreckage of the ark from the window with a calm, hypnotic detachment.

"Father, destruction is beautiful, is it not?"

"Not when it's your own, you fool."

"Are you saying there is a difference between the doom of others and your own?" Noah hovered over the shoulder of Ham, who still studied the cliff face out the window.

"My good father, you have slept for three days under the spell of your strange libations. For three days I thought you sick, and besides, no one has steered the ark yet this entire voyage. What good would you and your sick brain have done awake? By what powers would you prevent or assist our journey's end?"

"Out of the way."

Noah pushed Ham from the window.

Large mammals bellowed in the general chaos of shrieks and flutterings. I tried to listen for Plum Black or the other crows, to see if they had survived the wreck. But it was hard hearing anything over the sound of the sea rushing like a hundred spring waterfalls into the ark.

"Ropes! Lashings! Vines! Gather all you can!" Noah yelled to his sons and daughters. "Bring them up top!"

Noah ran about on the decks shouting nervous, angry orders that confused his family more than anything else. But they did manage to tie a few lines from the bulwarks to the rocky beach. Still, the ark continued to list farther down the side of the cliff face. The logjam of a vessel groaned under the tremendous strain of its own weight. The rocks used to fasten the lines were dragged into the waves, too, beneath the ark, bringing it even farther down. The one line that did hold stretched to an alarming thinness and wrung the water from its braids. Then that line snapped.

But the ark behaved as before.

Except the water at the bottom of the hull no longer rushed in but moved as a part of the ocean's tide, rolling from busted rib to rib with waves sloshing around down there on their own. A few cages were afloat in the slosh. But it seemed to Noah and his family that all was safe for now, and they retrieved the animals from the tide.

When it was safe enough, I flew to the window again.

Outside, all was a cloudy expanse without form.

If it was a mountaintop, you couldn't see it, covered as it was with rushing waterfalls and whitewater rapids and the mist they cast, shrouding the view of the peak and the sea beyond. The mountain was like an underwater diver who'd been holding his breath for much too long and just then violently plunged up from the depths, frothing at the airholes. The water rushed down its slopes and made a great crashing noise.

Constantly the beastmen walked up and down the ark, surveying it, kicking it, jumping up and down on its outermost extremes, so that if it was about to give way, they would only hasten the doom of all God's handiwork.

During their midday meal, one of Noah's sons spoke.

"Father," said Ham, who hardly ate but only dangled his long, wiry whiskers into his bowl of soup and studied how they soaked like tendrils of seaweed. "Father, how do we know if the flood is really receding or if the mountaintop is still filling the world up with water, so that its own peak will also soon disappear?"

Noah looked alarmed again and screwed up a bleary face.

"I will pray."

But instead he crawled down into the hull and scratched a mark into the ark's wood at the present water level. Noah did nothing but examine that mark from different angles, crawling on the beams for a different view, putting his finger near the mark and holding it there. He waved the foam of the waters away from his mark. He blew at it.

"Ah," he said. "I can't get a bead on this flood. Will it never end?"

Noah ran back into his quarters, his clothes soaked to his lank frame. He looked as wretched as his skeletal cattle with their hips protruding like sticks above their thigh bones. All of the creatures, in the new light of the day, looked malnourished and infested.

"You!" Noah pointed a crooked finger at the raven's cage. "It is time for you to see whether the floods have abated!"

The raven tucked and pulled at a loose feather and arranged it carefully as Noah opened the cage and thrust his hands into it. With his beak open and his head craned sideways into a question, the raven blinked his bone-colored eyelids in mock ignorance.

"So it is," said the raven, only after he was in Noah's clutches. "You wish my mate all to yourself."

"Evil One! Quiet. Cease! May God curse this beak."

All the creatures listening hissed, "Amen!"

"Isn't separating us into different cages enough?" said the raven. "Must you banish me from this world as well? Wait!"

The raven bit at Noah's hands, and the beastman thrust the dark bird back into the cage and shut the door. Then he sucked at his hand where the raven had struck him.

"Carrion." Noah spat.

"*Take a look at me,*" said the raven. "*Look at all the creatures aboard your most excellent ship. I've fed on nothing but seeds and grasses, hardly sustaining for a creature of such a rich diet as myself.*"

"This bird will need sustenance to fly. But where will I find something—dead enough?" Noah made an ugly face.

"*Many of the creatures we eat are murdered by methods other than our own—yours, other creatures', acts of nature. It matters not. Such concerns are not for the birds but for hairsplitters, of which your kind is the only lot, always in a delirium over your impulses verses the covenants through which you exist in a social realm.*"

"Ah, yes." Noah's features grew large. "The pomegranate, the worms."

"*Exactly,*" said the raven. "*To navigate by the stars, as you suggest, would entail a long journey. Would it not? I wish to eat a worm.*"

I recoiled in fear, expecting the raven to expose me to Noah.

"Worms." Noah laughed. "You like these."

And he extracted one worm from the heaping camel-thorn cake and held it just outside the ribs of the cage.

The raven gobbled it up quickly.

"*I wish for another. I demand it for the long and arduous journey ahead. It's the least you could do. I need at least a meal of worms to sustain me.*"

"Agh. Cease! My ears. Is there no rest from that beak?"

"*Just bring them, in bunches. For one condemned as myself, that's not too much to ask. A meal, a last meal. Not just for me but for my own species.*"

Annoyed at the horrid, squawking noises, Noah snatched up an entire section of the thorn cake, and to keep the precious worms from falling to the ground held it up with both hands. He could barely open the cage, which he did finally using only his smallest finger.

The raven took his leisure, eyeing the cake of worms before him, wanting to pick the largest and juiciest of them all. And just as he bent his head out of the cage, he hopped entirely outside it and lifted fluidly into the air. There was a dry whack and rattle to the clap of the feathers, dormant from flying for so long, but still the spread of them was monstrous and majestic and horrifying as the wings whacked at the air with an erratic speed and the raven slowly lifted.

Without looking at me, the raven gave a grim leer and one short blast of a laugh.

"Haw!"

Like a bat disappearing down into dark catacombs, he disappeared among the beams above the beastman's quarters.

"Shut the window!" ordered Noah. "And find him. Find the accursed one."

9. *Ruse*

Big woolly-bearded bird.

The raven's black feathers flashed out in the beamy dark. But mostly he lurked in the different decks without a trace, except for the dry rattle of his feathers. He flapped his wings repeatedly as if about ready to fly. I couldn't see him, but I could hear him flap. When he returned, he landed in the full light with the feathers of his trousers flared and his throat hackles enlarged. He tended to his coat, tugging and smoothing and rearranging himself, as if none of Noah's clan were watching, and walked with that stiff, exaggerated walk of a bird, holding his straight legs out to clear his back claws and throwing his head forward. He could have hopped or flown if he wanted. Instead, he leisurely walked to all the hiding places of my worms and ate them, one by one, shaking my precious stash down his horn. Over and over again he flew through the beastmen's quarters and perched just beyond reach. He laughed and jeered, especially at the clean farm animals that numbered seven. He whinnied, he mooed, he clucked. *"Come and eat. My friend, my furry friend. Eat up."* The raven used the exact words of the beasts as they dropped food into the cages.

"Father," said Ham. "I would like to have this creature when we return to the world."

Noah hurled a sandal at the raven, somewhere above him in the beams.

"Shut up."

"*Shut up,*" said the raven. "*My friend, my furry friend. Shut up.*"

All day the raven sang like that.

"But Father, this is a very skillful creature indeed. Perhaps we should not waste this one, not even risk it."

Noah held both of his arms to his son's shoulders. "Ham, I am glad you're on this ship. You remind me of how I used to be, or should be, anyway. And despite myself, I fear you are right. We should keep all creatures aboard and find some other way to save the world."

"*Shut up, my friend, my furry friend. There you go. Shut up. Eat up. Throw up. Soup.*"

"We should at least do something to make him stop squawking," said Ham.

All through the night, the raven kept at it.

Then, "*Ouch,*" the raven cried. "*Stubbed my toe. Why's it so dark in here? Got to do something about that.*" He flew into the beastman's quarters, stole the holy casting pearl, and flew away with it in his beak. "*Look at me. Glorious me. I light the way. Awake, my beauties, awake.*"

Unlike the slow-moving torches of the feeding cart, the light from the casting stone seared through the different decks, nearly as bright as day, shining from the raven's open beak, a magnitude of light unseen by the animals for months and months. The brightness pained the dim slits of their eyes, and they hid their round, black, startled eye holes from the glow of God's celestial pearl.

The raven's proud, sweeping journey ended right where it had begun. He brought the beastman's chamber back out of darkness and dropped the pearl on a beam just behind me, exposing my hiding place. Then he walked along one of the beams above Noah and his family, walking with his shoulders and trouser feathers puffed out as always, walking stiff-legged, with the exaggerated authority of some ancient luminary at the Roost. He paused and wiped his bill on his own shins and scanned all around him.

The sons and daughters of Noah held their blankets up before the companionway to their quarters.

"Now we have you," whispered Noah. "Insolent creature."

They tacked the blankets in place, and Noah made small hand movements to his clansfolk, who crept up on the balls of their feet as if hidden from the raven's view. There, they waited in strategic positions.

"Catch me if you can."

The raven swooped down before the face of Noah and gave a chop at his hair.

Then the raven landed right beside me, in my hiding place, three times my size. In the shadows he pushed me aside, just enough for me to be seen. He began extracting the beastmen's objects that I had cached there when they weren't looking, objects that were marvels to me, trinkets that entertained me, pieces of glass, clay, metal—bright useless objects of unusual beauty.

"My knife!"

The beastman's anger grew.

The raven hurled down the beastman's favorite, riddled with the pock-marks of salt and rust.

Noah picked it up and began to clean it with his robe as other objects fell, a comb, a fork, a braid of the beastman's hair.

"You awful, thieving bird!"

After all the objects fell, the raven pushed me even farther from my hiding place.

"Just go," he said with a nasty hush.

"Eiyyawwwk!" I had been silent up until then, but I howled, I shrieked, and bit him.

He speared me in the chest, and I flew backward, nearly falling to the deck until I caught myself.

I tried to fly back to my old hideout.

But the raven spread his monstrous wings and blocked my way. Then he tilted his powerful horn as if he would strike me even more fiercely. Completely hidden from the humans, he was silent and cunning, and he craned his head sideways in a question, answered by his own posture.

"*Go now, fodder,*" he said. "*I'm done with you.*"

I tried to fly free of the beastmen's quarters, but by now they all had sticks, and one of them held a stiff net of hemp.

"Careful. Don't hurt him," said Noah. "Though he's the Evil One, he's still important to us."

With the window and gangways blocked off, they cornered me, and, before the night was through, brought me down.

The use of birds to find land is an ancient maritime tradition. The raven was used by Babylonian sailors and later the Vikings, and according to the old Roman Naturalist, Pliny the Elder, mariners of Taprobane (Ceylon) also carried ravens aboard their ships and set course by following the raven's flight.

10. Atlantis

I thought the net was heavy, but their claws were bone-heavy and quick with an intelligence all their own, apart from those deep-set eyes that sleep-walked, animated by a logic that had ceased taking in the world long ago. Soon Noah had my wings pinned within the hairless, veiny bones of his clutches.

"He is a deceptive little one," said the one known as Ham. "He is much smaller now that he's in our grasp."

"That's because I Am smaller. I Am not the raven. The one you seek is still in the rafters."

"Who are you?" said Noah.

"I Am. A crow."

"Father," said Ham. "This is a crow."

"It is?"

"Yes. Both black-feathered birds. Both eaters of carrion. Look. This one is not the raven. Can't you see?"

Noah eyed his son, wheezing through his beard with a suspicious, worried look.

"Are your eyes that bad? Father?"

"What? What am I not seeing?"

"That he is what he is."

"All right, then. Go on. Check the crows."

It took a great long while for Ham to return, and I knew the news would be bad.

"What did you see?"

"I'm not sure," said Ham to his father, looking with lost eyes to his siblings as well. "There were so many blackbirds—brewer's blackbirds, grackles, red-winged blackbirds, dippers, coots, cowbirds, all manner of blackish-feathered things."

"How many *crows?*" said Noah. "It was the crow cage, wasn't it?"

"I—I couldn't tell."

Of course he couldn't, with the seven crows, along with all the other birds, but I said nothing.

"And in the raven's?"

"One."

Noah grunted. "I have no patience for this. Fool!" he said to me. "You try to deceive me a second time."

"Still, something is not right," said Ham. "Look at the white plumes around his eyes."

"I will dispatch him immediately, before he works some new treachery."

"Father, I thought you might save the raven after all, and not sentence him to the flood."

But as Ham spoke, the other sons unlatched the heavy portal, and Noah extended the hard, quick sticks of his arms.

"Fly bravely," he said to me, "if it is at all possible for a creature such as yourself. We depend on you for a sign."

Outside all was billowy whiteness. Then darker. I found myself in a deepening cloud as though the mountainside were afloat in it. Streams fell through the cloud stuff, then disappeared into their own noise. Whitewater rapids whirled through glacial ice flows, crystallized since the beginning of time. Waterfalls spilled noiselessly into nothing but cloud. Rocks stuck out into view, then hid again back in their own cloudy beginnings. I was happy to be flying free of Noah, though I doubted I'd ever find anything of the earth, or was anywhere near it. Finally I did find where flood and mountain met, and I followed the rocks and tide rips until I came upon the ark again and rapped with my beak upon the portal.

The latch opened.

I flew into it, and found myself inside a cage.

Noah dragged the cage angrily through his quarters until I was near his table. He did not speak but only smeared what was left of the crust of his dry, dense, figgy bread into a saucer of curdled milk, then, holding the mushy concoction up over his hairy maw, tried finding the opening between the shards of worn, skeletal teeth. The slippery, smacking sounds he made were loathsome, and when he preened himself, he only smeared the cheesy pudding more deeply into the tangled bush around his face.

He said, "I can see by the fear in your eyes that you did not even leave the mountain. You've been gone such a short time. Here. I give you one worm and one slice from my own table. No excuses. I will hear nothing from you but the sound of your wings as you leave."

Noah pushed me out the window again.

The next morning, before he released me a third time, Noah set me down and fed me from his table again.

My benefactor Hookbill the Dog Now watched him with her whiskery religious face seeing all, knowing everything, somewhat bored. Hookbill the Haunted tolerated the madness of Noah in the same way that she tolerated everything—the hyperactivity of orphans, and sad wanderings, and human food. Hookbill the Hound had the ever-patient eyes of an ancient traveler and so was never impatient to be anywhere, always in between places and home.

When Noah finished eating, he stood with me clutched in both of his hands and had his sons lift the window yet again, saying, "Do not return until you have found news from beyond sight of the peak."

I lit on a rock close by and looked back at the ark through the cloudbanks. There'd be nothing to eat while I was gone. Meanwhile, my wings grew heavy with water. I flapped clumsily until I was out of the lee of the mountain and there was nothing below me but seawater, and the wind grew steadily and blew away the clouds. I found myself beneath a formless overcast with a sourceless light. I turned around for a glance back at the mountain peak, but it was gone. All was ocean, only ocean, with its icy whitecaps breaking over the deep rollers. The more I flew, the heavier the seas became. They moved like great gray land formations, crashing, receding, repeating, and hardly moving, rising up to die, always renewing, always the same, icy, deep, and dark in their ongoing grayness, their frozen leviathan crashing.

Other mountain peaks rose up from the sea and disappeared again in the drift of the horizon, trying to emerge up out of the clouds they created and clung to. It was the mountains' last desperate attempt to get their heads up out of the water. One last gasp before they went under. I tried to fly to them. But the mountains kept their distance, drifting along the horizon. And the wind carried me away until I had to choose not to fly upwind. Mostly I glided, saving what little stamina was left in my wings.

The fight with the beastmen and the raven still pained my bones.

Above and below me, the gray-green elements darkened. There were no landmarks, no stars, no guidance. What I thought was the advancement of night was just me flying closer to the sea. Just above the waves, the deep waters absorbed the light. The air between the crests was cold and stung my eyes. Icebergs and their broken chunks were afloat, as large as the largest trees, close enough to throw out a dismal light all their own. For a moment I thought I was nearing land. But no, the ice chunks, after I flew near, turned out to be corpses. Large, washed-pale, and swollen like air-filled bladders, a flotsam of corpses rode the waves as if caught in a tide. I found one I could ride for respite. What kind of creature the corpse had been, I couldn't tell. It was white, large, and bloated like them all, smelling rank like a swamp in late summer but filled with near-frozen meat and pickled in brine. I plucked at it, a cow, or a human, it was too large to tell, and a venting rush of vapors hit me in the face. I ate. As I did, it began to sink. I flew to another fleshy, gelatinous island. I pierced it easily with my beak. It happened again. As I ate, the beast lowered until the waves washed over it. I survived that fleshy wreck to eat elsewhere. Here I was, the last of the last creatures caught up by the flood, the last of the unchosen, which was what most of the earth was, or had been, all of that gone now, and I going with it. I ate until I was fully engorged and bloated and listless, with my wings too wet and heavy to fly. I got my beak caught between the ribs of one of the corpses just as it sank, and the icy, stabbing cold covered me until I could no longer flap.

I would have sung my Parting from This Earth, except that the cold saltwater waves would have rushed down my horn and snuffed out both me and my song. It would be such a short song anyway, not varied and ongoing like the Mother of Many's, which took seasons to sing and looped round itself and colored that afternoon of afternoons when you found yourself basking in the tree of her song. My own song would be shorter than even the Old Bone's, or Hookbill's, blunted by their own Misfortunes. But I should have sung it anyway, back when I first entered the ark and actually did part from the earth, and my bird body had sustained itself only long enough to deliver me here to the hurling floodwaters. I opened my throat after all, hoping that the wind might catch my song long enough to send it back to Plum Black, the Beauty of our Aerie, and all the other crows of the ark, so that they might hear it caught up in the spirits of the wind and sing it above their new home of friendly trees, wherever that might be. Amen. My song was just a few bubbles that circled in the swill. The dark gray waters rushed down my horn, and looking up, I saw where the ocean met the rainbow, where God's good face blew upon the kindly waters.

I rolled like a soggy leaf in the depths of different hues and temperatures. I remembered the dream that my last meal had had back on earth. I dreamt the dream of a cow, where sunlight drenched the hills, and the succulent juice of grasses dripped from my mouth. When it rained, the water turned into a river that crashed over the valley. I bellowed in fear, and the water engulfed my bovine esophagus, open wide to the sky. Water spilled into my lungs and both of my stomachs and my bowels. I rolled slowly through the underwater ravines, and my enormous hoofed legs bumped into the jags of the valley below. Crabs, sand mites, and schools of tiny fishes took tiny bites from me. An ancient, warted flounder swam closer and studied my roiling tongue. Though both of its bubbling eyes were on the same side of its face, they worked and blinked independently, and the severe mouth tugged on me with its time-old, protozoic hunger. For months that ancient fish swam beside me, like my shadow. I saw its completely white underside without feature or eye, and this was its hunger, too. When there was too little left of me to eat, and the last vestiges of my identity dissolved with my scattering bones, I'd already become the flounder and enjoyed hiding beneath the ocean silt.

On the ocean floor there were still trees and bushes from the upper world, and I swam through and around them. I swam into an aquamarine village, and in through an open window, and into a human's hut. Chairs and billowing garments hung in the underwater chambers, bouncing off a wall perhaps once a new moon, gesturing, rolling. I swam in and out of dark-water windows and doorways, down streets, over walls, and between limbless tree trunks still lodged in the mud. I swam through the thicker element with a faint memory of those things housed in air. While the fine rain of expired plankton shells fell on me without event through the centuries and millennia.

V.

Covenant

Glad to see the floodwaters gone, Raven scanned the beach and eyed a gigantic clamshell. He walked up to the clamshell and discovered little creatures inside it. When they cowered at the sight of his enormous shadow, Raven figured he would have to soothe the fears of those inside.

"Come on out here, whatever or whoever you are. I will not harm you. The Flood is over. I am Raven, creator of the world."

The creatures emerged from the clamshell frightened and bewildered, but Raven played with the First People and showed them how to live in his shining, new world.

—RAVEN AND THE ANCESTRAL HUMAN BEINGS, *HAIDA, BRITISH COLUMBIA*

We divide animals in the Ark into good and
bad, but the crow doesn't arrive. We make
all the male porcupines and sloths sit on the
right side of the room, and the female
porcupines and sloths on the left side of the
room, but the crow doesn't arrive. The two
halves of Yin and Yang do not join.

—ROBERT BLY, *A Little Book on*
the Human Shadow

1. Diluvia

In the end, I was nothing but sea, surf, and spume, bulging and parting, leavened by the moon. Time flattened and grew expansive over the horizon, where I'd just lie and abide gravity and wallow upon myself. Where I was missing, I soon was filling myself in. I was the trackless depth of the sea and the ebb where rain and river stopped. I was the shore, and though there was much turbulence there—the jagged coastline made me gush and spout—I withdrew at the same time I advanced and accepted all things in my deepwater pastures.

But all too soon I felt a slight annoyance, more like an itch, and it grew into the frantic anxiety of survival all over again. The ocean above my head escaped by froth and runnels and in a rush I fanned sand up over my broken fins. I was the flounder again, caught beneath a disappearing slack tide without enough water to swim back to any depth. There I cowered and buried myself beneath the sand, which would keep enough brine in my gills to allow the high tide, once it returned, to rejuvenate me.

Above me I heard a growling pack of wolf-dogs in a fight over a fellow flounder, until one of the dogs had the stiff fish in its jowls, and the rest chased it down the beach. Then I heard the snort of another dog, this one just above me. Instead of fear, I felt the luminous presence of my benefactor Hookbill the Hound of the Two-Colored Eyes, and she too dug me up into the hot slather of her jaws and carried me along the mudflats that went on and on in the surf's nether mist. The light was still that of early, early dawn.

I'd washed ashore, out of the dream of a flounder and into my old form.

A crow in the mud.

Too muddy to cry out.

Above the surf, large predators stood guard, unmoving, like the stone statues once set before the temples of humans. At their feet lay enormous white carcasses, preserved in the frozen brine of the flood, melon-sized holes chewed out of the bloodless sponge. You couldn't tell what beast was what in the dull light. Cats three times Hookbill's size did nothing, not even turn their vacant eyes from their vigil out beyond the surf, as the dog, my old deliverer, passed right before them.

Hookbill, now heavy with pups, carried me through a land of utter desolation. Her mange swung in tassels of mud below her swollen belly, and the undersides of her legs kept a steady splatter going. We traveled neither rising nor falling in a land where the flood had wiped out everything and left only a sickly gray humus across the plain.

Occasionally we'd come across a heron or some great horned animal contemplating all the nothing in the vast, shadowless waste. As we approached, the bird would unruffle its wings and work them heavily without taking flight, the sun being somewhere, for the overcast was brighter in one part of the sky. Perhaps the wing movements were my own. I wasn't sure. I dozed in and out of sleep.

We came upon an upward slope furrowed deeply by a single path, and we slogged our way up the mountainside

· · ·

I shook myself awake when old Hookbill the Dog Now stopped trotting and bit on me a few times to rearrange me within the gentle pressure of her jaws. She stood looking up at the long pile of the ark and the huge rocks that had snagged the ship and held it fast. Its keel now sagged along the mountain slope, and it lay broken and caved in on top of itself, so it looked even more like a hill of black, shorn trees. Thin columns of smoke poured out through gaps that had formed along the ark's decking and sides. And in the ship's shadow, Hookbill the Haunted dropped me below the old bird body of herself still up there on the bulwarks, laminated by the weather and the pitch to a flat, grotesque shape, that of her screaming out the side of her face. Even the compressed old husk of her was growing weary, for this was one of her last acts in the crow realm. As I lay looking up, I could sense her powers taking leave of her own hound's body and entering into one of her pups, and by the way she'd delivered me—walking slowly with dropped shoulders, setting me on a rock—I'd thought for sure she'd made an offering of me. Especially when the first of the clan to arrive was Mona with her fat little fingers and her laughing teeth. She grabbed me up in her pink hands and groped and prodded me until her huge, gummy smile went flat.

"Here. Give it to me," said Noah. He spoke now with a solemn, reverent air.

"There's not much left, anyway," said Mona, slinging the muck from my wings off her fingers.

Cold, soaked, and crusty-winged, I could do nothing but allow Noah to pick me up in hands grown haunted and prophetic now that he had saved the world.

"Poor fellow. Run into trouble, did you?"

I wanted to spit back the bile of the sea he had ushered down my throat. *"Remember me? Eiyawwk!"* But my voice hardly carried.

And with old Hookbill the Intermediary gone to other purposes, the understanding between beast and bird grew cloudy and easily misconstrued. I cursed. *"Why don't you swim like a fish into oblivion?"* But my anger melted as I realized that swimming like a fish into oblivion wasn't all that bad. I wondered for what purpose I'd been pulled back into the broken, wasted world. My beak pinched down on the shells of soured grain that Noah held out for me.

"Father," said the son known as Ham, who took a handful of the grain and blew it from his palm. The wind caught it up and sent it beyond the mountainside.

"Not much left of that, you know," said Noah.

"With what will we replant the earth?"

"God will take care of that. What do you want?"

"Look at this creature, Father. Is this not the crow you sent into the flood?"

"No. This bird became so on its own. Why do you contradict me?"

"Why should I contradict you, when the truth does so on its own?"

"Insolent son, cease. After our voyage, our hearts need rest. Not argument."

Noah's grip around my wings tightened, and I thought he might hurl me to the ground.

"Here. You take it." He held me out to Nanniah, also heavy with child, who'd come near, hearing the rising voices of her husband and father-in-law in a quarrel.

In the gentle bones of her slender hands, I heard the lost Mother of Many beating her wings against the ribs that imprisoned her. Or perhaps it was the squirming of the unborn babe, conceived back in the lost world and carried in the strange sea of Nanniah's belly. Cursed or not, he kicked against her flesh as if to wake and be free. Strange animals, without the humility of an egg. She hummed, and her hands caressed me in the warmth of an entirely remote love, hidden inside herself. It would have been there even if the child were not. To her, I could have been a plaything or a shoe. As she walked, she carefully cleaned the sand lice, grit, and ooze from my tail feathers and wings.

2. Paradise

As if I were a fledge of the beastman, Nanniah the Madonna of Eden carried me everywhere in the sling of her arm. She petted me, she bounced me, she whispered secrets I could not understand into my scared and wrinkled ears. And soon, like water seeping through my feathery skull, my sea-filled dreams heard something like the warblings of the lost mother again and turned happy.

The heavy chaff-eating beasts, the goats, the yaks, the oxen, and so on, lived exclusively off the fodder of the ark, its hull busted open on the cliff face and the stores of grain spilled out, discolored and mildewed, already germinated in places. The roots and fresh spears of grass spread out of themselves, yellow, anemic, and thirsting. The mixed herd of livestock stood hoof-deep in the dunes of seed. Their jaws worked like grinding stones wearing down on what was left of the day.

The giant son of Nanniah remained seated there beside the rope ladder that had saved his life. Round-shouldered, naked, and pale as if still water-logged, he watched over the activities of the clan of Noah's with a confused, vaguely suspicious look as though he'd been slighted but was not sure why. He turned his perplexed face to his penis and flipped it around a few times and studied its reaction as would a naked toddler in the sand.

It was his mother's job to throw down scrap for the chickens and ducks, who seemed especially charmed by this, or by her, or both. The lap cat was always curling itself beneath the hem of her dress, until Nanniah tripped on the cat and it screeched. In her fall, Nanniah flung me to the ground. I flapped, but smacked hard against the loam, where I found the cat crouched over me, her tail swishing, ready to pounce. I cawed in anger. But the cat paid little attention, shifting her back paws side to side to gain footing for a jump. Here was a creature I'd usually imitate and taunt, especially back in the ark, and now I was helpless, until Nanniah caught me up again into the crook of her arm and carried me into the wreck's tired catacombs. We entered one of the newly broken cave-like openings, where Nanniah put me into a small, abandoned cage for protection until I could fly. Then she carried me in my birdcage into the compartments where the beastmen had slept during the voyage.

Except now their quarters were bright with flames.

The flood had left huge drifts of sand and rock throughout the ark, which the beastmen had formed into pits of fire, and now the smoke disappeared through holes between the black beams and branches. Here and there the pitch melted down from the logs and formed into black pools and stalagmites. From all the preparations under way, I was sure the old Hookbill had brought me back as a part of their offering. Mona came over to my cage and held out a sliver of fish gut between her pinched fingers and thumb.

"Fatten up, my sweet."

She dumped the rest into a bucket thick with slop. Most of what they prepared was seafood—or all of it, it seemed. The place had the damp, salty air of the hemp fishing nets that the Old Bone and I used to pick through on the beastman's idle boats. Ropes of seaweed were being dried on racks. All kinds of fishes and eels were flayed open and hung from the joists. The head of a lingcod as big as a bear's lay on a table, its filleted bones strung out, and the tail fin hung over the side. The beastmen must have found all the sea creatures stranded when the slack waters fell back. But from their talk I learned that they were forbidden to eat any kind of flesh whatsoever, sea life included, until the one known as Noah had invoked the

Everlasting All-Seeing Whom they referred to as Yahweh and they had made their ritual sacrifice to Him in gratitude for their deliverance.

Knowing this bothered me with increasing vividness as Mona, Japeth, and their mother, Namah, traded off dipping a ladle into the overturned shell of a giant sea turtle, eviscerated and propped up over the flames, so that the soup within gushed with a steady boiling. Through the steam, I saw the kelp, and the fish heads, and the turtle's own head and limbs, bobbing in the chowder of its own shell. There were other such kettles of gumbo and broth, and along with the pitch a sweet, salty moisture dripped down from the beams. Mona slurped at her ladle and swiped her face with her sleeve and leered at me with her small, nubby teeth set far apart.

"Here you go, *sweetie*. Want some bladder?"

I looked over to Nanniah for any sign of my salvation. But she only looked down, turning a paddle in one of their many steaming pots. I wished only to eat more anyway, since the more I ate, the more their sharp, narcotic potions mellowed, and in the magic of their sauces I yearned for the nearness of Mona's stubby fingers and the hypnotic knowing of her smile, which would bring me somewhere beyond this waiting. She held her hand out and I turned my head sideways through the wickets of my cage as if it were a kiss. It had been so long since I'd been anywhere near the black, bird-like beauty of crow wings, and I could mistake any sort of animal warmth as my welcome. As I lay listless from my bout with the sea, I wished only for more oyster drenched in their bloody opiate, so that the beastmen might hurry up and carry me over to their sacrificial chopping block, if that was what they were going to do.

When Nanniah finally picked me up, she carried the whole cage, and took no notice of me or her family, and left. Outside, she carried me serenely past the tents set up at the foot of the ark, as if a small village had formed in its shadow. Seeing her son—the naked giant—Nanniah placed my cage down on the sand next to him.

"Keep him safe," she said, and withdrew into the ark.

I wasn't sure whether she had spoken to him or to me, because the giant barely acknowledged me, but wore a cross, perplexed expression as he gazed out over the mountainside and the valley below.

"Crow," he said, still focused elsewhere. "Which burns hotter, the fire of bushes or the fire of stars? What becomes of the smoke from stars? If fishes drink, then what is it they drink? Water? Then why is there so much of it? And why can't I drink underwater myself?" And so on, he kept asking questions as Nanniah approached, balancing a ladle, filled to the brim. "Mother." The giant grew slobbery with emotion. He cupped the ladle with both hands, and soup ran down his soft, blubbering cheeks. He calmed himself, though, as he finished. "Mother. Why did you bring me here?"

She put her hand on his enormous, quivering side. "Because I knew you would not let go."

"Is Papa proud of me?" he asked. "Is he?"

"Yes. Very."

Because of his size, I could see only one of the giant's eyes at a time. His grief was like that of a whale, mute and lost within the vastness of his own flesh.

Now Noah had seen the feeding of the giant and grew fierce with displeasure. He hurled down the object of his toil, a rock about the size of a boar's head.

"Can't you *wait?*" He yelled across the muddy fields, his anger diminished only by the empty distance. "For even *a little* while?"

Nanniah answered with a quizzical look.

"I am piling rocks *for an altar!*" he said. "So that we *all* might eat, without spoiling everything."

"Then hurry up," said Namah. "Almost everything's overcooked anyway. You know how delicate fish is."

Japeth and Mona laughed and ran after each other in a game that involved throwing fish heads, fish fins, and guts at each other. Mona squealed with her bucket and tried to mash the glistening contents into the hair of her mate's younger brother.

"We're starving," said Namah.

Noah worked himself into quite a state of agitation, dragging his lame leg across the mud and piling up rocks for an altar. The rocks teetered over his head as he threw them into place. Soon he had a ram with him on the end of a rope, but grew weary of just standing there holding the tether.

"Shem, get over here. Help me hold this ram. And help me find rocks!" he yelled to anyone else around, which was no one.

"There are so few rocks in this land," Noah grunted, head down.

Soon the three of them stumbled up the rock pile, until the lank Holy Noah, God's Chosen One, stood poised over the ram, wielding his pock-marked sacrificial blade. He raised the knife.

But, "No."

He shook his head.

"No, no, no—this is all wrong."

He yelled out to the rookery, calling the names of his clan. They pretended to ignore him with wide, spooked eyes, immersed in their activities. His calls grew high-pitched and whiny, like a child's, until he individually ushered each of them into the service of his offering. "You stand here. And you here." They allowed themselves to be arranged with the patience reserved for children, as if the whole ordeal was simply to humor him, and because Noah moved so slowly with that hobbled walk of his. Soon all of his family stood as still as statues, it seemed, pitying him, his daughters and wife on one side and his sons on the other, each holding a crude earthenware jar. "Essence of Myrtle." Noah lit a stock of it and dropped it into one of the jars. "Essence of Pine . . . of Reed." He called out the name of each spice as he lit it and placed it in a jar. From where I sat, in my cage next to the giant, it seemed as though the stomachs of the beasts were on fire.

"To Namah!" he called. "Light of the Garden."

"What are you doing with that bowl?" she asked.

Noah was dumping out one bowl of fish broth into another in order to empty the first.

"We are gathered here——" He cleared his throat and turned his gaze upward, throwing his voice afar, "to give thanks for Your returning us to Paradise. And we shall need hearts and tongues, livers and testicles, and all the sacred flesh of divination to ask for Your Blessing." He held up the bowl. "Japeth."

The boy wiped the sacrificial blade on his own cloak and placed it in the bowl. And Noah held the receptacle with much aplomb as he limped past the two rows of incense bearers.

Now, all of Noah's excitement was not lost on the ram. When Noah grabbed the mane of its neck, it began to run. Japeth strained to keep hold of the reins while his father tried to cut along the panicked animal's neck. The ram ran in circles with the gimp-legged Noah hanging on to it. That was how the ram died, dragging the old man down the rocks. Noah continued cutting up the ram and digging into its flesh until he dragged it back up onto the rocks and set flame to it above the bed of straw.

As they all walked away from the burning animal, Ham spoke, under his breath: "Behold this offering!" He made soft gestures, as if gathering the air up to his face. "Sweet-smelling frankincense, galbanum, stacte, fresh spices of the morning, all for a murderous god."

Hearing his son, Noah cried out, and threw Ham onto the ground, though Ham fell more in deference to his father, or from ancestral fear, than from being physically overpowered.

Noah stood over him. "Take it back."

"Why should I take back the truth? How would that change anything? Especially what has happened?"

"You cannot dare to guess at God's way, nor make judgment on Him. Take back what you have said. Or will you ruin this world as well?"

Nanniah fell to her knees and cried out to Noah. For days she and Ham had crooned to me and fed me, suspicious of the rage of their father but wishing him back to good health, too. Noah must have forgotten himself in his anger, because he clutched the knife in a threatening manner and his fist shook.

"What? You too?" said Ham. "I thought that was God's bidding."

"Enough! Out of my sight!" Noah stood and limped away, throwing the blade into the sand. "How could I have made such a son? And how did we ever survive?"

Now the Everlasting All-Knowing beheld the twisting smoke and the sweet smells of bubbling flesh above the flames and landed not too far away, folding Its black, mighty wings. The Good God Crow took sidelong hops in the mud that covered the valley as far as the eye could see. The sun burned away the milky layers of cloud covering. And in a burst of brilliance, a rainbow broke out over the parted sky. The Magnificent God Crow burst out, too, with a few guttural croaks and caws. It preened Itself under a wing and hopped around, then pecked at an object lodged in the mud. Of course God would make many rainbows after this one, but this was Its first and for that reason perhaps Its most brilliant. The rainbow was so perfect and striking that even cattle stopped grazing to lift their heads. Every creature on the earth turned its eyes upward to behold this wondrous rainbow stretching across the heavens.

Then the God Crow flew above Noah, wracking the air with the might of Its caw, and Noah squinted upward as the Goodly Bird flew off and was gone.

In the majestic quiet of the sky, I saw a familiar far-off flapping, the only movement below the vastness of the clouds. The distant crow wings grew closer, and so did my hopes. Through the mesh of my cage, I saw her, the Beauty not only of the woods but of all the long-gone world. *Meet me in the sky!* My heart beat against the slats of its longing. I had to be near Plum Black and catch her mirror-like flashing in the sun. *"Plum Black!"* I called, or tried to. *"I Am!"* But my voice, like my heavy, sea-soaked wings, stayed lodged where it was.

Without a look at the wondrous rainbow, Plum Black lit on the ark. She clipped a loose twig from one of its untrimmed branches, exposed by the wreck, and flew away with it in her beak. Perhaps she was carrying it back to the aerie she'd found with one of the crows from the ark.

Seeing me suffer in my fight against the cage, Nanniah opened the door and reached inside it. Then she tossed me into the air. But my heavy, wasted wings brought me down into a muddy puddle, where I splashed through the wallow. "Oh, poor bird." Startled, Nanniah laughed and stooped to pick me back up, and she struggled to hold on to me. After pressing me against her face, she cradled me again in the gentle crook of her arm.

3. Vine Stock

From far down the sloping morass came the stooped figure of a black bird, hopping. It hopped with a crow's quick double hop. But why did it only hop? It was still too far away to tell. In my present state I did nothing but keep silent in the sling of Nanniah's arms. I'd burn with humiliation if any crow, especially Plum Black, ever saw me as a captive to those who had brought Our Mother of Many down. I hoped that it wasn't Plum Black, limping back to the ark after an injury. But who else could it be?

As the injured bird drew closer, I could see that it was a crow of some sort, maybe one of the seven clean crows carried across the waters. The bird wasn't lame but hopped just fine, and when something interested it down in the mud, it flew wonderfully above the object, making a low, banking turn and swooping back to take a closer look. Then it began hopping up the mountainside again. It was an extremely tall and lanky crow, God Crow–sized but wizened and raw with dull, split feathers and a world-weary manner. Noah was so busy gaping at the beauty of God's rainbow that he did not see this strange bird, though it took the traveler half the day to approach.

"*Good afternoon,*" said the Strange Crow, hopping up to Noah and inspecting the mud on its claws.

Noah only eyed the creature.

"*What is that in your hands?*"

Noah clenched the twig and looked down suspiciously.

The Strange Bird had that eerie otherness about him that brought both fear and awe.

Finally Noah spoke to him. "It is a vine stock."

"*Oh? Of what kind?*"

Nanniah also drew near, intrigued and alarmed, and the babe in her womb squirmed from skittishness.

"A vine from Eden," said Noah. "It will bear the grape." And he held it up to his face as if trying to inhale the future that would untwist from within the bark.

"*May I?*"

The Strange Bird flew to the blackened rocks and held up the outstretched points of its claws. The claw foot was thin and dry and cracked like dead root. Behind him, the rocks of the altar still smoked.

"No." Noah withheld the vine. "Begone with you. Haven't you ruined enough already?"

"*As you wish.*"

And the Wizened One hopped down from the rocks as if ready to hop all the way down the mountainside.

"*But it wasn't I who sweetened the juice of the apple,*" said the Strange Bird, beginning his long journey. "*Nor did I make your kind thirst to know more than can, or should be, known. I only point out the obvious.*"

"Obvious? Then why do you even come here? To pester me? To gain a foothold back into the world?"

"*Sir.*" The Strange Bird was sadly offended. "*Why am I here?*" He stopped and shot his glances all around him at the gray, muddy abyss that now had a wonderful sheen in the sunlight. He pecked at his shins. "*If I did not come* here, you would invent me, or someone just like me. Is there anything else you might wish from a mere servant?"

"Servant? Oh, no, I trust you not. I wish only to forget that old earth and all you accomplished back there. The knowledge you showed us from the tree has gone sour. I will let it ferment back to its beginnings, and yield wine, which will at least gladden people's hearts."

"Very well. May I help in any way?"

"Oh, no. No help from you. Begone. I wish only that this vine be fed by the sun and yield quickly. For the sooner I drink thereof and forget about you and how you ruined things, the better. This vine is from Eden, the old Eden, before you ever got there."

"As you wish. Though I'm older than the garden you speak of, I am, as I've already stated, nothing more than a servant. Farewell, Noah." And the Strange One hopped, lank-winged and weary, back down the long mountain.

Meanwhile, the vines Noah planted sprang forth with supple green shoots and luscious leaves before he could even attend to the next furrow in the mud, so that when he awoke the next morning, the vines hung fat and toppled over across the ground with bursting clusters of the opulent grape, and Noah laughed in his madness, already drunk in his anticipation, for he was the first and most accomplished vintner the world had ever known.

After pressing the grape that fermented that day, Noah sat on his rocks blackened by fire. He nearly had the potion up to his lips when he turned around, startled.

"Haven't you forgotten something?"

It was the Strange Bird again, perched beside Noah on the sooty altar.

"What? What could it be? Look." Noah held up his goatskin bottle. "Wine—already. Just look at how fertile this new world is."

"No, I meant an offering."

Behind the Stranger were four beasts, each tied to a heavy rope staked to the ground—a lamb, a pig, a lion, and an ape. These behaved as if already drugged by the heavy narcotic potions of Noah, whose face narrowed down to one eyeball as he studied the throat opening of his goatskin bottle.

I felt Nanniah's arms tighten around me, carrying me around all the time in the sling of her arms.

"*You!* Again? Did I not resist you yesterday?" said Noah. "Must you tempt me again?"

The Strange One hopped up to the foot of Noah.

"*I only remind you of your obligation to make an offering.*"

"But—I made one the other day. Everyone saw it."

"*Yes.*"

And here the Wizened One took it upon himself to remind the beastman known as Noah that if one is lame, as was Noah, especially in such matters as the ability to perform the marital act, then the firstborn must burn the offering in the supplicant's stead.

Noah turned to his sons, who had gathered around. All three stood at a distance, wide-eyed, like children.

"Father, it is true," said Shem, the eldest.

"But God accepted my offer yesterday," said Noah. "Did He not? Did you not see the rainbow? Did He not establish His covenant, that He would not curse the ground anymore on our behalf? No more flood upon all living things. No more wrath. Only mercy. He said, 'Be fruitful.'"

"*Yes,*" said the Stranger. "*To even God himself, at times, the particulars are not important. But, if you wish to pass on the ancient covenants, which is your duty and yours alone, now's the time for teaching, and also for alms. Your vineyard grows un-consecrated.*"

"But it grew so fast," said Noah.

"It is the Accursed One's work," said Ham.

"Nonsense," said Noah. "It's God's, just a little faster this time. Shem!"

And the eldest son obeyed his father and prepared the altar for fresh slaughter.

Ham withdrew and put his arms around the womb of his wife, who nurtured both me and the unborn babe, and he led us all away.

Seeing us, the Wizened One hopped up to her feet and spoke: "*What's this? A crow . . . Domesticated crows?*"

But Nanniah gave no answer, and Ham cleaved to her in such distress that I felt my wings in peril of snapping and I heard the sudden song of the mother inside her ribs tell me it was time. I worked my wings free and to my surprise, I was strong and dry and I took to the air. Nanniah helped by throwing me upward, as she'd been wanting to do all along.

In the sky, I flew. I flapped and flew away and found myself above a formless landscape without end.

"'Tis some visitor," I muttered, "tapping at
my chamber door—
Only this and nothing more."
—EDGAR ALLAN POE, "The Raven"

4. Sacrifice

From its ravaged origins, the wind had no name and no spirits that called out
for one. The gusts were barren and unchanging, formed from a world void of
form, and all of the sky was the same, one gray, abysmal murk. The sodden,
silty plains of Paradise still had pools of sitting water. Through the clouds, I
kept seeing strange skeletal birds in the vaporous depths, or the ghost of
them, rattling back into the dark vapors as soon as they appeared. They were
enormous, scaly, naked-faced birds in a hideous soar. Still, I managed to follow them, until they circled the same patch of nothingness in the sky. Not
only did that sky have the sweet taste of death in it, but it was a death that had
decayed and begun its rejuvenation, a taste I had grown to love, and used to
fly to with a sweet, happy singing in my heart. It was the vernal juices after the
winter melt, the decay where the germinating seed takes root.

I left the vultures and descended, only to find that they'd been circling
Noah's rookery. There, the old man was sitting on a stray log from his ark
and talking with the Strange Crow of the Withered Coat. Noah drank from
one of his goatskin bottles, in the middle of a loud discussion.

"No, no, you have it all wrong," said the Strange Bird. "It was the apple's plan
all along. Hence, the sweet juices. You poor mammals had no choice but to eat it. Besides, you must first know what it is in order to know why it is forbidden. For to choose
not to know, after having been given the choice, is to choose not innocence, which you
no longer have, but a docile, stunted life of ignorance."

"Ignorance?" said Noah. "I can remember back when farmers used to scratch the ground on their hands and knees, clawing through the dirt with their fingernails. For nine generations outside the Garden, they were like that."

"*Until you invented tools,*" said the Strange Bird.

"Until I invented tools." Noah smacked his lips around a good draw from his goatskin. "With that so-called knowledge of the apple, they'd still be scratching the ground." He squinted with glowing contentment out over the distance, completely unaware of the moon-eyed patience of the vultures perched on the far side of his fields.

Already the lamb lay like a limp sack with its blood spilled over the roots of the vine.

And Shem, the firstborn, busied himself trying to subdue the second of the sacrificial beasts. Though the lion was on a tether, Shem was mortally afraid of it. He tied the rusty sacrificial knife to the end of a long lance and repeatedly thrust it at the lion. I was hoping that the braided hemp might snap, for surely the lion would take his blood-fed revenge out on more than just one of them. Then there would be no one left to set fire to the bodies. Before its roar could escape the cavernous mouth, there was already an echo, like the molten bellows of the earth yelling back at the sad surviving lot. Soon the lion gained control of Shem's weapon. The young beastman dove after it, but stopped. The lion had it completely within his sphere.

"Father!" Shem came back and stood before Noah, breathing hard and yelling. "Must we sacrifice the lion? Alone he is like subduing seven beasts. No, seven of seven."

Noah shut his lopsided lips, and looked at his new bird friend in speculation.

"*Do as you wish,*" said the Wizened One. He had an easy lilt to his voice, sunny and lulling, a voice gained from basking in the tropics. "*As you say, I make no pacts. I only tell you what I know.*"

"I'm not sure," said Noah. "Can't we forgo the lion? Or replace him with a less troublesome creature."

"*Why do you ask?*"

"You were the one who brought these animals here fit for sacrifice in the first place, already on tethers and stakes."

"True." The bird lifted the skirt of his tail feathers and a small stream of excreta fell beyond the log. *"I brought the lamb mainly because a man can be as timid as the lamb before he tastes of the wine."*

"And the lion?" asked Shem, as if in a fight with his breath, half from his battle with the king of beasts and half from his increasing anger with the Stranger.

"Drinking yet a little more," said the Strange Bird, *"a man believes himself to be as strong as the lion."*

"Shem," said Noah. "I would have taken care of the lion myself, if it weren't against our laws. I have a personal debt against him."

Shem spoke. "No man will ever be as powerful as the lion. It is as the stranger says. Your drink alone tells you so."

"The sacred knife is within the lion's circle, is it not?"

"It is."

"Very well. You may use the bow," said Noah.

Shem withdrew into the tangled structure of broken logs that used to be the ark. Upon his return, he had a taut, curved bow and a sling of arrows. He stood just beyond the circle of the lion, which paid no attention, gnawing on the spear as if it were a slug of food. It seemed the lion had not eaten in days and lapped at his own blood.

Shem repeatedly flung arrows, and the lion kept gnawing as before but flinched with each new shot, until the great cat lay down as if readying for a nap. Shem watched the arrows rise and fall like porcupine quills, three in the lion's rib cage, one in the hip, one in the neck, and one that fell with the cat's last resonating breaths. When Shem walked near to pick up the sacred knife, the lion stood back up. But he buckled on his elbows, stood back up, and blinked at Shem with the calm, lucid knowledge of his own death, which he accepted. When Shem tried once again to cut the lion down with the blade, the lion roared, and Shem speared directly into the lion's eye. After clawing the lance free of his face, the lion lay back down with its good eye to the ground and fell asleep. Shem's own eyes leaked the water of the mammal. He walked past his father and spoke without looking up.

"I will rest now."

"Your work is not finished," said Noah. "Until then, all is for naught."

"I will gather my strength first."

And the lion's blood spilled down upon the sodden loam and fed the root of the vine.

Beside the lamb, they'd dug a hole.

Noah, the sad captain, limped over to that grave mound with a stiffened air made even more venerable now that he'd drunk his potions, and loosened the spade from the wet clay. It sighed, and water oozed up from the shovel mark. I begrudged the beastman's strange rituals even further, realizing that they were going to vanquish yet another sacrifice to the underworld. What Noah did not see were the three big, scaly birds perched back on the rows of his new vineyard, waiting with their naked, obscene skulls—faces without feathers so they could plunge right into the corpses and not have to worry about cleaning the bloody juices off their jowls. I flew over to wait with them. Alighting, I drew Noah's attention, and he hollered at us, thumping the ground and shaking the spade he had himself invented, now with a new, invigorated purpose.

We scattered, the vultures rising slowly with big, heavy heaves from their tree-branch arms, not scared, and not even concerned, but with a solemn patience that knew there would always be dead things in need of their services. They landed just a few rows back, and I flew up to the busted bulwarks of the ark. What did it matter if the spoils of another feast passed before our eyes by way of fire, or earth? There was always the ark, where I could peck at the last of the putrefied grain stores.

Noah looked down at the lamb. It had been a small lamb, about the size

of a cat, but was even smaller now that it was stiff and dry. The only movement around it was that of the flies, which seemed to have multiplied more
quickly than anything else in this new world. It was a whirling turban of flies
and the soul of the lamb rose with it into the air as Noah walked by. It circled in the air for a time, then swarmed back down on top of itself.

Ham walked up to his father, scowling.

Noah shrugged him off. "These we cannot burn," he said. "They are to
fertilize the field with our wishes to God. We must dig."

His son only eyed him as if he did not understand.

"Very well," said Noah, "if you will not help. Though I cannot perform
the holy rites, I can still work a shovel."

Nearby, the Strange Bird of the Sunken Posture pecked sharply at the
headless skin, looked up, squinted off into the distance, then tried to needle
his beak up inside it.

Noah turned his gaze upward as he paused on the shovel.

Everywhere in the wide bowl of the sky, the clouds retreated and all was a
clear, peaceable blue as if this was the sky's natural state. Everywhere the rejuvenation had begun. Beyond the vineyard, shoots of vegetable life rose yellow and green above the mud. Grasses along the ark's spilled grain stores
were taller and trembled in the new sun. Long lines of songbirds flew back
and forth between the seed piles and their new homes wherever they built
them according to the needs of their kind, and the winds also carried the
fresh pine sap of the forest where they lived. The old hound that had once
housed Hookbill the Seer now lay in the ark's shadow, licking clean her new
litter and nursing them as she breathed. The weary bitch's teats leaked with
the life juice of the mammal.

"*I Am!*" I crowed out the song of the new day, and the song of Our Mother
of Many, and of Night Time and Squall and Plum Black, I called, "*Plum
Black,*" working my wings, but with no will to fly anywhere, since I'd been

denied my own kind, but I flew along the sagging hull of the ark to the smashed body of Hookbill my Savior from the Lost World.

Hearing me, one of the pups lifted its head up toward the papery dead wings of the Old Hookbill. There was complete one-eyed understanding in the face of the newborn blindness.

"It's you!" I swooped down and threw my song out over the pup, who squirmed to return to the safety of the litter and its mother's brimming flesh, warmed from within and without.

5. Curse of the Wine

The pig saw Shem approach with the dull blade and squealed, straining against the rope. In anger against his father, Shem stood over the panicked animal and slit its throat in one swift rip. His elbow flew and the pig kept running, burrowing into the mud even after it lay down, squealing and gurgling and spilling hot blood down onto the root of the vine.

When Shem approached the chimpanzee, the ape raised his hands above his head in the most intelligent protest yet. He jumped and yelled and intimidated the beastman from approaching any further. Searching all around him, all the ape could find to throw was handfuls of mud and his own dung. Defeated, Shem walked back to the carcass of the lion, picked up the stick, and worked to splice the knife to its end all over again. That was when Noah walked near and handed Shem the shovel.

"Here. Busy yourself elsewhere. There's a matter I must discuss."

The son walked away, searching upward, where the calm, wide wings of the vultures circled without judgment. Beyond the rocks, he saw that the wild dogs had gathered.

"We must hurry," he said, "before nightfall and all is turned to carrion."

Then Ham spoke to his father, who still inspected the corpses. "Now that you have done this thing, and the offerings have bled on the vine, can't we just nourish ourselves and some of the other creatures who crave flesh?"

"That's a pig," said Noah. "We can't eat pig. And who would eat a chimp? So much like a hairy man."

"What about the lamb?"

"Do not ruin our sacrifice when you've done no work and have no thirst to quench."

Then Noah ran over to the charred rocks, where the Stranger was still perched, and took the goatskin bottle and lifted it to his face. His anger softened as he drank, and the Stranger sidestepped his way along the log, clutch by clutch, until the beastman had squeezed just about the last drop of potion from the bottle. The rich red color ran down his neck.

"Is it possible?" asked Noah, between deep breaths. "What must be done with the creatures?"

"Do as you wish," said the Strange Bird, still clawing his way side to side, up and down the length of the log, one claw at a time, changing which way he faced, lurching forward to catch his balance. *"These offerings were made to fertilize the field with your wishes, so that your vineyard might grow robust. For drinking the fermented fruit to excess, you will act as the pig. You will soil yourself as you drink yet more until finally you become like the ape. You will grope about in your own foolishness. Your wits will flee you. And you will blaspheme your Master, who keeps the garden."*

Noah stood openmouthed, in horror.

"It is as I feared," he said, downcast, and remote. "Shem, free the ape."

As Shem neared the beast, the ape strained against his rope, shrieking and scolding and ready to attack. Shem stepped back and turned to his father with a pleading look.

"All right," said his father. "Just feed him, then. We'll untie him when it's time."

Looking down, Noah buried his face in his hands. "Stranger, begone with you! Not only do you blaspheme God, you blaspheme me, and the dead. You mock the very nature of these animals destroyed on your own council."

"That is not so," said the Strange Bird, extending a wing and inspecting the ragged saw-tooth of his feathers, then folding it back into place. "That is the one thing I do not do. Take heed of my warnings."

And with much hardship, for there was little left to his frame, the Wizened One spread his prickly wings and used them to float over to the lion, where he lit on the stock of one of the arrows, which rocked back and forth as the Strange Bird hung on.

"Farewell," he said, looking down. "The sacrifice seems complete." Then he swooped down on the mud and began hopping as slowly as he had when he had arrived, stoop-postured and pausing often, heading down the long mountain, one hop at a time. "Do what you will with the remains. I leave you as I found you, except with more knowledge than before. My good Noah, you and your family shall live long lives for your hardship. May you enjoy your many years here on earth."

The gods smelt the fragrance,
Gathered like flies over the offering.

—*Atrahasis*, MESOPOTAMIAN
FLOOD MYTH

6. The Dead

Free of the leash, the ape lumbered using his hands across the open loam of the trail until he was a safe distance from the ark. There, he sat back on his haunches and brought the dried tuber that the beastmen had given him up to his mouth and chewed sullenly. Like the vultures, I waited—I up on the ark and they in the vineyard. Instinctively I avoided them, scaly-faced, pink-headed, and too death-like to assume the identity of the creatures awaiting their skills. I left them alone to stare with their lost, moony eyes at the feast sinking slowly before their sight. The young beastmen were still digging holes for the feast, where not even the God Crow Itself, for Whom such offerings were usually made, would ever bother to look. So it was a feast meant for dirt—dirt and the creatures that live in dirt.

During my confinement on the ark, I had learned more about the strange theories of the beastman concerning their voyage to the hereafter, but only their own voyage, since no other kind of animal can go there. The blessed human Soul takes leave of the earth by means of flight, given to it by a sudden sprouting of gauzy wings. Though no other part of the body has feathers, the wings do, and these beautiful wings carry the deceased up through their dirt mound and into the earthy air and the ether beyond, unsoiled.

While the sons of Noah dug, they made their staccato grunts and yelps with their usual excitement. But I found it hard to understand their barking. Noah sat on his rock and drank his potion with great contentment and did not concern himself with the nearing of the vultures, or wild wolves, or hyenas that circled outside his poor hearing and sight.

"Keeyaw," I complained, but without conviction.

The beastman simply lowered the headless goatskin bottle from his face. He let it roll from his lap, and the bloody potion spilled onto the rocks, until he clenched the opening shut with his fist and eyed me with a bleary, bursting look. I had the distinct impression he had something urgent to say. He had a desperate need on his face and in his grunts and searching gestures, as if he'd never laid eyes on a bird before, and was just then trying to figure out who or what I was. His attempt to break down the barriers between species completely rankled him.

He began to chirp at me, using his kind's poor skill at mimicry. Out of curiosity, I flew down onto the mud and looked at him. He leaned toward me on one elbow and sang. He had no actual crow's song in his head. He didn't even sing like a crow, but like a songbird, only sillier. He was enjoying himself. But it was the vain enjoyment of the self-satisfied, for he wore the air of the holy shaman animal-lover he was, Noah, who not only saved the world but saved me, the little idiot bird who loved his singing so much just then. In Noah's song, there were sounds I recalled from his sleepwalking days as he fed in the ark. "Come here, handsome fellow, pretty bird. Don't be afraid. Hello."

Then Noah sat up in a sudden lucid moment and called to someone behind me. I hopped back, and would have hopped farther, if it hadn't been my old benefactor the dog approaching with one of her pups in her teeth. She dropped the pup at the foot of the altar, and Noah petted her. Noah loved that old dog and pawed her with blind desperation, and when he spoke to me from his soused pile of rocks, I could understand him.

"Hey, bird. Why you? Huh?"

"You should know. You were the one who sent me into the flood in the first place. You did.*"*

But the beastman looked around with his bleary-eyed speculation. "How did we ever get here?" He motioned with a belligerent shrug to his sons, still trading off with that one shovel. "What is so special, or even noteworthy, about them that they should be singled out from the rest. Hmm? Was I standing at the right place, at the right time? Just look at this place."

Noah tried to take in his ravaged seabed surroundings. His weary mane and beard spread out from his face like flattened kelp in the sand, and I cawed back with all the bile of the sea. But it was as before; he was beast-man, I was crow.

Scratching himself, Noah stood and pushed his garments aside and made a great splattering of water on the rock. The sound decreased to just a trickle, and sitting down again, he hung his head, and fell asleep.

I lit beside him and tucked in my wings.

I tugged at the stitching of the goatskin bottle. What was left of the bloody potion mixed with the ash on the rocks, and Noah made the low rumbling sound of his kind during sleep. He just lay there, sprawled out, only half-covered by the many layers of clothes. The bluish-white color of his grub-like skin was obscene. The scar he had received from the lion was still a ravaged slab of meat nearly revealing bone. Much of him was missing. It appeared as though the dogs and vultures had already dug at him and left behind mealy, furrowed rows.

I hopped up and perched on the folds of his robes.

I thought of all the perished crows trapped within the ribs of man. After all, it was a myth that the Old Bone had freed any of the Perished; the job was left undone. And though the great Mother of Many was not singing there, perhaps a part of her song was, trapped and fluttering within the gaunt ribs of that beast. Not only would I get my revenge, I would be an honored Misfortune whose song would last beyond the wind as long as songs were sung, if only I could pluck a hole within the cage of the beastman's ribs and release not only all of the Perished but all the other birds and animals trapped within the field of human viscera. It would be a great outpouring of animal spirits in much the same way the ark perhaps was when the ramp door burst open from all the flapping of wings and poundings of hooves.

Then Noah's son Ham cried out as if I'd already killed the old man and was wing-deep in tasty innards. Ham rushed near and shooed me away. After I flew back a few hops, he ran his soft claws over his beard, trying to make sense out of the exposed, already-peeled state of nakedness his father had achieved.

Ham knelt down and spoke to his father.

He turned his father's face in his hands. Standing back up, he yelled, "Father!" But to no avail. "Father! The strange libations have claimed you!"

Noah snored away as before.

Ham picked up the headless, deflated goatskin bottle, wrung it dry, and walked with it across the fields. He stopped to talk with his brothers, who were just then rolling the lion down in the grave beneath the vines. The two brothers and Ham barked at each other. They growled, and Shem and Japeth dropped what they were doing and then barked at me and threw rocks my way, careful not to hit my perch, which happened to be their father. They ran up and waved their arms, trying to drive me away from my Holy purpose.

With great concern, they knelt over their father and splashed water from a bowl onto his troubled brow, all the while too ashamed to face the old man's exposed, wounded flesh and diluted spirit. Noah blinked and shook the narcotic sleep from his tangled seaweed beard only to behold Ham, standing there above him. Noah grunted, which startled Ham, curious Ham, who beheld his father in a quiet, detached way, murmuring sounds of astonishment, but also wearing that same scowling disdain once his father fully awoke.

"Here. Give it here." Noah wheezed through a parched throat, though he'd been dousing it all day. "The sweet wine."

Ham inspected the goatskin bottle in his hands. He pulled and twisted it into a painful shape. "It's empty."

"What?" said Noah, rising. "Either give me that one. Or one just like it. But full!"

Ham only stared through the opening of the empty, bladder-like bottle.

"Don't just stand there—gaping," said Noah. "Will not you partake with the old man on the day of our thanks? We have journeyed so far—to Paradise! We made it."

Ham cast his glance down the mountainside, and just then Nanniah appeared in her heavy, haughty robes and put her hand on her mate's shoulder.

She said, "This muddy valley that once held so much, Father, forgive me. We should not give thanks for what happened."

But Noah acted as if he hadn't even heard her and kept talking to his son.

"Can't you give thanks? For even a moment? For your very own life? Here. Drink."

Neither moved.

"Nor will you help out your brothers and sisters?"

"The time to help my own is gone," she said. "How can I possibly give thanks for this?"

"You ridicule me!" Noah's voice grew so harsh and loud that even the cattle on the grain piles stopped their chewing and lifted their heads, but this time for only a moment.

"Father," said Ham, "what have we done?"

"Begone! The both of you. If you won't make offerings or help."

And the two brothers, Shem and Japeth, had to restrain their father. While Shem held him down, young Japeth went into the ark and returned, dragging a heavy blanket across the sand. The two of them then covered the poorly healed scars of their father, and led the old man into the smoky caverns of a more secluded sleep, deep within the ark.

Later, in the fields, Shem and Japeth threw the last creature of the sacrifice down into its open pit, where the heavy sands of oblivion would fall.

"Out! Out of the way!"

I crowed at the lunacy.

"Let the crow do his work!"

I'd have loved to take a beast or two up flying.

And the Lord God called unto Adam, and
said unto him, Where art thou?

—GENESIS, 3:9

7. *Exile*

I knew enough about exile to know that Ham and Nanniah were being sent off under its curse—Nanniah seated on the back of an ass, and Ham watched over by a scowling father who stood on the decrepit gangplank that had once welcomed so many of the earth's creatures, summoned by the God Crow and led here by those most merciful wings across the water. The four of them, Ham, Nanniah, unborn giant, and ass, started down the long mountain. At the time I knew nothing of the extent of Noah's curse. I thought they were setting out to discover a better place, such as Ham's island of musical instruments, a place he'd only dreamt of back inside of the ark.

It would not be until the Old Hookbill now a Dog Pup had matured into a faithful farm hound and could apply her skills of intermediation that I would learn the full extent of Noah's curse and the many strange and odious explanations that it gave rise to. Stories of shame, ridicule, and castration, and other bizarre human acts, when it was the lion that mutilated Noah, and not Ham, nor his little boy, unborn at the time and still in the egg of Nanniah's belly.

Occasionally, as she and Ham retreated, Nanniah looked back at the home denied her in the shipwreck's appalling shadow.

When they were almost out of hearing, a horrible bleating, bawling sound came from the ark, as if from a monstrous lamb. It was the naked Giant Child, yanking against his rope, trying to untie it from the enormous log that held him fast. Giving up on the knot, he dragged the blackened tree trunk across the mud, and it was hard to believe that the world had been destroyed because of his kind. He stumbled down the slope, crying out for his momma, his skin flushed red where the knots looped around his neck and arms. His mother turned around, and her mule halted in the soft mud of a gully. No one moved. No one except the wild Giant Child as the tree lumbered and bucked, until soon the boy stood before his mother, whimpering. Then she and Ham turned back to Noah, who stood in the doorway of his broken ark, and they awaited his decision. For it was part of the deal for the Giant Child's safe passage across the waters that he would pay with lifelong servitude to the world's benefactor, Noah.

On the ark, this same Noah rose.

He gestured, about ready to speak, but averted his face and made a fluttering motion with his hand, as if brushing the last few crumbs from a table.

Nanniah climbed down from her mule and wrapped her cloak around the giant's wet, blubbering head, and she and Ham untied the ropes. Then they all resumed the slow journey down the mountainside, the Giant Child sniffling, and every once in a while letting out a long, quivering sob that gave him comfort.

"Come back!" I called.

But only the giant wild child turned around, filled with horror.

"Then *be* a slave to your giant slave—" said Noah, quietly, standing alone on the ark's ramp. "Blessed be the grace of God on your brother Shem, whom your generations shall serve. And may He also increase Japeth, whom your kind shall also serve."

And Noah withdrew back into the sagging, sunless quarters of his tree-heavy ark. Meanwhile, in Nanniah's womb, the infant beastman grew, innocent within and cursed without, pacified by the sway of the ass's shoulders and his mother's quiet, defiant song.

· · ·

I raised my wings to follow them beyond exile, since I was already an expert on it myself. Perhaps these two, Nanniah and Ham, were better off banished. Perhaps they'd find their own Paradise. On their island of musical instruments they could learn to be more like crows and develop expressive, resonant voices, taught to them by the great mother who just might inhabit the unborn giant growing in the sea of Nanniah's belly. Crows, with their own voices so pleasing and full, have no need for musical instruments. But after spending so much time imprisoned with the human, I could see now why the beasts might want to invent contraptions that sing, or dream of islands filled with them. Myself, I had only my own hunger and the song of how it had sustained nothing but sadness until then. *"I Am!"* I sang to the Lost Mother who rode within the banished. *"Why am I Am?"* I wondered, if I could not fly with my own kind, or free the Perished and fly in the wind that bore them along.

At least I could hope for a sign from Our Many, and so I swooped down before the beastmen's path, or landed out beyond their measly horizons, or hopped just behind them, and called out their inept calls. My visits seemed to give them a welcome break from the monotony of devastation, and even brought them joy, the Giant Child stumbling after me with open arms. Still, I grew impatient. They moved so slowly, they seemed immobile. They trod through gray ravines, past formless lands. Their thin trail of footprints shimmered as it disappeared across the floodplains.

"Will we never get there?" said Ham.

"Get where?"

"This accursed land."

"Enough. It's cursed too much already."

"Then curse whoever brought us so low."

Nanniah clicked her tongue. "Come along." And her beast quickened, stirring up stones. Soon she hummed and sang quietly to herself and, with one hand, rubbed the soft slope of her belly, and I remembered how she had once cradled me in the palm of the other. I remembered the dark, feathery fall of her hair keeping me warm as she nurtured the sea out of my hollow bones.

Seeing me, Nanniah would reach into her knapsack and throw seed down to me, and I followed, watching the seagulls and rock doves get to the offering before me. I watched and waited to see if these birds would be captured and eaten, or enslaved into the service of the obtuse beast who'd take their eggs and end up killing them anyway. But no. No harm came to any of the birds who took from their offering.

In the vast plains and valleys of the wastelands, I flew above the banished family, and strangely enough, they seemed to follow. Without even trying, I led them to water, and easy crossings, and suitable terrain for travel. While Nanniah clicked and clucked her tongue to me, only me. I landed on her shoulders, knowing I could fly off any time. She dropped offerings into my beak, and Ham walked beside us, smoothing down the white feathers of my face with his curled, bony clutches. I thought I might follow Nanniah and her family all the way to exile. But I figured we were already there, and flew off, knowing I could find them again at any time, even on their new island if they ever found it.

They've been able to handle anything we
throw their way. They don't just survive,
they benefit. Their numbers increase.

—JOHN MARZLUFF,
"Crow Mysteries"

8. Ghost of the Misfortune

For days I flew the depthless murk of the sky and had no home, while my wings worked only to find one. Below me was a stream or a river running through the morass, more like spilling across it in search of a bed where it could form itself. The water ran in such shallow sheets across the muddy floodplains, I couldn't see where it came from or where it went. Then I heard a sound that nearly dropped me from the sky. I thought it was my own memory, clearing its throat, a murmur sprung up from our own Lost Many's undying song.

I looked down.

It was Plum Black, hopping across the mud.

I cawed out her name and fell to the mud beside her.

But she took off, the instant she saw me. I heard only the whack of her wings as she left.

"Plum Black?"

I ached in a familiar fight with the sky, and found myself flapping in her path. It could be no other. In a liquid flash of her feathers, she was flying the other way.

I flew directly in front of her again. She threw her wings up in a panic and took off.

"Stop!" she cried. *"Good Ghost, spare me. I give up."*

This time she dove straight down to avoid me.

But I dove in before her.

"It's me. I Am! Didn't you hear me on the ark?"

"Of course, please. My heart stops." Her feathers rattled in her panic to escape me, and she pulled out of her dive and flew up high, and kept going, until she was in the clouds, and above them. *"My heart stopped back in the ark, too. Why do you torment me, calling to me from the dead, and giving me no reason. Why?"*

"No. It's me. I'm alive. I Am!"

"No, you're a ghost. Like the rest. All ghosts. Left behind in the flood with all crows."

We found ourselves above a dazzling whiteness. The tops of the clouds had ravines and mountain ranges all their own. Shifting cliff faces turned to ponds, then slow glacial drifts. Long billowing sheaves of the gaseous ice reached out into the sky as the sun boiled them up and they scattered. It was a spectacular airy earth above the old earth. It had been a forever since the sunlight spread its warmth through my wings while the air above cooled them. The cloudy depths below us moved along with the wind, and took us with it, so it seemed as though all movement had ceased. And there was nowhere to fly to anyway, since everything hung in the same suspension. We were adrift, Plum Black and I, like the drops of rain that formed before our faces and turned into tiny crystals.

"My eyes—" she said, and Plum Black flew in closer to me to catch a glimpse of my Misfortune, *"—my eyes want too much. I am afraid to fly beside you. Maybe the clouds will swallow you up."*

Up here Plum Black reflected all the hues a crow could ever have. I even thought the pale wash of Misfortune had formed along the spines and edges of her feathers. But it was just a dust of ice collecting on her wings.

"Didn't you hear me on the ark?" I asked. *"I called to you!"*

"Yes," she cried. *"From the dead. But I can't follow you to the Tree. I can't."*

"No. That was me. I'm alive. And you have no reason to follow me, since I have nowhere to go."

"How? How did you survive the flood?"

I wanted to tell her all about the Old Hookbill's prophecy and go even further back. But she must have had an ordeal of her own.

"It would take a Winter Roost," I said, "to tell it all."

"Yes!" she said. "Yes." And she flew up close. "A Roost, a long Winter Roost, when we're Crow Leaves, you and I!"

All of the sudden she swooped up below me and gripped my talons in hers. We each spun around the other, falling, and her beak opened in a screech of joy. We plunged beyond the sun, in and out of the half-darkness of the clouds, and let the weight of the earth spin us around.

Back on the fields of mud, I cried, "Again. Again."

But Plum Black leaned far into my face and gave me quick tugs and clips with her beak.

"Your feathers," she said. "The pale ones grow so thick. They curve around your face in a falling pattern. As if a hoarfrost had passed through you."

Instead of wanting to hide my face, I felt something entirely strange and new brew up inside of me. A heat rushed through me, but it was tempered by the appearance of Plum Black up close. She looked ravaged and thin from the passage across the waters, making her all the more precious, and the familiar old longing welled up in the hollow of my bones. We nipped at each other. We hopped and sang in the mud and passed pebbles back and forth, which were all we could find in the mud. Finally we found an oyster and broke apart its shell and fed each other the slippery meat. Her tail feathers twitched as she pulled them aside, and she crouched in a sad, shy invitation, twisting my anguish with the sight of her vulnerable folds of flesh beneath her crow-blue coat. But just as fast, she flew away, until soon she began pulling away again with breakneck speed, not looking my way but calling out occasionally, crestfallen.

"Please don't. Don't follow me," she said. "Please. This is as far as you should go."

I had to know why but feared the answer, and she cried out anyway, *"Gone, all trees, all crows, everything, gone."* But I could barely understand her, or her words. The reason she avoided me was to avoid a confrontation with her new mate, who had traveled across the waters with her on Noah's floating barnyard. Still, I followed her below the dismal cloud cover and across a formless land made dull by death. We came upon a crag along a gradual slope. And from a split between the rocks was a row of dormant trees. The last trunks on earth stood like mute Giants without heads or limbs, and here Plum Black lit. The twigs of her nest were covered in the bitumen taken from the nest of Noah, and the jag of it looked like something black and sooty, left over from a fire, precariously situated in a shallow crotch of one of the trunks.

She tugged at a twig of her nest as if getting it ready for something without noting where I landed. So I lit next to her and curled my hooks through the crude, misbegotten tangle. It seemed as if the nest was missing half of itself, and had no soft inner lining, and few smaller twigs to help weave it all together. I looked up—and gone, Plum Black was gone, as always, to where I couldn't tell.

And the birds are whispering

the elves are whispering to me,

I am, I am,

—JONATHON RICHMOND,

"Afternoon"

9. Season of Plum Black

How was it that fingerling twigs could sprout from the Giants that had drowned and lost all their branches in the flood? No more than trunks, the last trees on earth grew fierce tiny buds, and these shook their greenling heads in the wind that blew through and around Plum Black's nest. Gradually the winds returned with their spirits and names. It was as if all the birds that had drowned in the flood were just now rising from the mud to be carried off to the Bountiful Tree. I kept hearing them in the gusts that blew by, just a short blast of birdsong way back in my skull, or a howling through the jagged nest of sticks that Plum Black had stacked and pecked at and sat in with sad wonder. She kept waiting for the eggs to arrive, but seemed trapped already as if brooding for them to hatch.

"*I Am! I Am!*" I flew overhead, and lit on a tree, or what was left of one. "*Where are all the other crows?*"

"*What?*" she said. "*I'm waiting for the eggs to drop. Don't rush me. I don't know what to expect.*"

"No," I said, and hopped right beside her, and held my beak sideways so she could feed from my offering. "*I meant the other crows, the seven clean crows that came with you across the waters.*"

"*What?*" she cried. "*There were none. I was alone, in the dark, in a cage. I thought all crows would end when I died. Until I saw you.*"

"Then why did you tell me not to follow?"

"This nest," she said. "It's so miserable. Nothing like Our Many's. I didn't want you to see it. Until it was done. Even now I'm ashamed."

It was true; materials for the nest were rare in the wiped-out world. But we found many from the abated saltwaters of the flood, and slowly her nest took on a more hospitable form. Shreds of kelp and other seaweeds lined the nest's inner bowl. Dried seagrasses served as twigs, along with the limb of a crustacean, here and there. Even a starfish held up in the weave.

When she flew from the nest, I could fly straight into the dark dream joy of Plum Black. I'd be far off watching her, until she took off and I'd rush to be with her in the sky. She flew ridiculously high, pretending I wasn't there, and gave a turn of her head. She dove to escape me, and I'd anticipate her moves and fly in her way, until we were together falling from the sky. Landing, we fed each other insects or ocean clams still hiding in the sooty turf of the new plains. We locked bills and she crouched low in the fields of grasses and pulled her quivering tail feathers aside. In a rush I shook the heat of my anguish into her. Then we perched together, and for a moment everything grew peaceful. It was especially sweet for birds who'd finally found an aerie of their own to light together in the branches at sunset and let the best site for a nest come to them that night in their dreams. Except here we'd be long gone by sunset, and there were no trees anywhere. We stared out through the trembling grasses, trying to remember what woods were like. As always, Plum Black worked with her soft clippers at the Misfortune of my face.

"It's like a beard," she said. "Like a mask. Yet it hides nothing. Sweet sadness, it is you."

Then as quickly as it had begun, it was over, the feeling of flying back into the lost song of Our Many, made sharp by the grip of coitus, cut off from me, as if half of me had been sawed off and flown away. And we chased each other over the fields of the sun.

Then one day everything changed. The instant she saw me, she flew off, unable to cry out from all of the food stuffed in her pouch. I flew beside her, wanting to nip and tug on her feathers and have her chase me like before. But she let herself drop into the wind and hung on to it and was carried off.

And I followed.

In the cup of her nest was a brood of simps already too many to count, their gaping wound-like mouths all crying to the sky. Constantly she scoured the new earth to feed them, but never brought enough. Her nest was enormous, but her brood was even larger. Following her, I'd land on the pitch-covered nest and be nearly attacked as I lowered my offerings down to them. They nipped at my eyes and feathers as I found a beak, thin and veined like a new leaf, and felt the convulsive tugging of its infant hunger, pulling down on my food pouch as if yanking me inside out as only the ancient Hookbill could do. With others I had to push the food down their pharynx with my tongue. I moved quickly from simp to simp before I was emptied.

"*I am!*" they cried. "*I am!*"

"*Of course, you are. Which one are you? And you?*"

All of the world's flora and fauna was quick to replenish itself and make the world busy and robust, taking root in the rich humus of annihilation. At the wallows where the flood never left, water parsley, cattails, and all kinds of underwater leafy life curled up through the fanning layers of algae that soon formed a swamp. Loosestrife and brambles reached up over the sweet-grasses to lay claim to the banks and slopes beyond. I flew up over the greening hillsides. To get enough food, I had to return, nearer to the rising moon, on the banks of the nighttime flood.

Up on the shore, where the waves of floodwater could no longer reach, the trunks of the Giants were stacked up. The edge of the flood was littered with trees. Many still had their branches and roots, and around the rocks and the logs of driftwood, the ocean kept coming. The roar of the breakers was like the flood wanting to roll up onto the land all over again. But it kept pulling itself back down into the nighttime sea. I hopped nearer to the surf, and sang the song of our aerie back to the flood that had carried the trees of so many aeries here to its edge. I looked up into the distance between the stars and wondered if our songscape was still down there beneath the ocean, or if it was up above air again, on the shores of the other side.

What a perfectly New England sound is this
voice of the crow! If you stand perfectly still
anywhere in the outskirts of the town and
listen . . . .

—HENRY DAVID THOREAU, *Walden*

10. Lost Lore

Out of nowhere I found a strange crow chasing me through unknown skies, and he made it clear he would chase me to the ends of the wind. His broad old wings worked and rattled while I pulled far ahead, and when I turned around, he was nothing more than a desperate speck below the clouds.

"*Crow!*" he called out with a failing voice. "*Crow!*"

He told me to *rest my wings.*

Take heed.

His aerie was far off.

He had something he had to say.

The diminished ring of his voice would have been comic if it weren't so weathered and run-down. How could there possibly be a crow older than I? I grew oddly sentimental for the time when Fly Home would overpower the sky and send me off flapping. I made a sudden change of flight, which the stranger didn't see, and fearing he'd lost me, he flew in the wrong direction and cried out, "*Crow! Sing for me. So that I might know from where you fly.*"

I called him back to me and slowed enough so that when I turned around, he could see me. His face showed the strain of keeping up. The long bird paddled like the Old Bone now, with something strange about his size; his strewn feathers were lank and herring-boned.

He said, "*Strange bird friend. We are not much on this earth. Do away with your troublesome thoughts, and tell me, from where do you learn such powers of flight?*"

I leaned over, until my beak was just above his ear, and cawed, "*From the Mother of Many, I Am!*"

He nearly dropped from the sky, until he remembered to keep paddling. "*I Am?*" he said, as though he knew me.

I circled back around, and he dove before me so he could see the Misfortune on my face. Then he resumed flying, without any destination, as far as I could tell. I wondered how long he'd stay this aimless course, wishing only to speak with me.

"*Your mouth darkens with age.*" He flew, open-beaked, still in dismay. "*Surely you should have a name by now.*"

"*Aren't you one of the seven clean crows from the ark?*" I asked. I wondered if perhaps Plum Black hadn't seen them.

"*Clean? God, no. Being one of seven means only that Keeyaw can keep you in his stables, and sacrifice you, whenever he feels like it. What's so clean about that?*"

"*Keeyaw sacrificed me,*" I said.

"*And still,*" he flew, exaggerating his dismay, as if mocking me, "*you fly to tell of it?*"

"*He sent me to fetch news of land.*"

"*News—?*" The Stranger's shoulders worked heavily with each flap. "*No. That was the raven.*" He spoke like an old bird, full of dull knowledge. "*The raven claims to have found land. Except the raven never returned with any word. It took the doves to bring news—the dove, the dove, the frightened dove, in the form of a twig, they say.*"

"*No. That was me.*"

"*You? You brought back news of the Giants? To help Keeyaw?*"

"*I didn't bring back anything. Not even myself.*"

We flew in silence—except for the faint, odd wheezing of the air through his feathers.

"You're so old now," he said, "much older than your years, and, as the Hookbill foresaw, truly a Misfortune. Why don't you fly on and find your way elsewhere in the world?"

"I'm keeping a watch over the beastman," I said.

"Of course," he said. "Their kind must be watched. Much can be learned—no. Must be learned. I fear we have no other choice."

Just then it became clear that this was the Strange Bird of the Withered Coat. But he looked different now, in flight. It took him a great effort to work those large, elegant, ragged fans through the sky.

"You're the bird who talked with Keeyaw," I said.

"You were there, too?"

"In the arms of the beastwoman."

"Ah, yes. I remember it."

I stared at him with suspicion, because, if he knew so much about me, then surely he would remember me as the bird in Nanniah's arms, too shocked and sea-drenched to fly. But like the Old Bone, he could guess at my thoughts.

"Of course, I look different now. Around the beastman, I'm a curse, a pest, a malaise, am I not? But only because that's what he asks of me. When he's not around, what harm can I do? But you. You are moved by something other than your wings, I know, for I look down, for only a second, and then up again, and you are halfway across the sky. Before you take off again and leave me, I must ask one thing of you."

I watched him from the pale side of my head.

"At the Winter Roost," he said, "there we can abide by each other, you and I. And I hope you will stay 'til then and be the teacher of lost songs. You must, because here, on this side of the waters, I have heard you sing, when you thought no one was around—at least I know now it was you—and when you sing, you find the place where lost birds live. I want to call you Finder, the Misfortune of Lost Birds, or some such thing, I'm not sure."

"It's not hard," I said, "when we have no place of our own."

"It must be inside you, then. The songscape is in you, like no other. When I hear you, I'm there in the old aerie, with your Mother of Many above you in the nest, and all your siblings in the trees. Even crows you never met, they come back to me. I'll call you Memory of Many, if I may."

He stopped paddling and fell in behind me.

"Maybe it's your own memory playing tricks," I said.

"Perhaps. Still, your song pleases me. May I call you that?"

"How should I stop you? And who's here to care?"

"For the sake of those gone," he said. *"And those soon to come."*

He descended, heading for unknown skies. It could have been to the aerie, or Noah's wreck, or nearby foraging grounds, bursting with plenty. But all of these were the other way. As I watched the broad, fantastic fray of his wings rise and fall, slower and with greater effort than I'd ever seen, I felt that it was under such a flight that a bird journeys off to the Tree of the Dead.

"At the Winter Roost," he called back, already distant. *"Sing of us then."*

He flew beyond sight.

So every night I dreamt of the Winter Roost. I dreamt of a sky filled with birds. But what good was the old pull, when there were no birds anywhere to accompany me? Instead I found refuge with the spirits in the wind. The long lines of wind came in off the ocean with too much swirling energy and too many things to say. I tried to listen and become them. But in the winds, I was the absence of wind, and when I reached out to gather them in my wings, they were gone, just as more came. The spirits arrived in gales, in eddies, in mirthful pockets where they were strangely silent. The wind laughed and raced all around me and filled me with a longing for my fledgling days when I had tried to follow the Many, or Night Time, or the Old Bone, or any gang of youthful thugs, back when I couldn't gauge distances or updrafts and I fought against the currents and lost. As I flew into the winds, I flew into the past, and the winds matched my every move, winds of Old Aeries, of the Perished, of Loved Ones.

In the old songscape, I remembered how the winds had grown friendly, and even the furies that seized hold of my feathers also taught my wings how to reef closed and dive, and the same violent wind shot me wherever I wanted. A tuck, a plummet, a flick of my pinions and I'd just miss a tree, and for long days at a time, the spirits of the wind took me, as if I were flying back to deeper woods, where I'd learned how to follow the whereabouts of my family, not by sight but by their long-ranging voices. Is there any sound more beautiful and expressive than a crow's lonesome caw? Each elder had a larger repertoire in which this call note popped up with what seemed like randomness until you grew to learn that crow's song. And the way it was sung, from a distant copse of trees, or flying overhead, or anywhere in the distant echoey world, helped us to forage collectively over a great, wide expanse.

"What? What did you bring us? From far off? From far off."

"Open your beak, and I will show you."

In the spare trees of the new world, I found Our Aerie and flew into the black feathers of my dark dream joy and lit beside her.

"What? What is it?"

"From the flood banks. By the sea."

And I opened my beak and turned it sideways so that Plum Black could reach in with her sweet, ravaged hunger and clear my voice. Sometimes I bent down to the brood myself, where I really did feel like a ghost, missing the aerie while I was still inside it, looking over the dismal, blackened nest, and seeing how the piping, begging simps would soon fledge and take flight. How would these raw red mouths ever fly? And where would they go? I found myself either at the nest, or back to the edge of the flood, where I learned the austere beauty of longing held in check, and my heart filled with its ice floes, and the wind took me where it would.

At the close of day, instead of a Roost, I always wound up here at the surf of the flood. In the foaming sand I found a crab, scuttling sideways, trying to box me back with its slow, ancient anger. Stubborn, ignorant, wriggling its legs out the side of my beak, its prehistoric armor would protect it for maybe a few seconds more before I broke it open, trying to decide how much I would eat just then and how much I would hide or bring back to the nest. As I looked out over the flood, or the ocean, or whatever it had become, I saw the ghosts of lost birds, flying below the saltwater pastures and pushing up waves. The waves seemed to me like open mouths waiting to be fed, open like crying beaks with something to say.

And from the sky, down flew the God Crow.

It came down from the setting sun, and landed just above me on a tangle of driftwood with roots reaching up into the air.

It looked neither at me nor at the beach but made the soft, gurgling sounds of water flowing through a tube. It looked up and shivered as if drenched and made the clacking sound of wood against wood. It leaned forward for a better look at me, leaning so far that Its Mightiness almost fell, but It caught Its balance by extending the great span of Its wings the other way. Then the God Crow turned that magnificent horn to the darkening sea. And It opened that mighty horn, and above the vastness of the unabated waters came a light from Its parted beak—the light from the holy pearl hung in Noah's quarters, now throwing its sapphire cast over the nighttime sea. God the Crow kept opening and closing those mighty clippers, shedding light upon the foam and the breakers, and then sending them back into the approaching dark.

Then, right beside me, lit another bird, but how close I couldn't tell. It hopped and shuddered, and then made the sound of a barnyard kitty.

"Come here."

It spoke in a nasal mockery of Noah feeding the creatures of creation as if granting them the privilege of their hunger.

"Come here. Fear not."

I knew then it was the raven of the ark, the thief of my rightful place in lore, even if it was just the beastman's.

"I Am! I Am!" He jeered and mocked me. *"It wasn't I who made the juices of the apple so sweet. I'm only here to provoke you."*

He hopped across the mud with the same stooped posture as the Strange Bird with the Withered Coat. *"So sing. Sing a song for me, would you? Your voice, it's so beautiful—"* he began to hop right toward me, *"for a crow."*

"Really." I bristled and stood back.

Still God the Crow was opening and closing Its beak, casting Its sudden light, making it even more random by dropping and swerving Its head. Just as I was about to puff up and sing, the light from Its mouth shone straight into my eyes, and the crab was torn from my claws.

"Hah!"

It was the raven. Seeing his success, he flew away with my meal, just beyond me on the beach.

"Crow, remember," said the raven, his nearby beak busy and full, *"you are only a crow."*

I looked over at the God Crow. The slow opening and closing of Its mighty portal kept lighting the floodwaters, as vast and benign and distant as ever. Then, with a mighty caw, It spread Its majestic wings and flew out over the flood, Its open horn glowing like a falling star over the sea.

It was true. I Am! a crow, a crow hopping beyond the breakers, where the beach meets the flood. I Am only a crow, a crow you might hear *awwk!* Just the *eiyyaawwck!* of a crow, any day, outside your window.

But you should listen.

I may be talking to you.

Acknowledgments

The fundamental telling of this story is indebted to the work done by Robert Graves and Patai Raphael in their compilation: *Hebrew Myths, the Book of Genesis*. It is also indebted to the many marvelous, far-reaching sources I researched, all of which are included in the work's epigraphs. I am especially grateful to these, as they seem to talk to one another, and tell a story all their own.

You see crows every day. But to speculate on what I was looking at, and to think about the story I wanted to tell, I found the following works invaluable: Bernd Heinrich's *Ravens in Winter,* and *Mind of the Raven;* Konrad Z. Lorenz's *King Solomon's Ring;* Lawrence Kilham's *The American Crow and the Common Raven;* Candace Savage's *Bird Brains: The Intelligence of Crows, Ravens, Magpies, and Jays;* Catherine Feher Elston's *Ravensong: A Natural and Fabulous History of Ravens and Crows;* John Marzluff and Tony Angell's *In the Company of Crows and Ravens;* and the research of Dr. Kevin J. McGowan, at Cornell University, posted on the internet.

Special thanks to the King County Arts Commission for their support of a project entitled Bird People, awarded to Ben Jacklet and myself, which led to our increased interest in birds, i.e. Crows and those who watch Crows. Thanks to Professor John Marzluff for his open-minded yet sensible advice as I researched my protagonist, and thanks to John Withey who showed me what to look for when finding crow nests.

I can't consider the writing of this book without the constant encouragement and guidance over the years from my agent, Jeff Kleinman, and to both the keen and expansive vision of Fred Ramey, my editor at Unbridled

Books; and thanks also to Greg Michalson, Caitlin Hamilton Summie, and Alaine Borgias at Unbridled; special gratitude to Phil Bevis at Arundel Books. Ben Jacklet, Robin, Evan, Caleb, Squarehead Ed, Brian, Matt and Christi, and Misha—for the support over the years. Mom and Dad, and Isabelle Franklin, for the abiding inspiration.